When the World Falls Down

When the
World
Falls Down

Jon Bolitho-Jones

Matador
9 Priory Business Park,
Wistow Road, Kibworth Beauchamp,
Leicestershire. LE8 0RX
Tel: 0116 279 2299
Email: books@troubador.co.uk
Web: www.troubador.co.uk/matador
Twitter: @matadorbooks

ISBN 978 183859 285 1

British Library Cataloguing in Publication Data.
A catalogue record for this book is available from the British Library.

Printed and bound in Great Britain by 4edge Limited

Matador is an imprint of Troubador Publishing Ltd

Dedicated to my amazing wife Beth, and in memory of my grandad, Victor Jones.

Contents

One

DEAR READERS, YOU ARE ABOUT TO GO ON AN adventure. Through the pages of this book, you will be transported to a world of magic, space pirates, and adventurers; a place rarely visited by humankind. I must warn you, though, this journey is not for the faint hearted: we are heading for a place inhabited by monsters, orcs, evil villains, and beings that can rip a planet apart with a single word. Do not worry – I will make sure you are safe on your voyage. But before we depart, we must start at the beginning, with our hero, Bethany Hannah Morgan.

It was a cool and quiet night, and all was peaceful at 1½ Cordling Drive. This was a house unlike any other. With its eight floors and twisted structure, it looked as if it was on the verge of architectural impossibility. It was a house that looked as if it had come from another world entirely. On the seventh floor, Bethany was struggling to sleep, her mind racing, tangling itself into a mess – as was her long black hair. She shivered in her Star Wars pyjamas as she held her duvet up to her nose, with only her gleaming green eyes and pixie ears poking above it. Yet it was not cold – the spring air was rather warm. No, there was something bothering her, and she could not shake it from her mind.

You see, she had spent the day in mourning, dressed in black, at the funeral of her best and only friend. Bethany had never really had many friends; she enjoyed her own company. Indeed, she found her best conversations were always with herself. But there was one person she couldn't do without, and that was Grandpa Vic. He was gone, and as she lay there trying to sleep, all she could do was think about him. Every last detail raced through her head: he was born in the first half of the twentieth century, and he had worked in a steel mill. He had served in the Second World War, though his only contribution had been crashing a rickshaw taxi into the barracks swimming pool on a drunken night out with his friends, a story that Bethany always found hilarious. She knew him as a jolly old man, with wide-framed glasses, a big smile, and a big belly, who liked to get up to mischief. Bethany's parents, both being miserable sorts, did not like that one bit, but she didn't care. He would sing songs, most of which were rude, while joining his granddaughter on her many imaginary adventures. Otherwise, during the day they'd spend their time in the garden, telling stories or drawing pictures. At night they'd put on plays, eat pudding, and sing. School got in the way, but when the holidays came, he made her gingerbread dinosaurs and they got back to their usual fun. For the two of them, there was never a dull moment. When she finished secondary school, it was her grandpa she took to her leaving prom. They danced all night, oblivious to the world around them. It was a night she would never forget. She was then sent to boarding school for her A-Levels, and she missed him dearly. They wrote to each other every week. When she returned during her holidays, Grandpa Vic would always seem to change. At first it was only physically; he got slower and weaker, but he quickly ended up in a wheelchair or his favourite armchair. This didn't stop them, though, and they still had great fun together, Bethany sitting on the carpet in front of Grandpa Vic and listening to his stories, supplying him with tea during any intermissions. But then he began to change mentally; his memory started to go and he became argumentative, easily frustrated. Still Bethany would go to him, finding him in his usual chair every day. She told him stories, made him gingerbread, and drew him pictures, giving him all of her love. In spite of this, he ended up worse, but still she'd come to him, see him in his favourite chair, and put a smile on his face.

Then one day she returned from college for her Easter holidays to find the chair empty. Grandpa Vic had exchanged it for a hospital bed, and so she went to see him there instead. But that did not last long. He was in a bad state and so spent all his time asleep, and eventually it was a sleep he didn't wake up from. Her last word to him was goodbye. Whether he actually heard her, she never knew. What was certain was that Grandpa Vic had left her and that her life felt very empty indeed.

The funeral had been a grand affair, largely because many of his old friends had attended, sad to say goodbye to a very good man. It had rained all day, save for a brief moment when the sun had shone through the clouds, illuminating his coffin as it was lowered into the ground. When the whole thing was over, Bethany had returned home and gone straight to bed. And this is where the story begins, our skinny little hero doing her best to sleep; the house deathly silent, save for the gentle rustling of leaves; and the ticking of the Morgan family grandfather clock.

This clock had been with the family for generations. A tall, rather grand piece, it was claimed by Mr Morgan that it had never faltered or been damaged throughout its entire existence. It was, to him, an example of "perfect engineering, a constant and implacable certainty in a world of chaos and disorder". He loved that clock, perhaps even more than he loved his wife and daughter. But he was very much correct – the old clock was incredibly accurate and could show the exact time to the millisecond (well, if it had possessed the hand to do it with). Each second would be heralded by a click, each minute by a clonk, and each hour by a thunderous cacophony of twangs, dongs, and plonks. The noise itself was constant and would easily drive someone unaccustomed to it stark raving mad. The Morgans, however, were entirely used to the racket, and only when it stopped would they suspect something was amiss. The clock itself, of course, had never been so chaotic as to halt in its duty.

Bethany had had enough of the day and had proceeded to her room with the briefest of words to her parents, refusing to accept that her dear grandfather had passed away. Surely after she had awoken from her nightmare, she would run downstairs and find him in his usual cheery state, sat in his favourite chair, chuckling. The problem was that to awake from something, you normally have to be asleep first, and this was something entirely elusive to her that evening.

She tried everything: counting sheep, singing to herself, reading a book, and the classic method of simply closing her eyes. But it seemed that both her mind and body had forgotten how to fall asleep. Despite every attempt, she lay there in her messy, colourful room, staring into the darkness, doing her best not to think of her grandpa. At first she blamed her restlessness on her parents; they were still active and entertaining guests downstairs. This not only kept her awake but infuriated her too – how could people drink, chat, and laugh after such a day? She had every intention of charging downstairs and in her loudest and angriest voice telling them to shut up. But the potential of not seeing her favourite person in his favourite chair terrified her. And anyway, she didn't want to spoil her morning surprise of a smiling and very much alive Grandpa Vic. So she continued to lie there in bed, with her eyes clasped shut, desperately trying not to listen to the voices coming from downstairs.

Time, however, has a habit of rolling on and making things change. Before she knew it, the guests downstairs had bidden their farewells, jumped in their cars, and driven off into the night. The seconds ticked away and the minutes clonked ever on at their steady pace, announcing the lateness of the evening. Her parents, though, continued to chat on downstairs. They clattered crockery, clicked on the television, and munched on the snacks that had survived the day. But at last, they too headed upstairs to their beds, switching everything off, and putting away dishes. With everyone gone, Bethany half expected to hear her parents weeping, or mourning Grandpa Vic. But they didn't, and they, seemingly, effortlessly went to bed and quickly fell asleep. Still Bethany was restless, driven now by a frustration and anger aimed at her parents apparent calm. Everything was quiet. It was a silence that could only exist in the remotest of villages. One, though, that was interrupted by a steady advance of ticks, regular clonks, and hourly rumbles of clattering noise.

This grand timepiece continued its usual work just outside and to the left of Bethany's room. With no other nearby disturbances, she now laid the blame for her restlessness on the old clock. Grumbling to herself, she attempted to blot out the noise, smothering her ears with pillows. Still she could hear the ticks, clonks, and such, pierce through the restful night air. She had become furiously obsessed, counting each and every last noise it made as time marched on. By her calculations, she had heard the hourly rumble seven times at that point, meaning it was three in the morning. She'd had enough, and now had every intention of shutting the thing up with some form of grievous bodily harm (or extreme timepiece damage, as the case may be). But before she could pull herself out of bed, she was stopped by a huge crash.

Something – rather large and monstrous – had thrown its way through her cupboard door. The door crashed violently against the wall, almost smashing it off its hinges. In the face of such an unexpected and rather terrifying event, Bethany did what any sane person would do: she hid under her covers. Indeed, it is often believed that hiding under your covers provides plenty of protection from all sorts of monsters, fiends, and villainous characters. (What truth there is to this belief has yet to be determined by proper testing.) In this case, however, it proved sufficient and meant that our hero prevented herself from meeting an early demise. But it also meant she caught no sight of the monstrous intruder that had just charged into her room via her cupboard.

This surprise visitor did not stay; it charged out into the corridor, breathing heavily and quickly in a manner that suggested fear, pain, and a little bit of adrenaline. It crashed down the stairs into the house, each heavy step smashing into the floor in the direction, she now could guess, of the garden, her favourite place. Then, when the back door had been thrown open and the hammerlike stamp of feet had disappeared into the darkness of the trees, it was silent. Not even the grandfather clock continued to speak, for, as our hero would soon discover, it had been brutally smashed into three splintered pieces.

When one truly thinks about the saying "curiosity killed the cat", one realises that curiosity, as an emotion, could not have committed the murder, unlike other such emotions as anger and depression. It is presumably what the curiosity led to – the murderer, monster, or what have you – that actually committed the crime. (This is all assuming the murderer, monster, or what have you is not, funnily enough, named Curiosity.) For a moment Bethany thought this creature was just another creation of her overactive imagination. She was immensely popular among her imaginary friends, and she was always happy to add a friend to her gang. Perhaps this was just Norman, the blue penguin, returning from another of his wars. Still, her curiosity led our hero to follow her visitor, whether imaginary or not. Whatever it was, this being was clearly not human. If it ended up being some kind of bloodthirsty monster, she would take the proper course of action early enough to ensure she did not meet an untimely end. As you can guess by the fact that there are plenty more pages of this story ahead, she did not.

So it was that our hero leapt cautiously from her bed, suited up in a dressing gown and slippers, armed herself with a torch, and proceeded to track the journey and location of her very unexpected visitor. Carefully she crept out of her room, making sure not to trip on any of the special clutter and books she had collected over the years. The creature had left a trail of wreckage behind it; a number of her drawings had been ripped from her bedroom walls. Along with the broken body of the recently deceased grandfather clock, there were doors smashed off their hinges, furniture knocked over, and steps almost broken in two. Among the wreckage, a trail of blood spatters snaked along the route. It was clear to Bethany that this beast was neither graceful nor light, nor in the best of health either. But still she followed on, her curiosity and the beam from her torch leading the way.

She proceeded down the six flights of stairs, stepping over the debris as she went, taking care not to wake her parents. It was dark, but her senses were sharp and awake despite her current lack of sleep. She followed the trail and quickly arrived at the back door, which was wide open, letting the gentle breeze of the night stroke her face. Breathing deeply and plucking up her courage, she stepped through the door, into the garden and into the darkness. The cold night air was damp and clung to her like a huge, moist hug. The breeze sent only slight shivers through her body as she clasped her dressing gown around her with one hand and held her torch straight out in front of her in the other. The trail was now marked by huge footprints, created by monstrous feet pressing down and matting the long, dew-speckled grass, which was splattered lightly with blood.

The trail led her on through the untidy garden, right into the tree line, and further into the thicket. Beyond that, in the small forest, was a stream: Bethany's favourite place to get lost in her imagination. Watching her footing, she made quick progress, and before she knew it she could hear its gentle trickle. The trail in fact led there, through the trees, ferns, and broken branches, the destruction she passed created by an injured and panicked beast. She stepped onward quietly, careful not to attract the attention of her peculiar visitor.

It was then she began to hear it – deep, animalistic grunts, much like a gorilla's, in the near distance. It sounded like the low panting of an injured animal nursing its wounds. Despite the full possibility that her continued actions could lead to her early death, Bethany allowed her curiosity to get the better of her. All she needed was a quick peek at this creature, and nothing more. Creeping forward, she moved slower and slower, almost at a crawl, brushing branches and foliage carefully away as she went. It was close, just beyond some bushes. Its breath was calmer now, and Bethany could hear a mumbling of deep words in a gruff voice. All she would do was take a quick look and that was it. And so she did. Positioning herself in a low crouch, she slowly raised her head above the thicket.

There it was. Right in front of her was the beast, sitting quite calmly, nursing its wounds by her stream. It was huge, green, and hunched, with massive arms full of muscle and a gorilla-like posture. Its shoulders were square and strong, a hardened wall of flesh and bone. Its head was large and round with a huge gaping maw, the lower jaw sticking out slightly farther than the top, two jagged teeth pointing up over the upper lip. Its eyes, nose, and ears were tiny in comparison, perched at the top of the creature's head, almost hidden under its huge brow and the deep creases and wrinkles that snaked across its face.

What was even more remarkable, putting aside the fact that a huge green beast had just miraculously appeared from her cupboard, was what it wore. This creature was dressed very much in the fashion of an early eighteenth-century pirate captain. On its head sat a small black tricorn hat that was dwarfed by the colourful feathers sticking out of it. It wore a long, heavy red dress coat with gold lining and buttons, and a black trim. Under this were a pair of black hose, a frilled shirt, and a huge pair of black boots, studded with dull-edged metal work. It was quite an outfit, and apart from the wrapped wound on its left arm, it was smartly dressed. On top of this getup were all sorts of fascinating accessories. Stuffed in its belt were rolls of brown parchment, scribblings, and brass devices. Gold was everywhere, hanging from its neck as necklaces and stuffed on its thick fingers as chunky rings, bejewelled with sapphires and precious gems. Along with these there was a collection of weaponry. The main one Bethany had noticed was a huge slab of metal shaped like a sabre hanging from its left side. On the other side was a mean-looking axe. Finally, crossing over its chest were thick straps of leather stuffed with flintlock pistols in bizarre designs. To finish the beast's collection, there was a scattering of knives and daggers in all sorts of shapes.

Now, you might think this creature looked quite a sight. However, what looked more remarkable was Bethany. There she stood, as tall as she could (which wasn't that impressive at 5'1"), with her eyes wide open, staring unblinking, clad in a nightie and pyjamas and armed with but a flashlight. She couldn't move. Her whole body was rigid with fright and surprise, rooted to the spot like one of the great trees beside her. Her arm, though, sticking out in front of her, still held the flashlight. It was on and was sending beams of light in the direction of this unexpected beast.

Of course the creature could hardly miss her. Slowly it turned its head, still clutching its wounded arm, until its eyes met hers. For a moment, both our hero and this green stranger were motionless and silent, gazing at each other curiously. Then the beast's huge mouth opened, and words escaped:

"Well aye, hello there, young thing. What canne do fa yar?"

And with that, Bethany turned and ran back through the trees to the house. Scratched on the way by the branches, she dropped her flashlight in the bushes. Once inside, she closed the door behind her and quickly returned to the safety and security of her duvet.

Two

In the end, Bethany did manage to get a little bit of sleep, but she was awoken after not too long by her parents' uproar. Mrs Morgan had emerged from her bed, as she always did, to prepare her dear husband's breakfast of scrambled eggs on toast with a half-pint of orange juice. All of this would be laid out perfectly on his favourite tray and then taken upstairs. For her, the day began as normal. She awoke one minute before the alarm was set to go off at exactly 7.45. She hated the noise it made, and had no interest in taking the effort to study the manual so that she could change the sound. Instead, she had made it a habit to wake early to stop it before it could make any noise at all. Bleary-eyed, she put on her usual dressing gown and slippers and headed downstairs to the kitchen. It was then that she discovered something was very different in the house that morning – namely that the doors were all hanging off their hinges, the furniture was upturned, and delicate items had been damaged and destroyed. And with this began the uproar. Mrs Morgan woke her husband, who in turn began yelling and shouting at invisible culprits. These loud outbursts turned to sobs when he discovered the fate of his dear grandfather clock. Mr and Mrs Morgan were, like the timepiece, in pieces. Something had to be done, and someone had to be held responsible.

The police were brought around. From phone call to arrival, they made good time, but this did not stop either of the Morgans complaining under their breath at their sluggishness. Before long, the first officers to arrive had called for assistance and the house was full of police and detectives of all ranks. You see, there were a few problems getting to grips with what had happened. Mr Morgan blamed burglars, and his wife agreed. However, there were a number of issues with his conclusion – mainly that nothing had been stolen, but also that the amount of damage done to the house would be quite difficult to achieve by anyone of normal human size. The very fact that a thief would cause so much destruction, forget to steal anything, and then leave a trail of blood would mean that if this was a burglar, he or she wasn't very good at it. The authorities in the end blamed the crime on some kind of injured animal gaining entrance to the house. This conclusion could be correct in countries such as India, North America, or Japan, where injured elephants, bears, or robots might go on a rampage, destroy everything in a house they disliked, and then flee in disgust. But this was England, and in this country there are next to no native animals with the same destructive potential. Still, this was the idea they were committed to. As we know, however, it was not the case.

Bethany spent most of her time hiding upstairs within the walls of her room. She was a shy person at the best of times, but in front of people such as the police or decorators, she found it was best for both her and her parents if she just hid. Luckily, it wasn't long before all these visitors left and she could go about her business. She was relieved that no one had discovered last night's visitor and put him in any kind of captivity. She hadn't told anyone of his existence; no one would have believed her anyway. Still, she wanted to keep this as her special secret.

There was, however, a problem. What was to be done with this injured visitor, currently resting in the forest at the back of the garden? One option was to simply leave it there, but that wouldn't be right, she thought, as the beast needed help. The other option was, of course, to go and help it: for a start, it was able to talk, and that suggested it had sentience, maybe even intelligence and a moral compass too. After all, when the creature had discovered her, it had reacted in quite a friendly manner. It would be far more interesting to discover something utterly new than to run away and hide, something she felt rather ashamed of having done. So she decided it was best to visit the pirate at midnight and do her best to help it.

She spent the rest of the day making preparations: gathering food, drink, bedding, and medical supplies without attracting the suspicions of her parents. This was not as difficult as she had expected, as they were too distracted with the attempted burglary and grumbling about the incompetence of the police force. Before long, the day had passed, the sun had set, and the night had come with a full moon. She was anxious, almost scared, but she was excited too, and utterly committed.

And so she went out into the night again, wearing her pyjamas, dressing gown, and slippers and brandishing a new torch. On her back, she wore a rucksack full of food, drink, and supplies of all types. She had no idea what her visitor would like, so she had thought it best to take something of everything, just to be on the safe side. She was soon at her favourite stream again. There she could see the big, green beast clad in pirate gear, sat in the same place as the night before, nursing its wounds and grumbling to itself. Taking a deep breath and plucking up her courage again, she made herself known, stepping from the undergrowth with heavy steps and a deliberate rustling of leaves. The beast could not help but notice her.

"Well I never, you've returned, ain't ya?"

She took a step back cautiously, ready to bolt at the first sign of danger.

"Ah, no need to be scared, me girl. Not gonna hurt ya. Come forward, let me see you good."

She did as she was beckoned, stepping further out of the undergrowth into the light of the moon.

"There ya go! Smaller than I thought. Knew you'd be back. Bet you ain't ever seen somethin' like me before."

It chuckled, then pulled itself up with great effort. Bethany spotted another wound on its right knee – a bloody cut caused by something sharp, like a sword, which had ripped through the fabric of its trousers. For a moment the beast's eyes followed hers down towards it, and then after another awkward moment began to speak again.

"Ooooo, sorry 'bout that. Bit nasty-looking, that is. Lots of blood, not a good picture for a young thing like you."

It was clearly in pain as it struggled forward a few steps, limping as it went. She wanted to help, but her courage refused to return and she remained motionless and silent.

"You don't talk much, do ya? Well, tell me what kinda creature d'you think I am?"

Normally, Bethany would hazard a guess to such a question. She had a boundless imagination within the walls of her head. However, under such pressure, which her worrying had greatly increased, nothing of any use popped into her brain.

"I… errrr…"

"I don't mean to rush ya. Tell ya what, I'll give you a clue. I'm green, ain't I? And big —"

"An orc!" she blurted.

She had gone with perhaps one of the more common fantasy creatures, partly in desperation, and partly because she thought it might be correct.

"An orc? Now that is a right claim, that is. Kinda rude, might I say, too." The creature pulled its arms across its front.

"Oh, I'm sorry..."

Its hands were close to some of the pistols strapped to its front. Maybe it was annoyed and about to draw a weapon. Bethany backed away as fear built inside her. Her mind racing, she prepared to make a quick exit. She must have insulted the creature. Then the beast relaxed once more, breaking the tension with a hearty laugh.

"Hahahaha! I'm only messin' wit' ya! You should see ya face. Your answer there is, well, it's close. There are sum similarities. I guess in your world, orcs might be green. Come to think of it, most of dem in my world be green too... Try again?" he said encouragingly.

Bethany took another moment to think. The answer was obvious, she knew it. Problem was she couldn't find it in her head. If this was a test, she could very well fail, and then something horrible could happen, she didn't dare imagine what. A huge smile was creeping on the beast's face.

"I'm big, see, skin almost as tough as stone too. Don't stink up places like orcs, either. But I'd say you're on the right track, me li'l lady. Have anouder guess."

The beast seemed friendly. If it wanted to eat her, it was definitely taking its time. A small rush of relief started to run through her. Her wishes that her visitor would be built of some kind of wit and moral fibre were proving true. As she relaxed, the answer became all too obvious to her.

"A troll!"

The troll gave a heavy but merry skip. It seemed she was correct.

"That's right. Smart as paint you are. First thing of such ya ever seen and you know what it is after two guesses. Don't ya worry, though, I don't go round eating children, or hiding under bridges. Why'd someone live there, I must say! Though sunlight is still a problem…"

The troll in all its finery continued to mumble unintelligibly on. Now it was time for Bethany to take the lead. She felt they hadn't really been introduced, and that if she left out the formal and proper greetings, it just wouldn't be right. So, taking example from her father's many dull accounting dinners, she decided to break him out of his mumblings.

"What's your name?"

"Name?" the troll said with some surprise, trying to regain his composure and trail of thought. "Ah yes! Of course, me name. How foolish of meself for not properly introducin' me. Not everybody know me round heres."

Plucking himself up with an air of ceremony and extravagance, he prepared to properly greet our hero. He pulled off his feathered tricorn hat and, spreading his arms out to either side, bowed with a grace and pomp that contradicted his size and shape.

"Good evening, m'lady. My name is Grollp Pungdark, Troll Prince of the Darkmoot Marshes, Third Viscount of Vistalia, Earl of Dustmarch, Pirate Lord of the Seventh Quadrant and captain of the mighty ship the *Evanescence*. And, I must say, 'tis a pleasure to make your acquaintance."

Bethany giggled to herself nervously. All these words, places, and things, and not one of them made any sense to her! They were at that point just noises, but she knew that in her own world, the more names you had the more important it made you. It was probably the same in his world too. Grollp, as his name was, could not maintain his rather exaggerated bow for much longer and pulled himself up into a standing position again with a slight stumble.

"And so, what might I call you?"

She hesitated. What should she say? There weren't any fancy titles tacked onto her name. She could use her middle name, but that would hardly compare to Pirate Lord or Earl of Dustmarch, whatever that place was or that role entailed. But nevertheless, using her dressing gown to curtsey, she responded.

"Well, erm… my name is Bethany Morgan. It's really Bethany Hannah Morgan, if you include my middle name. I live here at 1½ Cordling Drive… I guess that's it really. Haven't got any fancy titles like yours, Mister, erm… Grollp Pungdark."

The troll captain chuckled to himself.

"Not to worry, young un, those sort of things don't mean nutin'. Why, where I come from, every runty Melkspawn has at least one fancy title. But you know what? It don't mean spittle, not never no. Nah, from all me travels, you know what really matters, aye? Is what's inside! And I can tell you're a good one, you are."

She was taken aback. This creature, or to be polite, Grollp, had given her quite a wonderful compliment. It wasn't something she was used to – no one really said such nice things to her, not even her parents. Most of the time, people didn't even know she existed. She blushed, fidgeted a bit, and quietly replied, "Thank you…"

"Why, jus' tellin' it like it is. See, when ya as old as me, well, you've seen a lot, done a lot too, not all of which I must say I'm happy about, but ya can tell a good 'un from a bad 'un right away. And you're right special, you are, and ya don't even know it."

She was now starting to get used to the idea of a compliment and so decided to press on. Grollp, though, was obviously exhausted. Bethany could see that his wounds were indeed taking their toll on him, sapping his energy. He slumped down again to sit against the tree. She stumbled forward in a vain effort to help him down. But it was useless – he'd have none of it, and through his own strength, he lowered himself onto the grass, letting the earth carry his immense weight. He waved her away jovially, dismissing her offer of assistance, while they continued their conversation.

"What's so special about me?"

"What is there to say… You've got your head screwed on properly. Know what's what. I guess ya kind, too. Many a creature woulda turned me in at the mere sight of me. Yeah, ya ran a mile first time, but ya came back. See, none of them uniformed fools could find me. This ain't the first time I been in your world. I know what most of your sort are like. All got their faces buried in screens, too ignorant, scared, or dull to really look and experience anything. That's why them fools couldn't find this ol' captain here. Cos their poor minds could never believe that I existed, even if they saw me mug. But in that head of yours, there's still a chance, no matter how small, that sumtin' as bizarre as me could exist in your world. And seeing that something of the sort did, you decided to help it, like any of your own kind."

"Help?"

It was true, that was exactly why she'd come to visit him that night, but so far she hadn't done anything of any real use yet. Maybe polite conversation was all a troll captain like him needed. It was likely that his adventures in piracy had led him to a life where it was rare for any creature to say anything good to him. Maybe trolls themselves were shunned in his world too. Branded as evil, secluded, and segregated into disadvantaged communities where the only alternative was crime. That would then certainly explain his move to piracy and would in turn see him shunned further as a criminal of the state, outcast by friends and relatives as a mark on their names and reputations. Maybe he'd escaped from his own world to hers in search of a better life, but whilst doing so had been injured by vengeful or hate-filled pursuers. To her, it was all such a tragic story, proving the evils of society and cruelty of mankind, or in this case trollkind.

It was then that Bethany realised there was a far simpler explanation for his remark. Grollp had spotted her bag and had probably guessed it was full of food, drink, and other helpful supplies. It could then be presumed that she had turned up in kindness to help this creature on the run.

"Oh yes! The bag..."

Grollp gave his almighty chuckle again. "Of course the bag. Got lost in your head again there. Now come on, let's see what you got in there. I'm starving, ya see!"

She passed the bag over, unzipping it as she did, offering up its contents. He took to it in a frenzy, grabbing each item from within it in quick succession. Every thing he produced seemed like a tiny morsel in his great hands, but this did not reduce his enthusiasm. She sat down next to the captain, watching intently. It was fascinating, seeing what things this creature ate and which he threw away in disgust: each time he ate anything and reacted positively, she made a little note in her head. He swallowed each sandwich in quick succession, including the clingfilm wrappings, which he ignored. The chicken drumsticks were also gobbled up quickly, bones and all. The loaves of bread were then consumed, after which he ate the sweet and dessert items, again often with their packaging intact. The fruit and cutlery, however, he gave a quick sniff and a grimace of disgust and then threw aside. The drinks she had packed were even less popular. The only one he gulped down was an old beer that had sat in the fridge for years and had belonged to her dad. She had picked it up partly on impulse and partly to get rid of the horrid thing. Grollp, however, seemed to thoroughly enjoy the brown bitter liquid, and he burped in satisfaction with such strength that the trees shook from the force.

"That was good, that was. Thanks muchlies."

He smacked his lips in satisfaction and then tried to pick hunks of food from his teeth with his thick fingers.

"I'm glad you liked it. Now I have some questions that I'd—"

She was cut off by a yawn that escaped his huge gob. It echoed off the trees, sounding like the satisfied calls of a blue whale.

"Not now. See, it's time to rest, yes."

He began to lower his hulking body slowly towards the earth, brushing away the bag. Bethany jumped up and out of the way as he collapsed on his side next to her with a great thump. He yawned again with the same intensity as before.

"But I need to know—"

"No time now. Time for rest it is."

Grollp's eyelids began to lower, a satisfied smile on his big green face. It was clear that he was quickly falling asleep, but there was still much to ask, still plenty she needed to know. It was rather infuriating really – she'd taken all this care and courage to come and assist this character, feeding him entirely at her own expense, and now he was falling asleep right in front of her without even attempting to answer any more questions.

"But... don't sleep—"

"Nope. Sleep now, talk later."

And with that, he gave one last loud yawn and fell into a deep sleep. There was nothing our hero could do. She felt lost, like the host of a party, standing in the mess after all the guests have gone home. A quick clean-up was in order, so she picked up everything that had been thrown aside, tidied it into her bag, and started to walk back to the house. Before she could get far, though, her troll visitor uttered a few last words:

"Bring more food next time and I'll tell you more."

Then he fell back to sleep to snore the night away.

Three

WHEN GROLLP PUNGDARK ASKED FOR MORE FOOD deliveries, he never expected the response he got. Our hero was the perfect host for her new friend. Using her allowance she popped to the local shops and purchased all kinds of food and drink. She'd studied her guest's tastes closely and bought a fine selection of things for him to consume. This ranged from whole chickens and joints of meat to wheels of cheese and fat pork pies. When it came to the drink however, she had to be more cunning. Carefully she pinched beers and spirits from her parents' dusty liquor cabinet – an item originally bought with much enthusiasm but only ever used to house bottles of alcohol given as presents that they disliked and were keen to forget. She'd then prepare it in the grandest way possible, spending hours reading recipes, cooking, and mixing drinks until she ended up with a variety of scrumptious items. For a day and a half, it attracted her parents' suspicion, but soon they simply passed all her excitable kitchen activity off as just another one of their peculiar daughter's obsessions. Bethany spent a small fortune in both money and hard work to satisfy her big green visitor.

Then, like clockwork, she'd go visit the captain in the forest down by her favourite stream at 2.00 a.m. exactly. It became her nightly routine for almost a month; she'd go with her bag full of supplies and see Grollp, who would promptly gobble it all up. She hardly got any sleep, but she didn't care; she was having a wonderful time and was always happy to see the captain. Grollp was also very happy to see her, and not just because of the food – Bethany was sure he liked the company too. He seemed to especially enjoy having someone to listen to his tales and adventures so intently. Not that he always told her his stories; indeed, often after being fed he'd tell her to come back the next day and fall into a deep sleep. Bethany found this a rather annoying habit, though she still loved her new bombastic friend. She found ways of tackling it too, namely getting him talking first before he'd even got close to stuffing himself to the brim, for, as she soon realised, once you got him talking it was very difficult for him to stop. In a few days, she had learnt all about him.

Her green captain came from a place called Edimor. This was not just a place as small as a city, kingdom, country, or world; no, it was a whole galaxy full of magic, monsters, wonder, and adventure. This vast collection of stars, planets, and so on was named so not for any real reason, but because Alberfungus Betswish Stunk, a goblin intellectual, had decided to start naming and cataloguing everything in known existence. He was the very first being to do so on such a vast scale, and so he was free to honour his recently deceased and much-loved pet cat Edimor by naming the galaxy after her. Where the name of his pet originated from is not known, and is just another of the great mysteries that exist in Edimor (that is the galaxy, not the cat, of course).

Edimor itself was made up of untold thousands of planets of various sizes and descriptions, both known and unknown. Some, like Golgotha and Manomora, were heavily populated, their surfaces almost entirely covered with huge cities. Others had no life on them at all and were barren wastelands of searing temperatures, boiling seas, and ice deserts, to name but a few of the extreme habitats to be found. There were paradise worlds, city worlds, factory worlds, forest worlds, worlds blighted by everlasting war, worlds of everlasting darkness, made of paper, stone, crystal, and gold, as well as those that were a mix of many types and those that were everything else in between. Of course Grollp claimed to have visited almost every single one of them and even claimed that he had a friend on each. Whether this was true Bethany did not know, though she was rather sceptical.

Edimor was also inhabited by many different races and creatures. There were those that Bethany had heard of before, through fantasy fiction and media. There were trolls, which came in many different types and subtypes – swamp trolls, mountain trolls, hill trolls, stone trolls (of which Grollp was one), and many others besides. Despite their names, they could be found on planets all across Edimor. There were also ogres, gnomes, orcs, goblins, fauns, fairies, lizardmen, werewolves, vampires, giants, and an elf or two, all names Bethany recognised from the many books she had read. A nice surprise was that these various races and creatures were in some cases rather different from what she'd been told. Orcs, for example, though green, muscular, and violent, were not necessarily evil. The reputation these creatures had as the servants of darkness had actually been created and spread by elven propaganda and their excellent PR team during one of their many wars. It had taken them a number of generations to dilute this reputation, and many peace movements had been created by orcs. However, things had taken a step backwards when the OAW (Orcs against War), whilst protesting the Demarcation War, had ended up in an extremely violent brawl with the OWYY (Orcs War Yes Yes) that saw casualties reach into the thousands. In spite of this, they made great police, dentists, and interior decorators.

The creatures Grollp enjoyed talking about the most were those that our hero had never heard of. To list but a few, there were gnobs, vulpines, rotscavs, grimps, volds, gresneks, phaggots, mulps, vicasprites, the nefarious scavii, red plimps, blue plimps, gors, rors, elegant protholtats, the deeply poisonous but adorably cute nibbs, and the enigmatic Andarins. To write about each of them in turn would be an exhausting undertaking and would be best put together in its own book. Grollp, however, spoke about them all in great depth, describing their appearance, shape, smell, colour, and temperament with a vocal energy and quality that would have put the greatest actor to shame. Bethany of course was fascinated and would curl up and listen intently, giving her new friend more food as he went on.

This vast galaxy, inhabited by these strange and wonderful creatures and filled with all types of crazy worlds, was dominated by the Alpharian Confederation. This was made up of a vast grouping of separate planets, empires, and kingdoms that promised each other mutual support. It was ruled over by the Oligarchy, a governing body of two constantly contradictory groups that ran everything from commercial prices and trade to matters of war and civil rights. This body was made up exclusively of a race called the smargs, who made the perfect politicians at both their very best and worst. They were assisted in their duty by a vast bureaucracy that owned endless libraries of documents, forms, and written procedures managed by an army of scribes, assistants, and other servants and workers. They had ruled so for thousands of years, and though they weren't a force of evil, they weren't necessarily one of good either.

The Oligarchy was housed on a planet called Goldensmorg, found in the galactic centre of Edimor. It was covered by a vast city, full of chimneys, factories, and banks, where fortunes were both made and lost, and where many careers were ripped abruptly to shreds. A massive world full to the brim with those seeking wealth and trying to make a name for themselves. The sad fact was that though the potential and opportunity were there, often a bright-eyed hopeful faltered, fell by the wayside, and generally disappeared amongst the vast crowds of inhabitants. The entire planet smelt horrible, and a layer of yellowish smog hovered in the air. Some claimed this could be seen from space, and some even went so far as to say that this was all created by the general population's stench of desperation. Grollp disliked the place and hated talking about it, and though it was a nice planet to make some quick gold, he never stayed too long.

For the troll captain, there were far more important places to be explored and adventures to be had. It was his exploits across the galaxy that Grollp enjoyed talking about most. These were Bethany's favourite stories too, and so the pair got on perfectly. You see, if you haven't already guessed, Grollp Pungdark was quite a man of the world (or troll of the galaxy). In Edimor, he was a bit of a celebrity and was much loved – or hated, depending on who you asked. One of his favourite stories was how he had recovered Grand Emperor Sentra's treasure from the bowels of a great grimwhale. This vast collection of wealth had not always been found inside a horrifically unpleasant space monster but had resided on the immensely ornate tomb world of Thar. Sentra was both ridiculously rich and hideously vain, and so to honour his own death, he had an entire planet made to house his bones and his belongings after he passed away. The planet had been constructed and his body laid there to rest upon his death, its location hidden. But his remains had not rested there for long, as the planet was swallowed whole by the grimwhale. Grollp, upon hearing this news, was rightly annoyed, for he had been searching for the treasure for ten years. Now, when such an event occurs, the average person calls it a day and goes home, but this was not the case with our brave and foolhardy troll captain. He took the helm of his ship the *Evanescence* and piloted it, much to the horror of his crew, right into the jaws of the grimwhale, which swallowed them whole. This spacefaring monstrosity was truly humungous in size, which meant Grollp had ample room to pilot his ship through the digestive tract, find the treasure, and then leave by a hole at the other end. He had done the unbelievable and had become an immensely rich, but smelly, pirate captain. Though much of his crew had retired on the earnings of the voyage, Grollp, like many pirates, was rather foolish with his gold and had spent it on the high life in the space of five years.

Grollp's adventures had also made him many enemies, and not just with the law. The crew of the *Abomination*, made up exclusively of the rat people rotscavs, were constantly prowling the sea lanes for the *Evanescence*, looking to set straight an ancient grudge. Their ship was actually the repurposed carcass of a gulpwhale, a smaller cousin of the grimwhale, and was deeply unpopular at ports due to its sheer unpleasantness and stench. The crew of the *Swordfysh* was after Grollp too, but this was merely because of a slight insult he had unintentionally made to the ship's captain by not bowing low enough. This had set the captain Lokar Felkharth the Resplendent on a blood feud that could only end with the decapitation of the troll captain.

Grollp, however, found his many predicaments all rather amusing, and thoroughly enjoyed foiling his enemies' best-laid plans. Not that he had always escaped his adventures unscathed; in fact, the ones in which he had taken a wound or two were his favourites to boast about, and these were the adventures that he told Bethany of most frequently. She knew she was meant to be impressed, but she couldn't help but worry about his well-being, for she had grown rather attached to her new friend.

In fact, it was Grollp's current wounds that concerned our hero the most. Apart from the two already mentioned, there was a deep stab wound in his lower abdomen that stained the white of his shirt a frightening blood red. She tried her best to dress and treat the areas, but he simply pushed her away. Grollp refused to acknowledge that he'd been wounded at all; it was hardly fitting for an adventurer such as he to be suffering from a weakening injury. To him, they were little more than scratches that would soon be gone, leaving marks that would expand the rich history that was etched onto his skin. But it was evident to Bethany, and would be evident to anyone that saw them, that these wounds were fatal. He visibly got weaker – he found it harder to move and stand, while his breathing got heavier and even his appetite began to disappear. Bethany tried to attend to his wounds but he'd just wave her off jovially, batting away all the fuss. He continued to tell his stories with great enthusiasm, seemingly ignoring his own frightening physical state. Sadly for our hero, her new best friend would soon be departing, leaving her, again, very much alone.

Four

THE FATEFUL DAY CAME MUCH LIKE ANY OTHER. It was a weekend, and Bethany's parents had booked a short holiday for themselves in Torquay (without their daughter, of course). On this particular day the weather was miserable.

The rain had been falling quite lazily as a light drizzle all day, the sort of rain in which you don't realise you are getting wet until you are completely soaked through. Our hero prepared herself for a long day outside and cloaked herself in a huge yellow raincoat that looked on her more akin to a tent. Bethany, being a wonderful host as always, had decided to spend most of her day keeping her visitor happy. She was armed with a pair of hefty umbrellas and flasks full to the brim with hot whisky – Grollp's favourite drink and a rather difficult habit for Bethany to satisfy. The captain was as pleased as always to receive her company and praised the quality of his drinks whilst gulping them down with reckless abandon, finishing off the first one in short order and then moving onto his second. However, he didn't appear to be his usual jovial and energetic self, and what he had to say made our hero deeply concerned.

"Now see here, lady. We've become right proper friends we have, ain't we?" Grollp's weary voice ill suited him.

Bethany knew something was bothering the troll – maybe it was his wounds. She tried to raise his spirits. "Why yes, we have, captain, sir. Think I've heard all of your adventures. I bet there's more to be told, though…"

The response was slow to come, and she stood in the drizzle with a big black umbrella in one hand and a collapsing smile on her face.

"Ain't nuthin' ya haven't yet heard, li'l lady," he said, shaking his head slowly. The rain clung to his face, pooled together, and slid down through the ridges. Bethany's smile was all but gone. Raindrops pattered on her raincoat.

"There's something I think I needs tell ya. You've been a marvellous host an' all, a right proper person you are, knew it from a pinch."

Bethany couldn't think of anything to say. She knew that something bad was coming, people only talked like this if it was. It felt colder, and she tried to hug herself warm, despite the damp. Her only response otherwise was to let him speak on.

"Now, you can probably tell I ain't in the picture of health. Got some pretty nasty wounds here. But you know what, I've 'ad worse, I 'ave. Not gonna stop me, I can tell. Remember that time when I fought the three-headed daemon on—"

"What is it?" Bethany blurted. She was getting frustrated with her visitor and his stalling. Immediately embarrassed by her outburst, she dropped her eyes sheepishly to the damp grass beneath her.

Grollp continued to say his part, though he sounded a bit taken aback. "What I'm trying to say is, yes, these injuries may seem bad, but they ain't really nothing at all. But no, that's not my point. See, it's where I got them and the manner of them that's the key. I'm a wanted troll I am, and it ain't cos of the usual stuff, it's cos of something I've taken. Something real important."

He began to pull himself up to standing, using a tree as support. His sodden coat unfurled and sagged, pulled downwards by gravity and the sheer volume of rain soaked into it. After a few pulls he was up, though it seemed for a moment that he would fall again into his sitting position, dragging the tree, broken, with him. He stood, though, if unsteadily.

"Now Edimor, it's changed, see. I know you love the sound of the place. Ya eyes light up, see, wheneva I mention it. The problem is it's all gone wrong. There's no room anymore. It's bloated, stuffed to the brim, and things are just getting worse, slowly but surely. The rich are getting richer and the poor are getting poorer. There ain't no adventures for me anymore neither, not really anyway. And there's only going to be so long before it's gonna all be sucked into this great purple hole, see."

She felt uneasy. The lines and scars that marked his body began to change, change from marks of adventure to lines of world weariness. It was clear he was exhausted, but he refused to properly accept the matter.

"It'll suck everything into oblivion. Turned up when this kid appeared. Fellas think it's all his fault, though some don't. Big arguments all over, just made it all worse. I think it is him, or her, or it, some kind of practical joke. Ain't done anything for ages, but that don't mean you should leave it. So I took it upon meself to get things sorted, got some wonderful advice about what might sort out the big ol' hole or that kid."

He then rummaged through his jacket pocket with his stubby green fingers. Bethany watched as he produced a small, slightly damp cloth and began to unwrap whatever was inside. She could make out something small and delicate within.

"I went travelling, all over I did, looking for this item, see, an item that is said to bring all our troubles to an end. Everything will be sorted. Wasn't easy to find, might I add. Seemed like everyone and anyone was trying to stop me. Like Mother Nature herself didn't want me gettin' hold of it, but I did, see. And here it is…"

He opened his hand. And there within the folds of the cloth Bethany could see a small, rather plain silver tear-shaped locket on a simple silver chain. It looked ridiculously fragile and dainty in his great hands.

"Well, it don't look like much, do it, but it's said to be full of unimaginable power. Daren't open the thing, don't know what'd happen. But it's special, see, and everyone knows it. That's why I got these scars. Sell swords, the law, and pirates too, all trying their best to rip it out of me cold, dead hands. But that ain't ever gonna happen. Nothing can stop the great Pirate Lord Grollp!"

The last words came out as a small shout that shook the branches slightly with its force. At last Bethany realised that Grollp truly believed he was untouchable, utterly invulnerable to everything that the world could throw at him and anything that would lay any other person low. His adventures, many that they were, had created a truly remarkable character with no understanding of his own mortality. It was also clear that her friend had been neglecting his wounds and, despite her best efforts, was getting weaker by the day. There was the most awkward of silences, only interrupted by the steady droplets of rain. A silence that anyone but the most stubborn of sea captains would understand. But like all silences, it had to be broken.

"Why are you showing this to me?" Bethany said in her most emotionless voice.

"Well, see, you's my mate, ain't ya? Taken good care of this old space troll. Never forget I will, never will, mark you that. Properly repay you I will, one day—"

Bethany knew that, left to his own devices, Grollp would just end up wittering again, and so it was down to her to lead the conversation.

"There's something you want to say, isn't there?"

For the first time, Grollp seemed nervous. The patter of rain counted out the seconds while the troll captain constructed his thoughts. They were both wet now, soaked through; even Bethany's waterproof could not hold back the dampness.

"See, m'lady. I've never been good with goodbyes, but I think it's time for me to go. Those beasts that are tryin' to do me in will stop at nothing to get me. They'll follow me all the way here, and Ior knows what damage they'll do if they find you wit' me. It breaks me heart, but I gotta go. Can't let 'em get hold of this either, not now, not ever. Otherwise everythin' in Edimor ain't gonna last much longer. That's why I gotta leave today, and soon. I can sense them coming, I don't know how, I jus' do. You understand, right?"

Bethany just stared right back at him while Grollp waited for a response. She didn't know what to say, or even feel. She just felt numb, her body refusing to take it all in. Refusing to accept that her best friend was soon to be leaving her.

"You won't forget me, right?"

"Forget you, m'lady? Never! You's a special friend, ya are. Bethany Hannah Morgan! Well, I ain't met none like her. I do rightly believe by the laws of dramatic effect, if they exist that is, that we were destined to meet and become as thick as thieves."

And with that, Bethany crossed the short gap between them, arms open, and gave him the strongest hug she could manage. His body was tough and wet like raw stone, but she didn't care. She needed to hug him. Perhaps for the last time, for who could know when two such beings would ever meet again, especially in a galaxy as large and exotic as Edimor. He hugged her back, enveloping her with care in his granite-like arms.

"There, there. Getting all emotional there, ain't ya. You'll see us again, ya will. When all this stuff blows over, I'll be back. Make a li'l holiday in this green here. You'll feed me again, won't ya?"

Bethany chuckled. "Always!"

He let her out of his grasp, ending their embrace, and stood looking into her eyes, a huge smile on his face.

"Good. Well, you know what, could ya get me another flask of tha' whisky? Nice and hot with a few of them spices. Like you always do. For the journey, that is. Make sure I return that flask when I come visit agains."

He laughed quietly. Bethany nodded to him, with a sad but warm smile on her face.

"There's that smile! Bursts through all the cold and wet of a day like today, it does! Anyway someone mentioned something about a bit of drink…"

Bethany chuckled to herself quietly.

"Right away, Captain!"

She made an about-turn and a quick dash back to the house and was soon in the kitchen. It was starting to get dark, and the room was cloaked in shadow. She would have turned on a light, but there was no time for such unimportant things; Grollp had to be on his way. The best she could do was to send him off with his favourite drink. She grabbed a huge saucepan from a cupboard and placed it on the stove, then turned to head into the living room's liquor cabinet and collect the rest of the whisky. Before she could move, a claw suddenly burst from the darkness and grabbed her violently by the wrist.

"Wellsss hello theresss, Bethany Morgansss. Youss been out a lotsss and longsss, you hasss."

She would have screamed if she could, but she was shocked motionless. She remained silent and turned slowly to her left, her hairs prickling upwards. There, on two feet in the gloom of the kitchen, grasping her wrist with a leathery four-fingered claw, was a figure. Standing just a bit taller than her, it was heavily cloaked, with a frightful rat face and sharp eyes with red-slitted pupils that fixed on her face, examining every line. She couldn't see much of this creature, as its black cloak hung long. What she could see was part of its face, the sinewy muscled arm that grasped at her wrist, and a long pink tail that ended with a blade, all of which was covered in patchy rotten fur and scars, most notably one that ran downwards across its left eye. She knew what this had to be – a rotscav.

"Sssshhhhh… sssshhhhhh, li'l ladysss," she said as she brought her left hand up to her face, resting her index finger mockingly against her lips. Bethany noticed that one of the rotscav's fingers was missing from the knuckle upwards. "No needsssss to make a noisssssseeee, isssss there? No screamingsss, all right. Cos if you do—"

She wrenched Bethany's arm sharply and painfully, bringing her to her knees in agony. She stifled her scream. As she looked up again at her cruel assailant, she could see that its right claw now held a dagger that was pointed straight at her, right between the eyes.

"I'll breaksss your arm, and then gutsss you like a stuffed fish!" She chuckled to herself.

"Who are you?"

The rotscav yanked her roughly towards its face, smiling as she did.

"Why! Wheressssss me mannerssss? My name'sss Scrawlsnit, former captain of the mighty vessel the *Abomination*. I isssss here to make businesss with an old friendsss of mine."

Bethany felt the creature's hot breath on her face as she spoke. Scrawlsnit still held her hard by the wrist, but slowly lowered the dagger.

"Nowsss tell me, do yousss know the whereaboutssss of a big green pirate named Grollp Pungdark? I won't runsss through all hissss silly titlesss and such. But see here, he'ss an old friend of mine, and I'm wantingsss to see him," she said in a sickly sweet, sing-song voice.

There wasn't anything Bethany could do – but she could never betray her friend. She would just stay quiet. And so for a few short moments, in the dark of the kitchen, Bethany stayed absolutely silent whilst the terrifying creature grasped her. The silence, of course, was soon broken.

"Oh, there'sssss no point in keeping hussshed, I knowsss he'sss here. I knowsss he'sss out theresss, lyingsss by a tree wounded, waiting for you to return with dem vittelssss. Am I right?"

Bethany stayed silent. Pain shot up her arm as Scrawlsnit tightened her grasp. She brought her face closer to Bethany's, staring deeply into her eyes, transfixing her in her gaze.

"I knowsss I'm right!"

Then, with a twist, she wrenched Bethany's arm, bringing her down to the floor again. Bethany stifled another scream, a bit of noise piercing the air around them. Tears began to form in the corners of her eyes, and her heart began to race. Her breath started to come in short, panicked gasps.

"Let'sss go see himsss, shall we?"

With that, Scrawlsnit tugged at Bethany's arm again and pulled her outside, dragging her roughly through the garden. The rain was now far heavier; it splashed down on her yellow raincoat and drenched her hair in a second. Lightning flashed, and thunder rumbled not long after. Bethany noticed the weather only dimly, for there were far more pressing matters at hand. Before long they had crossed the patio and the garden and were entering the forest at the end of it, getting closer and closer to Grollp's location. The rotscav knew exactly where her target was.

It was not long before they were in sight of the troll captain, though he hadn't noticed them yet, as he was still busy collecting together his belongings. Scrawlsnit's delight was evident as she painted her face with a huge sinister smile, turning back to Bethany with a look of murderous glee on her rat face.

"He ain't seen usss. Now, no screamingsssss from yousss, or I'll runsss you right through."

It hadn't occurred to Bethany to scream – in fact, she had no idea how to do so in such a situation.

"Let'sss play a little game, ssshall we? I want you to ssstep out there where you can be ssseen and sssay, 'Here'sss a friend for you, Grollp.'"

Bethany had no choice but to agree. She had to do something, maybe make some sign that something was amiss, a hint as to what was really going on. It soon became difficult to think, though, as she felt the dagger lightly pressing against her lower back. Scrawlsnit kept one claw firmly on her shoulder and guided her through the undergrowth and into the open. Grollp turned and saw Bethany immediately, a big warm smile appearing on his face.

"Well, hello again. You've been a while, ain't ya? This weather's a right pain."

At first she couldn't say anything – she could hardly breathe. She stuttered and shivered a bit. Grollp, starting to realise something was wrong, began to move forward as best he could. Scrawlsnit, growing impatient, pushed the dagger slightly harder into Bethany's back, and the claw on her shoulder tightened uncomfortably.

"Is something wrong, m'lady?"

Still she couldn't summon the words. The dagger pressed harder than ever; a spot of blood trickled down her back. The rat's breath grew heavier on her shoulders, but still she struggled to speak. Grollp drew closer, a hand reaching for a pistol.

"Here's a friend for you, Grollp!" she declared, nervously, her voice cracking.

The troll captain looked confused. Bethany felt the pressure on her back reduce and the grip on her shoulder loosen.

"Hello there, Grollp. It'sss me!"

For a moment, all was still. Then lightning crashed and Bethany was pushed to the side as all hell broke loose. Grollp drew one of his pistols, but Scrawlsnit was quicker, leaping up and landing on a branch with catlike reflexes. The troll captain aimed and fired his pistol. A bright green blast shot through the air, evaporating the rain as it went. It smashed into the tree branch, ripping it into splinters, but Scrawlsnit had leapt out the way with ease. She charged towards Grollp, a dagger in each hand. Bethany watched as Scrawlsnit rushed past the Captain, who struggled to keep track of her. A split second later the rotscav slashed at his left leg. Despite his tough skin, Bethany saw the blades break through his flesh. He groaned in pain, collapsing onto one knee, all the while aiming his next shot. Bethany pulled herself up and watched in terror.

"Stay back!"

She stayed in her spot. Grollp fired again, ripping apart another tree with a flash. Another miss. Scrawlsnit leapt to the right and returned fire with throwing daggers. He dodged one, but the other two landed in his chest, ripping through his coat. He groaned in pain again, weaker this time. He wobbled, barely able to stand, but drew his blade regardless. Scrawlsnit cackled.

"What'sss thissss? Had enough already? You are ssslow, you are. And patheticsss."

The rotscav fiend approached the captain confidently. Grollp raised himself and swung his huge sword towards her. Bethany looked hopefully on but was disappointed. He had missed, but only just. A chunk was ripped from Scrawlsnit's cloak, revealing the patched rags and leather armour underneath. He swung a second time, and yet again the rotscav just managed to dodge the blow. But Grollp was gaining some momentum, swinging with a satisfied grunt. This time, Scrawlsnit was nicked across the upper left arm, a new scar for her collection. Grollp went for another swing, missed, but broke a nearby tree in two. Thunder cracked.

It went calm again. Grollp looked around, breathing heavily. It was quiet but for the heavy patter of rain. Steam rose from the damaged trees and he seemed lost as he turned this way and that, desperately searching for his enemy. Bethany felt herself doing the same, her heart pounding with cold, fear, and worry for her friend. He was injured, and even worse than before. She wanted to approach the captain to treat his wounds, but before she could take a step, a bright blue blast burst from the undergrowth. It slammed into Grollp, sending him flying and driving him into the ground. His coat was charred and steam rose from his burnt skin. Fear turned into terror, as her friend lay squirming in agony. Her body went numb, and all she could do was watch on. He was still alive, but only just.

Scrawlsnit appeared, striding confidently through the undergrowth, and Bethany watched as she threw her pistol away. She then drew two long blades from underneath her cloak, brandishing them in her hands. She approached Grollp, who lay helplessly writhing and groaning.

"Hehehehahararar, you almosssst got me there. But I was alwaysss gonna win. Now it'sss time to finisssh the job I sssstarted..."

She stepped up onto the captain's stomach and then onto his chest. The blades twitched in her hands. Lightning flashed again.

"Gonna finisssh yousss quickly. Nice likesss that I am. Then I'm gonna grab your new friend theresss and kill her ssslow. Proper sssslow. Rip her apartsss limb from limb. Like you knowsss I can. Keep her alive long enough that ssshe startssss pleadingsss to die. But then I'm jussst gonna keep going and going—"

Grollp let out a huge roar and surged to his feet, grasping Scrawlsnit's tail in his hands. A look of terror splashed onto the rotscav's face. Using his immense strength, he began to swing his smaller opponent by her tail, smashing her into the ground repeatedly. He kept swinging, reducing the rotscav to a bloody mangled bag of broken bone and flesh. Grollp smashed her into tree, earth, and rock alike, not stopping even after it was clear she was dead. Bethany screamed in terror, begging him to stop – it was horrific. Grollp could not hear her as he roared triumphantly, using every last bit of air in his lungs. Then, as if finally hearing his friend's screams – he stopped, dropping the mangled corpse at his feet, and everything was still.

The thunder roared as if in echo.

Quiet returned but for the continuous patter of rain. Bethany could do nothing but stare in utter terror. She'd never seen this part of him before. His full destructive power was obvious – he could easily crush her like a bug. He stared back, murderous ferocity still blazing in his eyes. But then he saw her properly once again and it all ebbed away, a smile returning to his face. His jolly manner bubbled up despite his clear exhaustion.

"Got her I did. No need to be 'fraid, lady, 'tis all over now. Really showed her I did. Better head off now. Should rest first, though, mind. Only a few scratches, but she's left me right tired. Hahahahaha! Didn't I tell ya! Nothing can stop me. Nothing at all! I'm Grollp Pungdark, greatest pirate lord ever to exist!"

With a crash, he collapsed on his front, smashing into the ground with a loud thud. The rain kept falling, and Grollp Pungdark was dead.

Five

OUR HERO BETHANY DID NOT VENTURE BACK out into her favourite little forest for quite some time. She was shocked to say the least, spending most of her time in her room with her thoughts. Anyone who really knew her would have been able to tell that she was behaving erratically, getting frustrated by minor things like the sugar getting stuck to her teaspoon or the repetitive colourings of the local butterflies. However, as she did not really have any close friends, no one noticed anything. Even her parents noticed little; to them, she had always been an eccentric girl, so they left her alone to her thoughts. Even her imaginary friends provided scant help for her state of unrest.

She did not do much but think over the following week. At first she thought of going back outside, to her favourite spot, where Grollp liked to sit. Where he sat every evening waiting to greet her with that huge smile on his face and a story to tell. Maybe that stormy night had all been a nightmarish dream. What if he was still there waiting, wondering what had happened to Bethany Morgan and the refreshments she always brought? But she decided against it. The events of that night had felt all too real. Images of the fight stayed with her: the mangled corpse of Scrawlsnit, the charred trees, and her best friend lying flat on his face, dead. It felt real, but at the same time it didn't. Perhaps this character Grollp was just another friend she'd conjured up in her mind; perhaps the entire experience was just her doing what she always did, living in her imagination and forgetting what was really going on around her. For a few days she did in fact believe this, that none of it, not Grollp, not Scrawlsnit the rotscav or Edimor, existed at all. It could very well have been the case, except for one little thing: the locket. She didn't know what she had been thinking, the moment had passed by so quickly, but she had decided to take it. Reaching into his huge pockets, she had grabbed the wrap of fabric which held it and taken it back with her into her house at full speed, hoping maybe to hide it from those whom Grollp had mentioned in hushed tones. She'd locked it away in the top drawer of her bedside table, where she hoped it could not be found.

Eventually she did venture back into the garden to head to the little stream in the forest where Grollp had always sat. It was a warm day, and the sun was out. The grass was especially green and healthy, with a gentle breeze blowing in the air. It was the perfect day to meet old friends, so she dressed up in her best flowery dress, tidied her hair as much as she could, and wore her favourite sandals. On her back she carried her usual backpack, full to the brim with Grollp's favourite foods and flasks of whisky. In a small front pocket sat the locket, freshly cleaned and wrapped in a new velvety cloth. To her parents she was a peculiar sight, but they, as they usually did, thought little of it and got back to their daily business.

With a nervous energy, she bounded out into the fresh early-afternoon spring air. Butterflies danced whilst the birds sang their happiest tunes. She made her journey in quick time, pushing through branches until she reached her favourite spot. But it was disappointment that greeted her. Grollp was nowhere to be seen. In fact, there was no evidence there of his presence, or the events of that night. A few trees lay broken apart in several pieces, but the corpses of her friend and his cruel attacker were no longer there. In their place were two large rocks and a new thorny bush. It was then that she came to the decision that nothing had ever happened. It had purely been a flight of fancy to keep herself occupied, and there was in fact no Grollp, no Scrawlsnit, and no Edimor. Heavy with disappointment, she made her way back to the house, her backpack still full of food and drink.

It may seem that our story ends here. That all this time, the troll captain and his rat-like nemesis were just creations of a lonely girl's mind. However, the truth was that this was not the case, whether Bethany realised it or not. It would only be a week before our hero was greeted again by two interesting strangers.

The first rather unexpectedly came during the middle of the night from the very place Grollp had emerged: Bethany's cupboard. She was wearing her favourite dinosaur pyjamas when she was woken by a new, rather short visitor as it pushed through the door. As she opened her eyes, she saw right before her a little green creature who was smartly dressed. Bethany recognised what it was in an instant, remembering Grollp's stories: it was a goblin. This was first evident by its green, mucus-like complexion and its height of four foot five. Its face was rather lumpy, with two smallish, sharp yellow eyes which sat either side of its long pointy nose. Just underneath this was a large, toothy mouth, which curled in a business-like frown. This was a peculiar enough creature standing just beyond the end of her bed, but what it was wearing was even more surprising. The goblin was dressed in the finest suit gold could buy. It wore a long black tailcoat, under which was a fine silken grey waistcoat embroidered with an immensely intricate pattern. Beneath that, it wore a dress shirt with fine gold buttons, topped with a black bowtie. A red cummerbund was wrapped around its bulbous protruding belly, while its smart black suit trousers hugged its spindly legs. To finish it all off, a small black bowler hat sat on its head, a shiny brown cane was tucked under its left arm, and two huge black dress shoes covered its feet. This was indeed a goblin, and a very proper one at that, for as Grollp had told her, goblins had long since given up on a career of mischief and villainy and had settled for lives in big business and politics, which some say are far more evil occupations.

Bethany was surprised by its sudden appearance, but she wasn't the only one to feel that way. The smartly dressed green creature too had a look of shock, disbelief, and embarrassment across its face, an expression that hinted it was expecting someone else. Unfazed, however, it seemed to come to a decision to begin formalities. Clearing its throat with a sharp cough, it removed its hat and bowed in her direction.

"Good evening, mademoiselle…" The goblin spoke in an odd, high-pitched voice with an accent that sounded ever so slightly French. "I do not mean to disturb you from your rest, but I am here on an errand of an urgent nature."

Bethany sat up in her bed, the covers reaching to her waist and hiding her legs. She quickly forgot that she had been disturbed from her sleep and was wide awake staring at her visitor. But unlike the smartly dressed goblin at the foot of her bed, she had forgotten her manners.

"You're a goblin, right?"

While this was indeed true, as the green visitor rose from its bow quickly and looking slightly shocked, it retched a bit in disgust. Putting its bowler hat back on, the goblin stood rather rigid with annoyance.

"Why yes, I am, but I don't think that's all quite relevant, do you? Now, I am here in great urgency, and—"

"Who are you? You must have a name?"

Bethany could barely hold in her excitement. Here was a new and wonderful creature, probably from somewhere in Edimor. What made it even more wonderful was that this pompous little creature was exactly how she had pictured a goblin would be when Grollp described one to her. She needed to know more, even at this hour of the morning.

This interruption flustered the creature again, and it searched for words, looking embarrassed somewhat at its own behaviour. Its eyes darted all around the room, avoiding hers, as it took its hat from its head again and held it to its chest.

"Please forgive me. I should not have been so brutish and forward in my manner. Will you accept my deepest and most heartfelt apology?"

After searching the entire room, its eyes landed on her face, awaiting forgiveness. Bethany didn't know what to say, for she had little clue as to why the creature was so flustered. This pause seemed excruciating for the goblin, and it nervously fidgeted on the spot. You see, for these green creatures, manners were everything. After choosing as a species to change their working speciality, many of their priorities also changed, amongst which was the subject of proper manners and etiquette. The world of banking, finance, and law is full of villainy, backstabbing, and general selfishness, as well as all-round unpleasantness. All in a purely legal manner, of course. It is far easier to get away with such things if you are polite, for as it is well known, good manners are everything. So as a species, they had decided to perfect this into a finely crafted and manipulative art of gestures and words.

In the moment, however, Bethany forgot all of what Grollp had told her, and so she lost her opportunity to really wind up this snivelling little creature, choosing instead to use her own good manners. Putting on a posh little voice, she responded, "Why, of course you are forgiven, good sir."

Realising how ridiculous she sounded, she stopped. The goblin, though, responded quite well to it, taking it as a cue, and continued on with the formalities.

"Ah, very well. Thank you, mademoiselle. Let me properly introduce myself." The goblin again performed its grand bow towards her. "My name is Monsieur Obglarp Denepom XVII. Count of Bullen Marsh and Grand Lord Exchequer of the Yellow Moon Bank."

Bethany couldn't help but giggle to herself. I say to herself, but a goblin's ears are very keen, and so Monsieur Denepom picked it up quite easily. Irritated, he waited for a response, trying to peer up at her whilst holding his bow. Bethany took her time, pushing the covers aside and climbing out of bed. When she had reached exactly the right spot, she responded with her own bow, imitating as best she could the goblin's own.

"And my name is Mistress Bethany Hannah Morgan, first of her name, erm… Daughter of a Round Stuffy Man and errrmmm… ah yes, Countess of Mouldy Cheese and Pickles!"

She laughed loudly, rising from her bow, enjoying her own jokes. Denepom, however, did not. Rising as well, he placed his bowler hat back on his head, a large, indignant frown upon his face.

"Enough of this tomfoolery!" he said in his sternest, and squeakiest, voice. Bethany couldn't help herself and laughed more, tears forming in the corners of her eyes. Denepom grew more impatient, his manners straining to their limit.

"It is on a matter of great urgency that I am here. If you would please stop fooling around! Edimor and, heaven forbid, her whole financial sector are on the cusp of utter annihilation!" He was getting louder and more agitated. Maybe it was time to stop laughing and listen. Bethany's ears had prickled at the mention of Edimor.

"Go on... I mean, please continue, good Monseur Denepom."

Nodding his head in satisfaction, he continued. "Thank you, good Countess of Mouldy Cheese and Pickles..."

Bethany kept her giggles as quiet as she could.

"It seems that things in Edimor have taken a turn for the worse. There is this hole, you see, right out in the centre of our galaxy, ready to consume everything. That is why I am here on such urgent business."

She thought of Grollp and everything he had told her. Of his warnings and stories. About the polite villainy of goblins, the stagnation and crumbling of Edimor, of purple holes and sinister figures. And then she thought of the locket, which at that very moment was locked away in the top drawer of her bedside table. She thought of going over and retrieving it, but then her goblinoid visitor continued on.

"Yes, very urgent. That is why I must demand that you take me to Mr Frederick Holland at once!"

The name meant nothing to her; indeed, she knew of no one who owned it. Despite that being no fault of hers, she apologised. "I'm sorry, I don't know anyone called Frederick Holland."

The goblin's brow furrowed, and he frowned again. He looked from side to side, not making eye contact, and stroked his chin. He was clearly very disgruntled. After a brief moment, he addressed Bethany again.

"This is 1½ Cordling Drive, is it not?"

Bethany diligently replied, "Why yes, it is, but—"

"Well then, take me to Mr Frederick Holland!"

"There's no one here with that name. I'm sorry, but—"

He reached into his inside jacket pocket and pulled out a small wax-sealed envelope. On it, written in ink and in the fanciest handwriting imaginable, was the name Frederick Holland.

"I have a letter here with the name Frederick Holland on it. It is also addressed to 1½ Cordling Drive. Normally such an errand wouldn't warrant my participation; however, it is a matter of great urgency that I deliver this letter in person, to a Mr Frederick Holland. So please, answer my questions with the utmost honesty and truthfulness. Will you promise to do just that for me?"

It was clear that this was incredibly important to the goblin.

"I will, I promise." She nodded firmly.

"Good. Now please, mademoiselle, tell me, is this location that we currently stand in 1½ Cordling Drive?"

"Why yes, it is."

The goblin nodded to himself. "Well then, as this is said locale, please will you take me to Mr Frederick Holland. I have an urgent letter here that I must deliver to him in person."

Bethany wasn't sure how to proceed; they were simply going around in circles. They were indeed at 1½ Cordling Drive, she knew that for certain, but as for a Mr Frederick Holland, she did not know how she could help this goblin gentleman find him.

"I'm sorry, there is no one with that name here. There's me, my mother, and my father, but no one—"

He waved his other hand at her face to silence her and then put the letter back into the inside pocket. "That is of no import. I see some kind of mistake has been made. It shall be rectified in due course." He straightened up his jacket, smacking his lips and looking sheepishly around the room again. "I won't waste any more of your time. Good evening."

With that, he tipped his hat in Bethany's direction and swivelled on the spot to face the cupboard door. He then dragged a nail in a pattern across the wood, opened it, stepped inside, and closed it behind him. Bethany gave him a moment to leave – whatever that involved – and then made to follow. But when she opened the cupboard door, there was no one to be seen, let alone a short green banker.

This brief visit had left Bethany all abuzz with excitement – she felt alive once again. She missed Grollp yes, but things were happening now. But what to do with this new energy?

The next few days saw nothing exciting and no other visitors, which just made her ever more restless. Most nights, she slept on the floor right in front of the cupboard, getting barely a wink of rest. This was broken up with thorough investigations behind the door, searching for some kind of entrance or trap door hidden amongst the clutter. Sometimes she even called out, shouting, hoping for someone, anyone, to respond. But there was no response, and her searches yielded nothing remarkable about the inside of her cupboard. Her parents of course thought she was mad, but made no effort to intervene; surely this was simply another of her hobbies and would soon pass. So for a week and a half, Bethany's adventures were on hold, as no other interesting characters came to call.

Her next visitor was even smaller and came not from the cupboard but from a window.

It was on another beautiful spring afternoon that our next character met our hero. The sun was out, and a cool breeze was blowing. It was so nice that Bethany had decided to leave the window open so the air could circle the room. On this Sunday afternoon, Bethany had resigned herself to sitting in front of the cupboard door and waiting in slim blue jeans and a loose pink t-shirt. Most people would have given up after a few hours, but not our hero. She did get incredibly bored, though, so she spent the time singing through the soundtrack of the *Rocky Horror Picture Show* while she waited.

She was just finishing her eighteenth rendition of "Time Warp" when her new visitor flew through the window. He was a very small thing, looking much like a stick insect but with wings and a tiny leather satchel under one of its front limbs. This little creature was rather enjoying her singing. He flew into the room, landed lightly on her left shoulder, and as she finished her song, finally piped up.

"What a luvely singin' voice!" he squeaked.

Bethany almost jumped out of her skin. But caught herself, though, as she had started to grow comfortable with all these interesting new visitors. The stick-insect creature sat quite comfortably where it was.

"Oh, hello there! Thank you very much, by the way."

She looked at the creature resting on her shoulder, where it stood nodding its little head in satisfaction.

"Right luvely voice, I mus' say. And it's a right luvely pleasure to meet you, me dear. My name is Knit."

He extended a limb as if to offer a handshake. Bethany took it and shook carefully.

"A pleasure to meet you too, Knit. My name is Bethany, Bethany Hannah Morgan."

He nodded again, quite happily. "Ooooooo, that's a lovely li'l name, that is. Now tell me, why have you been sat inside on this very spot doing nothing, when you should be outside in this luvely weather?"

Bethany blushed, turning away to avoid what she thought were his eyes. "I guess you're right. I've been waiting for someone."

Knit looked from side to side, perhaps for anyone else that could be there in the room. "Who?" he squeaked.

"Oh… I don't know. Someone, anyone. A lot of funny things have been happening around here lately. All kinds of people and creatures have been coming through that cupboard door. Just kinda waiting for the next someone or something to arrive."

He turned to the door and then looked back. "I wouldn't expect many to come through there. Ain't a very busy wizard's door, that. Only really ever li'l me comes through there, and that's only to come here and have a little rest on the trees by that nice li'l stream outside."

She turned back to him, her eyes wide and full of energy again. "A wizard's door?!"

"Of course, a wizard's door. It can take you to lots of places all across Edimor. Not all of them, mind. There's still many places locked away and hidden."

"You come from Edimor?"

He nodded his little head. "Why yes, of course. Well, I come from Greendale really. Luvely li'l green planet, full of trees. Away from all the bustle. It's all funny there at the moment. Lots of people getting all angry and frustrated about all this nonsense."

"Oh, I do want to go there. How do I use this wizard's door to get there?"

"All you 'ave to do is write the name of the place you want to go on the door with your finger, and go straight in—"

Bethany stood up quickly in excitement. Knit leapt up from her shoulder, his little wings flittering.

"Oh, I would really like to go there!"

Knit flew back into eyeshot in front of her, coming close so that she could see and hear him clearly.

"Tell you what, I'll take you!" he squeaked. "You can come round for tea. Meet the missus. She makes a luvely cheese casserole, she does. Live in the luveliest tree on Greendale. You could meet my son, he's training up to be a doctor, see. A right catch he is."

She nodded in affirmation. "Yes, that sounds wonderful."

"Right, well, gather your stuff and we'll be off. Just got to pop out and grab me book. See ya in a bit!" he squeaked as he flew towards the open window.

"See you in a bit!" Bethany replied.

With that, Knit was gone. Bethany did as she was told, grabbing a bag and beginning to gather up her things. She then proceeded to pull a big purple hoodie over her head and put her rainbow flats on. Finally, she grabbed the locket from the top drawer of her bedside table and placed it in the outer pocket of her rucksack. Then she stood, waiting.

The problem was that Bethany had just about had enough of waiting that day. Her curiosity was taking over, edging her closer to a rash decision. So impatiently, she walked up to the cupboard door, intending to go in. The next problem was that she had no intention of visiting Greendale, or not yet, anyway. She was far more interested in visiting Goldensmorg first. So quickly she wrote it out as well as she could on the cupboard door and stepped right in.

Six

TRAVELLING BY WIZARD'S DOOR IS UNLIKE ANY other experience you might encounter. Many expect the process to be as simple as walking through a door into another room, with the proviso that the new room is actually in an entirely different location. The whole experience, they think, must be quite relaxing; with one step, you go from a warm living room or bedroom to an enchanted snow-covered forest, where you are greeted by a local faun who is naked save for a little red scarf. It is expected to be quick, painless, and in no way stomach churning or distressing. In reality, this is not the case.

The door is an incredibly powerful enchanted item, flowing with magical energy. Once activated, the area around you will go utterly black as the device dematerialises its contents, transforming it into tiny bits of living matter. These are then thrown at ridiculous speed through time, dimensions, and space to the location which has been pre-ordained as the drop-off point, either through the choice of its creator or its user. During this process, any living thing using the door feels an unnatural sensation of travelling impossibly fast. This is accompanied by a disorientating pure white light and an unnerving hissing. When the user has reached the destination, the light and sound subside as the items being transported are put back together piece by piece. Then, once fully constructed, whatever undertook the journey can continue on with its regular existence.

This whole process may appear dangerous, life threatening, even suicidal. In fact, in the early days of its creation, this was the case; the items and people transported would sometimes reappear as a congealed mess of matter, or if they were more lucky, not reappear at all. But over the years, this mode of transportation has been completely refined and has become a thoroughly safe mode of travelling from point A to point B. Theorists believe that it is indeed the safest; for even though the traveller's form is completely broken up, dismantled, and in some ways destroyed, the whole process and reconstruction occurs so quickly that the body of the user doesn't even realise what has happened, and so cannot act accordingly and die. However, even though on a purely biological level the process happens extraordinarily quickly, at the psychological level it takes much longer, roughly five minutes. For those used to travelling in such a manner, this is all but a mild irritation. But for first-time users, the whole experience is extremely distressing and stomach churning.

As you can guess, this was the case for Bethany. At first, everything went pitch black, and it quickly felt like she didn't exist anymore. This changed quite suddenly to a startlingly bright white light, an uncomfortable hissing sound, and the feeling that she was on the world's fastest rollercoaster. After about a millisecond in real time, which felt like an hour, she started to slow down, regained a sense of being, and then stopped. All the discomforting sensations faded as she rematerialised in a new location, left with an incredibly uncomfortable queasiness in her stomach. In actuality, she had made the journey from 1½ Cordling Drive to Goldensmorg. So to honour such a significant occasion, she proceeded to release the contents of her stomach all over the floor in front of her.

Seven

UNFORTUNATELY FOR BETHANY, AFTER disgorging the contents of her stomach, she discovered she was not in the location that she desired to be in. She was on Goldensmorg, true, but it was a very dark and horrendously smelly part of it. Instead of the tall buildings, narrow streets, and hectic bustle of an overcrowded city, she found herself in the darkness of what she suspected was its sewers. She was right – not that her correct answer could improve her mood.

Nonetheless, the place was magnificent in its own right. The sewer system itself had been constructed from the huge labyrinth of tunnels and caves that had always stretched and twisted underneath the city. After they had done centuries of service as catacombs, Greevus Gotsnarch (another wealthy and eccentric goblin personality) had decided it was best to repurpose them as the grandest and most ornate sewer system in Edimor. Using his great talent and immense wealth, he saw to it that the rough granite caves and tunnels were carved away and replaced with endless smooth concrete passageways and canals that stretched deep into the planet. These were improved with locks, bridges, and gateways through which the amassed filth of Goldensmorg could be managed by a dedicated team of workers. It was dark – very dark indeed – but not pitch black, much to Bethany's relief. The ingenious Gotsnarch had introduced the fluorescent blue Gumbon slugs. Fed on the fumes of rotting and decaying filth and refuse, they naturally glowed, providing the hapless sewer workers enough visibility to operate. The fact that the sewers were almost always full meant that the slugs were very rarely hungry.

As impressive as her surroundings were, Bethany took little interest in them. This was partly because of the smell, but also because she hadn't the faintest idea where she really was. Wherever this place was, it was not the place she wanted to be. She came to the conclusion that if she were in fact lost deep underground in a city's sewer system, the only thing she could really do was go up. So after recovering from her initial sickness, she took a few large gulps of water from the bottle she had brought with her and latched her right hand over her nose in an attempt to block out the smell.

Looking both directions into the semi-illuminated darkness, she could see she was in the middle of a straight stretch on one side of a sewage canal. This meant that there were only two viable routes to take, unless she wanted to swim to the other side, which she knew was not a good idea. With but two options, the chance that she'd pick the right route was pretty good. There were far more of the fluorescent slugs to the left, and so it was far brighter. The brighter the route, Bethany thought, the less threatening it looked, and the more likely that the light led to an exit. So, she turned to her left and marched off along the path.

She continued on into the semi-darkness of the sewer tunnels for hours. First she took to her journey with a degree of confidence, striding quickly forwards along her path. She was starting to get accustomed to both the darkness and the smell, and began to sing showtunes to herself as she went. This did, for a time, alleviate the monotony of her journey. She was lost, that she knew, but at least she was doing something to resolve the problem, and there was no point moping over her predicament anyway. The slugs continued to appear at regular intervals. At some points she would find them in huge clusters. This at first she took to be a good sign. However, she quickly realised that these gatherings of slugs meant that instead of an exit, she would find a particularly rancid and noxious section of sewage.

Still, she continued marching on, her legs growing tired, her confidence fading, and her showtunes taking a sad air. At some points she would come to a bend, a junction, or a fork in her route. These at first both interested and beguiled her; the choices she had to make at such junctures were of the utmost importance to her adventure. But soon, much like with the slugs, she was met with disappointment, as whichever route she picked meant the same old routine, more trundling along endless tunnels. Not that it was all the same; indeed, she was quite surprised by the art plastered on the walls. Despite some faded colouring, it was clear that these were fantastically crafted pieces that were drawn, painted, and otherwise made by very skilled artists. These ranged from vast landscape pieces to portraits of prominent individuals, none of whom were human. Gotsnarch himself appeared frequently, sometimes as portraits or marble busts, or within great pastoral scenes, relaxing. Apart from the famous goblin himself, the majority were short comic strips about comical defecation. Even in a completely different galaxy, with an utterly alien culture, history, and identity, it was clear to Bethany that the denizens of Edimor, or at least Goldensmorg, appreciated the crudeness of toilet humour.

Despite the vast collection of artwork and scatological comics she encountered, after another hour of trudging along concrete gangways through the endless sewer tunnels, she began to feel tired and rather discouraged. Gone was her early, slightly queasy enthusiasm to escape. Gone too were her showtunes. Instead, she made little noise but for the dragging of her feet and the panting of exhaustion. Everything looked the same and the tunnels just went on forever, with little change and no hint of an exit. So in the middle of a hexagonal sewer chamber which branched off into a series of tunnels, she slumped down one of the walls and sat exhausted, trying not to fall asleep. It was time for a rest, so she took her flask and some snacks from her bag and began to consume them. Looking lazily around the chamber, she searched in vain for anything new, an exit or even something interesting that would perhaps fill her with some sort of hope, imbue her with the energy that would help her continue her journey. But it was identical to five other chambers she had already passed through. Thankfully the smell was weaker here, but this did little to lift her spirits. Indeed, there was nothing she felt she could do that would be able to stir her into action. Instead, she stayed slumped against the wall with her legs aching, taking occasional bites of her snacks. She needed to sleep, just for a bit at least.

Before she could close her eyes she was hit by a sudden noise. It was a quiet one, but still she sat bolt upright, hoping to find its source. It was entirely different to anything she'd heard for the past couple of hours. There were footsteps, from another living thing. They were coming from the tunnel to her left, which was particularly dark, almost devoid of the slugs.

But soon enough it got louder, the thud of pounding feet echoing down the tunnel. Something was heading her way, and it was unlikely to be human. From the sound, it seemed to be running, too. This noise was all that was needed to rouse her from her exhausted slump, and she jumped to her feet, ready to meet this new character. Her heart thumped and a lump formed at the back of her throat as the sound of running got closer and closer. She could hear the heavy panting of breath, the sort that hinted exertion and distress. Her bag still rested on the floor, its contents scattered around in a mess, but Bethany took little heed of it. All she could focus on was the sound of running and panting, and the imminent arrival of this new being from the gloom.

And appear it did. When it seemed like the footsteps could not get closer or be any clearer, a creature appeared from the darkness. It was short, even shorter than Bethany, about four foot five inches. The first thing that caught Bethany's eye was that its dark brown skin appeared to have a wood-like texture. In the middle of its large head was a short trunk that drooped over its wide mouth, above which it had two big, jittery black eyes with stubby eyelashes. What it had for hair, which seemed to have a green, leafy quality, sat messily on its head, on top of which rested a long, green felt cap that drooped down behind its back with a little orange bobble on the end that bounced with every hurried step. Its body was tiny, hidden under a neat green tunic with a thin rope cord tied around its podgy belly. Sticking out of this torso were a pair of stubby arms and four-fingered hands, with fingerless gloves. It also possessed two stubby legs, dressed in light yellow trousers and finished off with reddish-brown boots, each with a metallic grey buckle attached to it. The creature ran in panic through the tunnel from some unknown assailant, all the while holding the side of its hat with its right hand so that it wouldn't fly off during its desperate flight. Bethany took it all in with wide eyes and fascination, so much so that the creature ran straight past her, paying her little attention and almost getting completely out of sight before she made any attempt to move, let alone introduce herself properly.

It had almost disappeared into the darkness down the tunnel to her right before Bethany finally gave chase. Breaking into a run, her body bursting with energy, she made her pursuit. Her exhaustion weighed her down, but a burst of adrenaline hurtled her forward. She had to know who this creature was. Luckily for her, its stubby legs meant it was unable to move particularly fast, and she began to catch up with it. It was leading her along a route she was confident she hadn't ventured through before, for the tunnel seemed to be going uphill. Though it was hard work, it filled her with hope that maybe this creature was leading her to the exit. However, it was also running in panic and fear, and she dreaded to think of what terrifying thing was perhaps in pursuit of both of them now. As she ran, she noticed the slugs started to become few and far between. The stench of sewage began to subside too, though the tunnels progressively grew darker and darker and she could hardly see in front of her. She was gaining on the creature, though, and that was what was most important. When she was close enough, she tried to talk to it.

"Hey!" she shouted in between breathy pants.

The little stubby creature continued running, but turned its bulbous head over one shoulder. With a look of abject fear on its face, it gave a high-pitched squeal, turned its head back, and began to speed up. Bethany kept running, but just as she was about to reach the little creature, she tripped and stumbled forward onto her front with a painful thud. This was all it needed to escape her; turning a corner, it quickly disappeared from sight. Bethany pulled herself up in an instant. She ached all over, the slabbed floor taking a toll on her body. She was only a bit bruised, but it was enough to destroy her momentum. Frustrated, she grumbled to herself, her body coursing with a fury she could barely contain. Why was this happening to her? Why had she fallen at such a stupid point, too? She brushed herself down and, with aching limbs, began to build up speed to continue her pursuit. Following the creature's path, she burst around the corner it had just taken.

What she found was another tunnel, just like the countless others she had passed through already. A rough painted plaque adorned the wall to her left, featuring a smartly dressed goblin with a wide toothy grin. But this was not what caught our hero's eye. There, a couple of metres in front of her, illuminated by the green glow of a sewer slug, stood what she guessed was the creature she had been pursuing so eagerly. There was something dreadfully peculiar about it. What was certain was that it just stood there, partially illuminated and utterly and eerily still.

With a marked hesitance, Bethany approached, one step at a time. It still didn't move. So she continued to walk closer, her footsteps echoing down the silence of the tunnel. Still the little creature did not move. She tried calling out to it:

"Hello..."

But still nothing happened. The thing continued to stand still, in the same position, not even breathing. Something was amiss here. Swallowing her fear and letting curiosity get the better of her, she continued forward. As she grew closer, she could see the creature was now all misshapen, posed in an awkward position. Its right arm twisted out and up towards the ceiling, as if reaching desperately for the sun. The other gripped on to the wall, its stubby fingers latched on tightly. What surprised her even more was that its feet had taken root, breaking through the concrete floor below. Most bizarre of all was what seemed to appear from the top of its head. Ripping through its hat, a twisting brown branch reached for the ceiling, at the end of which were three small green leaves. It seemed to Bethany that if this was the creature she had chased through the sewers, it had not turned into a statue but taken root and turned into some kind of tree. Maybe this was what this kind of being did.

She decided to venture around the other side of the creature and look it squarely in the face. "Hello?" she hesitantly called again, knowing it would be in vain. As she expected, the creature remained motionless. So with great care, she moved around it in five small steps and confronted the short creature. It still had a face, with its two big black eyes and small trunky nose, but it now looked sunken and withered, as if it was slowly transforming into a skull. It was an unflinching face, as motionless as the rest of its body. Lifeless, it could be said, with an air of dread and gloom about it. Instead of a panic-stricken expression, it now looked utterly sad. So sad, in fact, that it almost looked as if it would start crying at any moment and never stop. To Bethany, it appeared to be an amalgamation of all the sadness that existed in the world, now come together in this one form in front of her. It reminded her of something. Something recent that she had yet to properly understand. Something so utterly sad that it had broken some part of her. Her jaw clenched and her hands tightened into fists as she tried to make sense of this sadness that now stared at her, lifeless. She was about to shout and scream her frustration to the world, but before she could, another voice came from the darkness behind her.

"I don't think you're supposed to be here."

She would have responded, with something witty or exciting, but the words just could not escape her mouth. Our hero had not expected to end up in the greatest sewer system in the galaxy, to chase a panic-stricken creature through it, and then to find it had been transformed into some kind of tree, most likely against its will. And she certainly had not expected that something else would appear in the darkness and accuse her, with an emotionless and rather sinister voice, of intruding somewhere she wasn't meant to. Unable to respond to the situation verbally, gripped as she was with what could be fear, she turned around to try to get a look at this new character. To her surprise, in the darkness of the tunnel not too far in front of her was not one person but two. She could barely make out what they were – all she could see were their silhouettes, standing side by side. One was tall, almost seven feet, and slim. It seemed to be draped in some kind of cloak, from which poked a thin neck topped with a round, hooded head. The other was far shorter and childlike in stature and shape. It held its taller companion by the hand, as a six-year-old would hold its parent's. It was wearing a mask. More worrying, perhaps, was that it appeared to be human. Apart from this, Bethany couldn't make out anything else in the darkness.

"Yes, you. You are not supposed to be here." The voice had an almost monotonous manner, picking up its consonants and diction with a certain precision. It belonged to the taller silhouette. "We've been playing down here for a long time, waiting for someone interesting to turn up. So long, in fact, that we had to find other activities to keep ourselves busy."

Bethany tentatively turned to glance at the rooted creature behind her, then returned her gaze to these two new characters, wary of losing them from her sight.

"But now you're here. We haven't seen one of your kind for a long time. As such, I believe it's best that we get things sorted."

Our hero still felt frozen to her spot, almost in a trance. She had to say something, anything at all.

"Who are you?"

A perfectly reasonable question, one might say, but the taller being seemed quite taken aback, its shadowed silhouette flinching in response. It turned its head downwards as if to look at its companion before focusing again on Bethany.

"I do not believe that is important right now. What is important is what we do to you."

It spoke in the same smooth, emotionless way, but now with what seemed like the hint of a threat. Bethany was not oblivious to this and took a ready position, prepared to take flight if this being approached or did anything further with aggressive intent.

"What shall be done about this young being?"

It turned again to its companion, this time kneeling so it could lean in to hear it. The smaller figure responded with a short giggling whisper.

"If that will please you."

Bethany was ready to make a run for it, get out of sight. But her curiosity got the better of her once more. The taller figure again addressed her.

"I'm sorry about what must happen. It is his wish that this should be. Mind, it could be worse, though I must say it could be a lot better. We know the trouble that is coming. Trouble that would be made a lot deeper because of someone like you."

Before Bethany could say anything, the taller silhouette reached out with its right hand. Instantly she felt queasy again and dizzy, stumbling and wobbling in position. Then all was black as she felt herself falling forward.

The brief nightmare she had was terrifying and disorientating. She was surrounded by hundreds of the little wooden trunked creatures, and they sang her a melancholic tune as they wept profusely. Their song bore into her brain uncomfortably, and so, unable to stand it, she began to run.

The creatures followed her in pursuit. As she fled, the tunnels twisted and morphed into a series of unbearable shapes. The creatures seemed uninhibited in their chase, but she was beginning to slow as her feet turned into roots, which started to latch her violently into the floor. Then in front of her, from out of nowhere, an old man appeared. He was sitting in a chair, wearing thick-rimmed glasses, and though she couldn't quite see through the shadow that covered him, he seemed to be smiling. He gave a short, warm chuckle. There was a warm smell of gingerbread in the air. Before she could work out who he was, she had tripped and fallen onto her front. The roots on her feet finally latched into the slabs beneath her as the creatures reached her. All sobbing, they pounced on her, and she opened her mouth to let out a blood-curdling scream. Before she could make a sound, she awoke.

Then there was light again, warm and yellow, though her eyes were pulsing and bloodshot. Her vision was blurry. She looked around frantically. Her head felt different – in fact, her whole being felt entirely alien, as if she'd been placed into a new body. She tried in vain to do something, to find out where she was, even just to move. Finally, as her sight returned, she turned enough to find someone standing over her. To her relief, this was a new character, some kind of hairy, bearlike creature, not one of those sinister silhouettes that had thrown her violently into a disorientating stupor. A voice came out of whatever it was, a tired and nervous voice, but a normal one, all to her relief.

"You finally stopped, then? About time. You know you shouldn't be down here?"

She made an apologetic nod as she tried desperately to reach out for comfort from this new character. Before she could, it continued.

"You know it's illegal for anyone of any means to be down here. Especially a young gropscrub like you. I could get in

trouble for finding you. That would scupper everything...
Erm, so, I must say, I'm very sorry for what I have to do..."

With that, it went dark again as whatever it was placed
a sack over her head. She felt it lift her onto its shoulders
with hairy arms. Bethany again blacked out, this time with
exhaustion.

Eight

BETHANY DID NOT KNOW HOW LONG IT HAD been. Neither did she know where her journey on the back of this big, hairy character took her. The hessian sack on her head meant she was in utter darkness, and she felt incredibly disorientated; it was giving her both the worst headache of her life and an unnerving sensation of not quite being herself. Neither did it help that along with her giddiness she was exhausted, and as a result she was spending most of the time travelling drifting in and out of a deep sleep. So with all this, she had no idea where she was or what was happening – a most unpleasant sensation, especially when one knows that they are in an alien world. In the brief moments she managed to get her bearings, she'd hear voices and the sound of footsteps and feel the lurching, heavy movements of her captor. Later, she felt herself being passed from one pair of hands to another, the discomfort of close, inspective eyes, and the unpleasantness of dry breath as her journey seemed to continue in a new direction.

When Bethany finally came to, she found the sack had been removed from her head. It was nowhere to be seen, nor was her captor either. What she did find, rather disappointingly for her, was that she was yet again within the confines of a gloomy concrete structure. She yearned to get to the surface of Goldensmorg and feel the sun and wind on her skin. But here she was, in the confines of one of its dull manmade structures. She found herself on a plain and thoroughly uncomfortable wooden bench in the corner of a small cell, with her wrists in metal cuffs, tightly linked and chafing. This room did not look like part of the sewer. It looked like a prison cell, and she was one of its prisoners.

What she had done to warrant being treated like a criminal she did not know. She must have done something illegal, but exactly what was still a mystery. But there she was, a prisoner in a cell, likely located in some huge dungeon probably designed by some eccentric goblin. It just seemed to be her luck as of late, Bethany thought, to end up in such situations. Trying hard not to let her frustration get the better of her, she decided to inspect her chamber. Not that there was much to investigate, but at least it would draw her attention away from her current situation for a few seconds. She decided to undertake this activity in good order by checking each of the four corners of her cell in turn. The first she inspected, to the left of the door, was completely unassuming. Like the rest of her room, and much of the sewers in fact, it was grey, smooth, and solid. Right at the bottom, tucked tightly into the corner, was a crumbling little hole. But that was all that interested her, and so she turned to her left. This was much the same, but with the bench attached and without even any crumbled plaster to catch the eye. She moved rapidly on to the next cell corner, which turned out to be as exciting as the last two. Finally, she turned to the right side of the door, which to her surprise had a mirror resting on it. When faced with such an item, it is very difficult not to notice your reflection.

What she saw standing in the mirror was not the slim and tiny, messy-haired young person she knew all too well, but that very same little trunked creature she had met during her time in Goldensmorg's sewers, albeit wearing her own clothes. She couldn't believe it at first, moving this way and that, taking her eyes off the mirror and walking away to then return and check again. But there it was, right in front of her. Fear started to grip her tightly in the stomach. She thought she felt different, as if she were in a different body, but she had attributed that to her giddiness rather than to some actual physical change. She looked down at herself, hoping to find herself looking very much normal, but to her continued shock and fear she had, as the mirror had shown her, very much changed into that creature. Those sinister strangers must have transformed her. With her body tight with shock, she fell onto her bottom, hitting the floor with a soft thud. Then with her mind racing, and her heart pounding with panic, she screamed. What came out however was a mix of a squeak and a snort, unlike any noise she'd heard before. Not that this made matters any better. She felt nauseous, cold, and entirely hopeless.

Everything had gone completely wrong. Her attempt to visit Goldensmorg by magical means had backfired and instead of finding herself in some exciting fantasy world, she'd ended up lost in endless, noxious sewers. Then she'd been accosted by sinister figures who, from her understanding, had transformed her into another creature. Upon which she then seemingly got herself arrested for some kind of misdemeanour and thrown into jail. She couldn't imagine how the situation could get any worse. It then dawned on her that her bag was missing. She must have left it in the sewers. A sickly lump formed in her stomach as she desperately scrambled to find it in her cell. She quickly realised how hopeless her search was and slumped down once again rubbing her head – a dull, tired ache beginning to form in the middle of her skull. It wasn't the bag that was the problem, but what was inside it: the locket. The exact item that had mattered so much to her dear friend Grollp. The exact piece that she had promised herself to look after, and yet she'd been careless and lost it at the first opportunity. She did not dare think who or what was now in possession of it. Continuing to wind herself up she began to shake violently in her helplessness, her headache getting worse. She realised she must have been a depressing and miserable sight, but she didn't care. Things were so hopeless that tears began to form in the corners of her eyes.

But before she could start sobbing, she was interrupted by the heavy clank of bolts being unlocked. She stood straight up, her headache forgotten, and stared patiently at the door. The locks clanked away, the heavy-duty iron shuddering with the precision and routine of an old gaoler at work. It was not long before the noise stopped and the great metal door swung open outwards with a weighted moan. It was bright outside, especially in comparison to the confines of her cell, and Bethany winced, shielding her eyes. In a second or two they had become accustomed to the light, and there standing in the doorway was her gaoler. It was an orc – well, if her information from Grollp was correct – a big green toothy face, a heavy-set lower jaw, and small, red, sunken eyes. But for an orc, this gaoler seemed to be rather decrepit. It stood with a hunched posture, much like what Grollp had described to her, but this one seemed to own it as a deformity, more akin to the stance of Shakespeare's Richard III than to the power stance of a gorilla. It was covered in a ragged black cloak that obscured its whole body, under which she caught glimpses of a patchwork uniform made of leather and chains that hung

off its misshapen and shrunken frame. A scar across its right
eye, blotches on its face, and big, stompy, hole-riddled boots
completed the picture. Bethany stared at the creature with
fascination. The orc stared back in utter disinterest.

"Come on den," it grunted dully.

Bethany could think of nothing to do but nod. The orc
turned around and started hobbling slowly down the prison
corridor, its shoulders heaving awkwardly with each step. With
both her hands manacled, she followed suit, easily keeping
pace with her slow gaoler. The corridor was much like her cell,
minus the bench and mirror, of course. They passed door after
door, each a perfect facsimile of the wrought-iron one on her
chamber. It was light, unnaturally so, and the glow appeared
to emanate from a series of glass boxes that lined the walls.
Bethany hazarded to guess there was probably something like
the sewer slugs stuck in them. In short order, the hunched
gaoler had led her to an iron-barred gate guarded by two other
orcs. These, though, were tough-looking beasts at the peak of
their health. They stood as straight and erect as their bodies
would let them, clothed in a mix of boiled leather and metal
plating that gleamed in the light. In their right arms they each
held a long blunderbuss weapon covered in cogs and servos
and ending with a huge meat cleaver of a bayonet. They looked
straight forwards in that unflinching guard kind of way, paying
no heed to our transformed hero or to the orc gaoler, who was
now pulling a ring covered with an uncountable collection
of intricate bronze and silver keys out from its cloak. After
slowly and carefully examining each in turn, it found the right
one and placed it with a shaking hand into the keyhole of the
gate, which opened with an exhausted creak. It then led the
way again, taking her into an octagonal chamber with a raised
platform in the middle, full of orc guards. This in turn had a
tall lectern in the middle of it, with polished steps leading to

the top. The whole thing seemed to be some sort of lift, held in place with chains that hung from the ceiling in four corners. It reminded Bethany of a medieval pulley system. Above it was a hole through which it could enter the room above. Bethany could see the light coming through this opening, and more importantly could hear the roar of noise that was descending from the chamber. She had a horrible feeling that it was going to be her next destination.

She was right. Her orc gaoler gestured to her with its right claw.

"Stand on dat," it grumbled, barely coherently, as it pointed to a space in the middle of the raised platform.

Dutifully she did as she was bid, and with small shuffling steps, still uneasy with her new body, she moved up onto the platform and stood right in the middle of it. The light now shone down on her from the chamber above. It was warm and musky, and the air that came with it thick and sickly. The noise was clearer now: it seemed that there were numerous creatures above her, all in a thoroughly heated debate. Even with all the ruckus she could hear insults and curses coming through in low and bitter voices. She had a feeling that she'd be the object of their attention in a few moments; whether she'd ellicit such angry rhetoric was another matter.

Awkwardly she waited on the platform, no one saying a word. Bethany tried to listen to the arguments roaring above them, but could not make anything out from the din. She understood that she would be going up there in a second, but what she couldn't understand was why she was still waiting. Her manacles rattled as she fidgeted impatiently. She just wanted to get things started. It was then that she could hear footsteps that clipped and clonked down the hallway to her left. Turning she could see the silhouettes of several creatures approaching through the semi-darkness. From the noise, one was clearly leading the way, whilst the others were struggling to keep up. A short, sharp, high-pitched voice echoed down the hallway, issuing commands and instructions to the servants attending it. When the character finally entered the light, Bethany could see it was a goblin; in its smart dress coat and trousers, it looked much like Denepom. What made this goblin different was how fine its clothing was. Its jacket was covered in ostentatious medals, whose gold and silverwork glittered in the wall lighting. Along with these items, it had a long brass chain around its neck, much like one that a mayor would traditionally wear. Bethany could only assume it was an object of office, and one that had been used for centuries, for the metalwork was rather beaten and worn, lacking any real shine. The goblin also wore fine silken gloves on its thin, bony hands. The frills on its shirt were far more ornate than Denepom's too, puffing out in such a glorious and obscene manner that the fabric almost dwarfed the creature in large velvet ruffs. What little hair the goblin had was all greasily slicked back across its scalp. There were a number of other differences from the previous goblin she had met – this one looked older, with more wrinkles lining its face. It was also taller and slimmer, and with no podgy belly to be seen, appeared rakishly thin. It walked with a grace and authority that Denepom had somewhat lacked.

Attending to this goblin were five little fleshy sprites. They were grubbs: diminutive creatures made of pure magical energy to attend to their masters, or so Grollp had told her. Obedient and utterly loyal, they were also cheeky and mischievous, getting up to all sorts of tricks, though never at the expense of their masters, of course. Indeed, their appearance was entirely suggestive of this mischievous side, as they were smiling creatures bouncing with frenetic energy. They had no bodies to speak of, just rather round and lumpy heads with limbs attached. Each sported a big toothy grin, above which sat a tiny little nose and a pair of jittery and colourful eyes. Their four limbs – two arms and two legs each, of course – were long and gangly and appeared ill suited for the bodies, or should I say heads, they were attached to. At the ends of their arms were misshapen hands with four fingers, some with claws and others with sucker pods on their tips. Their legs ended in large bare feet, all of which were a fleshy pink colour, making them stand out starkly against their grim, greyish background. These five creatures frantically attended to their goblin master: one brushed the goblin down with a little wire brush, another was holding and passing over papers, whilst another jotted down the goblin's sentences on ragged brown paper and another advanced in front of the party, sweeping the ground with a broom as they approached. The final grubb trailed a few paces behind, with a weird-looking white judge's wig ill placed on its head and an enormous, heavy-looking leather-bound book in its arms that seemed to slow it down considerably.

In a few short moments, the goblin and its attendants had reached her on the platform. It finished off its last sentence, and with a gesture of its right claw sent four of the creatures scurrying away to the walls. At another gesture and a short sharp cough, the fifth grubb brought the book up to the lectern and placed it open upon it. Relieved of this weight, it scurried quickly over to its master, taking the wig off its own head and placing it neatly onto the goblin's. It scooted away quickly to join its mates, giggling as it went. The goblin, standing just in front of Bethany, closed its eyes and took a deep, deliberate breath, accompanying this with a gentle upwards movement with its arms, then exhaled with a long squeaky hiss, its arms gracefully descending. It opened its eyes and looked inquisitively up and down our hero in her manacles.

It rolled its eyes, scoffing to itself, then took off its glasses. Pinching the end of its long pointy nose, it began to wipe them with a cloth it produced from its inside jacket pocket. Bethany did her best not to stare. Her body curled and hunched together, as if trying to desperately hide itself from any further looks. After a few awkward moments, having finished cleaning, it placed the glasses back on its nose and stared at her again – this time with a small smile creeping onto its face.

"Name?" it ordered in a refined and sharp little voice.

"Bethany," she answered. Given her current situation, she thought it was best to behave and do what she was told.

"Bethany, aye? That's a funny name for a gropscrub," the goblin blurted rudely.

"Well, yes, I guess, but I'm not really a gropscrub, whatever one of them might be!"

The goblin scoffed and proceeded to laugh to itself, capping off its chortle with a disapproving tut. "You are a funny little thing, you are. But I would say this isn't the best place for humour."

It stared unblinkingly at her, straight into her eyes. She felt immensely uncomfortable but could do nothing but stare straight back, her body motionless.

"Do you understand what trouble you are in?"

Bethany shook her head sheepishly. It was likely a lot, going by the goblin's temperament.

It turned away, breaking its stare, tutting to itself disapprovingly again.

"Well, my young gropscrub, Bethany, you have been caught loitering in a restricted area, and the due legal process has taken effect. You are about to go in front of the Council of Elder Smargs, the highest power in Goldensmorg, and they do not look favourably on such ill-considered breaches of the written law."

Bethany turned away, looking anxiously into the darkness, lost in her thoughts whilst her body shivered in fear. The goblin climbed the short flight of stairs to the top of the old wooden lectern, stood in front of the open book, and set about its business. For a few seconds all was silent, apart from the distant roar of debate coming from above.

"Well, I think it's time to begin. Stay quiet, except when you are asked a question, and do what you are told. Achieve this, and things shouldn't be too bad for you," the goblin said, feigning compassion.

With a swift turn of its head, the goblin looked out into the darkness, presumably to some underling out in the chamber somewhere. Then at its quick barked order of "Up!", the chains started moving with a heavy and continuous clatter and clunk, and the platform jerked and began to ascend towards the hole above them. As they approached the light, the noise got louder and more ferocious and the musky, warm light enveloped them. The smartly dressed goblin calmly gave itself a final brush-down and took a ready stance behind the lectern. Bethany stood as still as she could, trying to control her fidgeting, a lump forming at the back of her throat.

Within a few moments, they were entering the room above. She was immediately enveloped in thick, sickly air, her nostrils filled with a rich and stewed stench of sweat and bitterness. The noise was almost unbearable, hitting her like a stampede of angry bulls. There were so many voices and so much anger that she could barely make out any of what was said. It was bright, too – unnaturally so. She tried her best to inspect her new surroundings, looking around with squinted eyes, taking in every detail of the vast chamber. It seemed to be a coliseum-like circular structure, with ring after ring of seats that stretched endlessly upwards away from her. At the bottom, where she stood, was the arena floor, round and made of sandy-coloured granite. Not far from her were the arena walls, made of stacked concrete slabs that ringed her in, punctuated by archways that were barred with ancient iron gates. Each space was numbered with polished bronze numerals, which were mirrored on the other side of the arena with copperplated ones. These numbers, beginning with two, seemed to get higher and higher the further up the coliseum they went – some kind of ranking system, she thought. All this was punctuated by the occasional banner, pulpit, or desk which added a dash of colour to Bethany's surroundings. Right in front of her on the lowest tier was a particularly large and ornate throne, covered with fine cushions of red and purple, and with the number one plastered on the granite pulpit in front of it. Sitting on the throne was a huge, dark purple, prune-like creature, finely dressed but fast asleep. Indeed, behind every single number that ringed the room was one of these creatures, all of varying size, expression, and garb. Bethany knew them in an instant. They were the rulers of Goldensmorg, the smargs, and this was their courtroom.

Grollp had described these creatures as the most repugnant, vile, and corrupt beings in the whole galaxy. He had also said that they were the perfect politicians. This wasn't just because of the aforementioned attributes but because they took great pleasure in law making, maintaining order, and the endless paperwork that goes hand in hand with politics. Not that this gave them any real pleasure at all, as they were the most miserable of all creatures. These prune-like beings were in fact just great slimy masses, with protruding thick, flabby arms and legs. You see, when a smarg is born, it is tiny, and indeed is often considered the cutest creature in existence, with big sparkling eyes and adorable little chubby cheeks. But with age and professional progression in politics, soon these enchanting attributes disappear. Their eyes become small and sunken, their noses go all shrunken and pig-like, and their cute little mouths become great cavernous maws full of saliva and mucus. Once giddy and excitable, they become foul, bad tempered, and immensely lazy, as their bodies wrinkle and shrivel into huge sweaty mounds of purplish flesh. These beings, even more so than the goblins that adored them, were into the finer things, especially clothes, and so often dressed themselves in the finest velvets and silks money could buy. Unfortunately they had little taste, and so their outfits came in various garish and nauseating colours and designs.

It was these, the smargs, that surrounded our hero. Each sat behind one of the numbers that ringed her position, roaring and shouting at those around them. This was the Council of the Elder Smargs, the most powerful politicians on Goldensmorg and the rulers, to some degree anyway, of Edimor itself. There were two thousand altogether, one thousand per political party. The smargs with the number 2 had the highest authority and power within the party, tending to be the oldest, largest, and foulest of their kind. So it follows that the smargs with the number 1,001 had the least authority and were of the lowest rank – also being the youngest, smallest, and least foul of the group. Each smarg had a counterpart in the other party, and the rank that had to deal with an issue was determined by the seriousness of the crime. The two parties had very clear policies: the Bronze Party stood by disagreeing with everything the Copper Party said, whilst the Copper Party stood by disagreeing with everything the Bronze Party said. Between the two parties was the smarg that inhabited the position of 1. This creature was affiliated with neither party and spent most of its time asleep, looking for all the world like a disgusting, overripe fruit. It was the wealthiest, foulest, largest, and most slovenly of all the smargs whose word was the law. Anything that it said had to be acted upon, for it was in a position of almost complete omnipotence and omniscience. It was therefore the creature of the highest authority in Edimor, though it very rarely expressed its opinion or exerted its will. It was through this creature and the two parties that made up the Council of the Elder Smargs that Edimor was run, and though the brave, the foolhardy, and the determined could escape their orders, they possessed a huge amount of political authority and clout – though this had actually been given to them by default, simply because no one else could be bothered to rule on such a vast galactic scale. Grollp had described them well to Bethany, mainly because he had plenty of experience standing before them as the guilty party. Each time he had used his wits to escape, and these had been some of her favourite stories.

Though the smargs dominated the arena our hero had risen into, they were not the only ones there. Along with the goblin next to her, she was surrounded by a dozen orc guards clad in hardened leather armour. They all stood on the arena floor with her. However Bethany could not help but notice a tall, slender, cloaked figure that stood mostly hidden in the archway to her left. It seemed mysteriously human, as well as surprisingly familiar to her. Up amongst the smargs crawled hundreds upon hundreds of grubbs, attending to their immense and slovenly masters. They scaled and descended wooden ladders between each tier, brandishing books, papers, accessories, huge goblets of drink, and plates piled high with all manner of food and treats. All the while the smargs angrily bawled at each other, the more capable standing and throwing their arms up in disgust or pointing accusingly to their counterparts across the room. All of this created such a din that neither the smargs nor in fact anyone else had noticed the rising platform or the arrival of our hero into the room.

For a few moments they stood there on the platform whilst the smargs surrounding them argued on, oblivious to their existence. The goblin, however, refused to let this bother them. With a small gesture, an orc guard bowed and disappeared down one of the gated tunnels. Moments later it returned accompanied by a troll, dark green in complexion and twice the size of Grollp. Hunched, much like her orc gaoler, it was dressed in the same manner as the orc guards. It brandished in its right hand a huge bone horn, which it positioned purposefully on its stand. Then, with a huge intake of breath, it blew into the instrument, creating a primal, droll sound that was almost deafening. In a few moments, when all the troll's breath had gone, the noise stopped. The creature looked exhausted from its efforts, but it had clearly done its job, for as Bethany turned back to look at the smargs, she saw they were all now deathly quiet and every single pair of eyes was staring straight at her. The silence hung unnervingly in the air, as if it were part of the warm mist that loitered in the arena.

The goblin broke the silence. Clearing its throat with a few sharp coughs, it began to speak, its volume far superior to what a creature of that stature should have been able to manage.

"Ladies and gentlemen, counts and countesses, masters and mistresses, barons and baronesses, madams et monsieurs…"

The list went on, seemingly forever. Bethany noticed how perfect the goblin's diction was and how effective its projection. It was also pretty clear that it was really rather enjoying the whole routine. Finally, after the goblin had read through all the titles, some of which were unrecognisable to our hero, she continued on.

"Smargs and smargesses, who inhabit our glorious court of Elthabar the Magnificent today, I, Vice Arch-Count Delphi

Shagratti III, Princess of Haberdash, Lord of Menier, Mistress of Stationaria…"

Delphi listed her own titles much in the same manner as before, with the same mix of bravado, theatricality, and pride that seemed to continue with full enthusiasm for what yet again felt like an age. Bethany began to forget how nervous and tense she was and started to become bored, sneaking a quiet yawn so as not to interrupt. After a good amount of time, but not quite as long as Delphi's original address, she continued on.

"…and Creator of the Obsidian Phallicai, come to you today with issue GSSI8894963582623X217…" And on she went, reading from the pages of the book in front of her and listing off a long collection of numbers, letters, and glyphs. Her list was so extensive that she had to turn the page three times. Fighting her boredom, Bethany noticed that every single one of the smargs, except for number 1 who was still fast asleep, were sitting in their positions listening attentively and excitedly in total silence. Delphi finally came to the end of her list.

"…22467745135ZP. The issue at hand takes into account the intrusion of the party present in restricted governmental territory, namely Goldensmorg Sewer Complex, Section 27B, on which lockdown was placed upon the sighting of the Carer and the Mysterious Child, exactly three weeks, two days, seventeen hours, twenty-three minutes, fifty seconds, and one hundred and ninety-nine thousand, two hundred and eighty-seven Gobbinus macro-seconds ago." (Goblins, of course, upon achieving positions of authority, thought it prudent to include their own extra unit of time, which only they could understand in any detail.)

There was a mixed response from the court. Whilst some tutted and puffed in disappointment, higher up in the seating area there was a wave of eager excitement and frantic movement. Delphi continued on in the same manner, her audience captivated with every word.

"The offending party stands before you here. One gropscrub, of the name Bethany Hannah Morgan, of unknown origin, likely however from the second planet of Originatia. The offended party being the governing body of every suitable and civilised planet of Edimor, in particular those of Goldensmorg, as well as the peace and harmony of every good and honest citizen."

A chorus of angry groans and boos erupted. Some kind of half-chewed amphibian snack was thrown from the assembled smargs in the direction of our hero, landing only a few feet away from her. This was followed by all sorts of other detritus, but all fell just short of hitting Bethany. Of course, it was a capital offence for such detritus to hit an offending party before they were proven guilty – such an event would mean the immediate release of said prisoner. Therefore, Bethany knew, it was proper practice for every smarg in the court to throw short until the verdict was passed. With such a reaction from the arena, our hero did not have the greatest of optimism, and the smirk she could see on Delphi's face was even more disconcerting. The goblin continued:

"Now, due to certain urgent and disconcerting circumstances that currently threaten our very existence, the category for this intrusion offence has been upgraded to level two…"

There was an all too obvious change in the court. Those on the higher tiers now groaned in disappointment, whilst those on the second tier of seating sat up, abuzz with excitement, some even licking their lips in anticipation.

"…and so I must call to attention the debating persons, these being of the number nine."

Another groan rippled through the arena. Some of the smargs spat in disgust at each other, sending huge dollops of greyish-green mucus flying across the room. Other detritus also flew from one place to the other as the smargs sought to take out their anger on each other and anyone nearby. The entire court again descended into a furious roar of angry noise. The only ones not joining in were the number 9 smargs from each side of the room, who were now being attended by colourfully dressed grubbs. Each one carried something: papers, books, quills, sweetmeats. Others carried towels, gaudy accessories, and what appeared to be perfumes, which they liberally applied to their masters. All of the servants looked to be giggling to themselves at some kind of joke that only they understood. Apart from this, everything seemed to be in utter chaos. With the tired precision of routine, Delphi gestured to the troll, who took a huge intake of breath and released it into the horn, again producing the horrendous racket that brought the smargs to order. The corners of Delphi's mouth curled up into a smile as she raised her hands to calm the court.

"Elders of the Goldensmorg Court, Oligarchy of the Civilised Worlds, now is the time to render justice on this miserable offender. Let the debate commence!"

With that, both number 9 smargs clambered to their feet as quickly as their bulk would let them. They each reached out an arm into the air as if desperately clawing to win the race to be first upright and speaking. Fate would have it that, groaning and panting for breath, the member of the Bronze Party reached its feet first. Its opposite, perhaps hindered by its huge and heavy velvet cloak, grumbled in defeat as it leaned breathless on the desk in front of it.

"Bronze Nine! As you are the first to your feet, you will choose, as is usual protocol, the argument you wish to represent."

Our hero knew, as Grollp had told her, that the first smarg always chose to argue against the accused, for they always took the greatest pleasure in arguing to prove someone guilty, no matter how innocent they were. Bronze 9 was just about able to stand under its own weight in a black tailcoat and trousers, exuding confidence from its vast bulk. It was rather smartly dressed, with a bow tie wrapped around its thick, almost non-existent neck, a frilled shirt, gemmed cuffs, and a leathery brown waistcoat whose buttons looked like they were about to burst off. What was peculiar was its accoutrements; a white powdered wig sat on its head, laced with ribbons and bows. Its fingers were stuffed into gaudy golden rings that were engraved and covered in jewels. Upon the breast of its suit was pinned a line of medals and badges, which all sparkled. What was more unsettling, though, was both the bright red lipstick that painted its chubby protruding lips and the greasy stains that soiled the front of its shirt. After taking in the whole room with its small beady eyes, making sure everyone was focused on its person, it began.

"Dear friends and acquaintances of the court," it said with a deep guttural voice, globules of spit and mucus flying from its gob. "What stands before you is a gropscrub of the most nefarious nature, who, with full knowledge of the law, decided to commit the most hideous of crimes: that of trespassing on public property, which we all agree—"

"I object!" bawled its Copper counterpart, an even larger specimen who seemed to be dressed as a Roman emperor, with a toga of thick red velvet and shining gold brooches. It looked even more peculiar with a little golden wreath on its head, a white powdered face, and what was clearly a fake mole painted on its sunken right cheek. "My friends, this argument put forward by my compatriot is clear folly of the highest order. This smarg is of the most dubious nature to suggest that this gropscrub of the name Bethany actively chose the sewage catacombs of our great city, for as we all know, this species is more at home in—"

"I object!" the Bronze Party member replied. Spittle sprayed everything in its immediate vicinity. "To suggest that this creature here does not enjoy dark and murky surroundings such as the sewer complex of our fair city but only the habitual locations of its race is clearly offensive and breaks the Oruk Malgia Charter of—"

"I object!" the reply came, the debate starting to properly heat up. "It is clearly an act of utter desperation for my colleague to suggest I am breaching the Oruk Malgia Charter, for without full character analysis of the defendant, we must refer to the habitual nature of its species. This means, of course, that my Bronze Party opposite is—"

"I OBJECT!" The sheer volume and force of the reply sprayed spittle all across the room and even knocked a few attending grubbs off their feet. The energy of the arena became frenzied again as other court members began to jeer at their fellows while they too prepared detritus to use as missiles in the coming moments. "This foolish youngling of a smarg clearly does not have possession of the particularly vital information of the recent establishment and registration of a new gropscrub community. They have inhabited the dark and dank dwellings in the caves along the River Nien. With such registration comes a vast selection of records, meaning we do indeed have the relevant information to—"

"I OBJECT!" came the response, with even more grubbs losing their footing. Bethany herself stumbled slightly as she seemed to be hit by the full fury and anger of the reply. The room was almost at boiling point, with snide comments becoming ever more audible as each side prepared to burst into a rage. Our hero could do nothing but stand there and wait for the inevitable. Indeed, as she looked around, the other creatures on the arena floor with her seemed rather relaxed, as if used to the chaos of the court.

"To suggest I am a mere youngling is rash and erroneous, especially when such remarks come from a highly unfashionable being such as my opponent—"

"IIIIIII OBBBJJJECCCCTTTTT!" yet again came the response with even more power than Bethany thought possible. "To call one such as I unfashionable is ridiculous. Especially when the one using such insults is but a common scuttlespawn!"

"Pussmarg!"

"Hagwart!!"

"Feggle peasant!!!"

"Gnob jockey!!!!"

"Grubb cleaner!!!!!"

"MEEEEELLLOOOONN HEAAAADDDD!!!!!!"

At last the argument boiled over and exploded; the room broke into chaos again. Missiles and insults flew as all sense of order disappeared. Delphi smirked and tutted to herself. Before she could gesture towards her troll servant to interrupt the squabble again, the mysterious figure that had until now lurked in the shadows moved towards the centre of the arena.

This being was tall and thin, striding forward with an aura of dignity and authority. It was human in appearance, but at the same time it didn't feel human at all to Bethany. It was clad in a long, dark, fitted cloak, under which was an ornately patterned black surcoat with a silvery tint that covered its lean, muscular body. Its legs ran long, covered in similar black and silver fabric, as well as knee guards that shone as though made from the finest metals. Its hands were covered in black gloves, and it wore glimmering metal vambraces and segmented shoulder pads strapped into place with dark brown leather, dull buckles, and metalwork. The only bit of flesh that Bethany could see was its head, which was hairless and chiselled, a dull grey in colour. It was very similar to that of a human. Its ears, though, were small and pointed, and its eyes were almost entirely black, apart from the strikingly red irises. Black geometric shapes sat neatly on the creature's forehead and framed its eyes. Its face was severe and almost emotionless, with a slight frown plastered just above its somewhat pointed chin.

Bethany shuddered away from this being, as if she were a mouse cowering from a circling cat. It strode towards the platform whilst the whole court continued in disorder. Its eyes were fixed upon Bethany, and in a few strides, it stood right next to her. Delphi sheepishly shrank away from her platform as it passed. Bethany felt its attention clearly upon her, like it was staring into her soul examining every fibre of her, like a doctor inspecting a patient with a yet-unknown illness. After a few moments of this motionless examination, it swiftly turned to face the court, raising a hand. With a monosyllabic utterance and a hiss of noise, the courtroom went quiet. Every single smarg was giving this being its undivided attention. Bethany could not draw her eyes away from it; an unnatural aura seemed to radiate off its person, as if this creature were not made of flesh and blood but something else altogether.

The goblin managed to pluck up the courage to continue proceedings.

"Friends... o-of the... c-court, Grand High Inquisitor Malakia takes the floor..." she hesitantly said as she ascended and then quickly descended from her plinth.

For a few moments, it was completely silent. The Inquisitor stared back at our hero, this time with confusion and wariness, then turned back to the court, moving its head in a slow, controlled way, scanning each smarg as it went. It began to speak in a voice that was deep, cold, and emotionless, full of authority and command and all too eerily similar to the shadowed figure she met in the sewers.

"Members of the Elder Court, as you know, we live in perilous times. Since the appearance of the child and its carer, our very existence has been under threat of annihilation. Life and everything that we know could soon end. The eye of darkness grows each day, and twelve different planets have moved into position, ready to go over the brink any day now. True, nothing has happened for some time, but still the threat from evil forces lurks, ready to cast everything into oblivion."

For the first time since Bethany had arrived in the court, the smargs seemed nervous, even scared. They began dripping with sweat, their once bullish nature shrinking away as they squirmed back in their seats. The Inquisitor addressed them unblinkingly, its eyes darting from one to the next, holding their attention in what appeared to Bethany to be some kind of hypnotic spell.

"At first many refused to accept our own mortality, but approaching the matter in such a way is futile. We must strive with the full fury and vengeance we can muster to rid ourselves of this problem and all the agents of evil that continue to corrupt our society. Surely you must all agree?"

The smargs nodded and murmured hesitantly in agreement. With this response, the Inquisitor turned to his right, staring down at our hero again, with the same wary, questioning eyes. His gaze was focused on her face, making her tremendously uncomfortable as it lingered for a few moments too long before he turned back to address the court.

"I have stood attentively today, watching the proceedings unfold. The accused by the name of Bethany Hannah Morgan who stands here is not just any normal gropscrub. There is something different about her – indeed, all my powers detect a mysterious quality to her. A quality that I cannot ignore. I hope you trust my suspicions, as you have done so many times in the past, for have they not always led to the benefit of every honourable citizen of our great intergalactic community?"

Again the smargs mumbled in agreement, nodding their huge, neckless heads. With a sweeping gesture, the Inquisitor pointed directly at our hero and began to speak again, his voice full of hate.

"Therefore, I beseech you to agree with me in calling this creature guilty, not just for her intrusion of private government property, but for conspiracy against civilisation and order itself! She is undoubtedly an agent of evil, a spy for those forces that desire to see our world destroyed and plunged into darkness. If we let her leave here today innocent, we will have signed not only our own death sentence but the death sentence for all existence! She is one of those agents that would be happy to see our total destruction and our consumption by the great darkness!"

The court began to grumble angrily once again, though now their anger wasn't directed at their opposing party but rather in her general direction. It was clear to Bethany that the entire court had turned decisively against her. Even the Copper Party, her defence, were baying for her blood. She didn't dare imagine what would happen if the guilty sentence was passed, especially in the light of the extreme accusations the Inquisitor was putting forward. Everyone was clearly angry, full of hatred grown from a fear of change, no matter how immense or inconsequential. She seemed to recognise the emotion. Indeed, their rage seemed contagious, as she felt it start to boil up inside herself. Why was she here? Why were they picking on her? Could they really be that idiotic, jumping to such a ridiculous conclusion? She'd hardly been on

Goldensmorg for any time at all, and here they were blaming her, a stranger to this world, for all their troubles!

The Inquisitor, happy that he had won over the crowd, seemed content. "Therefore, I not only ask that you vote for her guilt, but that she be left under my care, to rehabilitate her as required and find out what we need to know."

Rehabilitate? Bethany knew what that meant – she wasn't ignorant. She knew he had designs to torture her, or do something unspeakable to her, transforming her into some kind of mindless servant. Grollp hadn't really mentioned much about the Inquisitor, he had never been troubled by him, but she knew it was bad.

"Those voting against incarceration, under my care of course, and in favour of her unequivocal innocence, so that she may go free today to do what evil or otherwise she desires to undertake, raise your hand now."

Unsurprisingly, not one raised a hand. The courtroom was uncomfortably musky and quiet for a few moments while the grubbs checked and then double checked their count of the non-existent votes. After such proper practices, the Inquisitor continued. Bethany had just about had enough. She felt her face starting to go red with rage, and her heart pounded furiously.

"All those in favour of her incarceration, for an unspecified time, under my—"

"NNNNNOOOOOOOO!" blurted Bethany. She had found her courage. "No! No! No! No! NO! No! No! NO! No! No!"

She hadn't found any more words yet. Her outburst had the desired effect, though; everyone was stunned silent. Even the Inquisitor seemed taken aback (the court hadn't seen an argument like this since Lord Cuthbert "One Word" Von Hotzendorf stood accused of gross public indecency and defended himself successfully by repeatedly shouting the word "Bum!" at the top of his voice). Bethany was now struggling to find a convincing argument whilst her opponents were all stunned into inactivity. Before she found one, a series of utterly unexpected events occurred in quick succession.

First, without any obvious reason, Copper number 9 exploded. Bits of the repugnant creature splattered all across the court. This was greeted by a chorus of disgruntled moans from the Bronze Party to the left and a series of cheers from the Copper side. You see, to combat uncontrollable assassination at court, which was used as a tool to remove particularly strong opponents and weaken the opposition, Clause 33881772736454t had been passed. That had been a particularly bloodthirsty year – the entire court had been mysteriously murdered five times over, with the exception of Bronze and Copper number 13. The new clause stated that if any such tactics were used again, the party of the victim would immediately be declared the winner of any decision currently debated. The clause was rather successful, though it did mean that both parties occasionally assassinated their own members as a means to win almost impossible arguments.

Delphi looked shocked, and the Inquisitor seemed disappointed and frustrated, charging quickly back to his corner of the court. Bethany, however, greeted the explosion with a huge smile. Grollp had told her plenty about the clause, as he himself had used it regularly as a tactic to escape the court. As you can imagine, our hero was rather relieved. Perhaps she would finally get outside and see all the wonders of Edimor. Delphi took her position again on her plinth, ready to continue proceedings.

"Members of the court, errmmmm… in light of… current events, and due to the protocols put forward by Clause

33881772736454t, I declare the defendant, Bethany Hannah Morgan, in the light of the law, completely—"

Bethany closed her eyes and waited for the word to finally fly through the air. But it didn't come. She waited for a few moments more, but still there was nothing. Nervously she opened her eyes.

Each and every member of the court stood or sat (ability depending), staring, in bemusement and utter silence, right at court member 1. The slumbering smarg was stirring for the first time in almost two hundred years. It wriggled, brushing off stale crumbs from its garish attire. Then it wriggled the other way, smacking its wrinkled lips and giving off a huge, deep yawn. With great effort, it pulled itself up, assisted by a number of grubbs. When the vast bulk of the creature was in an upright sitting position, it started to scratch itself curiously, peering around the room slowly with squinting, tired eyes. With a deliberate move from its right arm, it plucked from beneath its bottom a hapless squashed grubb. It flung it aside carelessly. With an immense groan, and the assistance of even more grubbs, the prune-like creature pulled itself to its feet. Seeing it unable to hold its own weight, its assistants remained, desperately trying to hold it in its upright position. Satisfied, it properly opened its eyes, which seemed magnificently small in comparison to the rest of its body. It looked around in a daze, searching the room as best it could, as if it were blind. In quick order, a pair of grubbs arrived carrying a pair of large, thick, and dusty-looking glasses, placed them upon the bridge of their master's nose, quickly dusted them, and rapidly made themselves scarce. The ancient number 1 finished searching the room and found our hero standing, now rather sheepishly again.

The beast, breathing heavily, leaned forwards as if trying to get a better look at the accused. The grubbs grunted miserably as they struggled with the extra movement. Its eyes were now huge, magnified by the thick glass of the lenses. It focused on our hero – she could feel it staring straight into her very soul. Not only that, but she could feel herself staring back into it, mesmerised by the creature's aged eyes. She could sense every change the creature went through. It was examining her, using some other mysterious sense to do so – much like the Inquisitor, but this time in a slower and more deliberate manner. First it looked at her with an air of disinterest and boredom, as if it were looking at a bare list of information. In a few moments, however, this changed; it became interested, fascinated perhaps, by something it had found deep inside her. This was then replaced by terror, unequivocal and abject fear, as if it had stared into the very fires of hell and seen the demise of itself and everything it cared about. As if it had stared into an endless nothingness.

It trembled and shivered. Slowly it began to lower itself back into its seat, sweat pouring down its face. It settled with an ungraceful thud, breaking its throne, whilst the attending grubbs fled out of the way of danger. It continued trembling whilst desperately searching for something to say. After a few painful moments, it yelled its verdict:

"GGGGUUUUUIIIIILLLLLTTTTTYYYYYYY!"

The court gave out a huge, spiteful cheer, breaking into chaos again. Detritus now flew through the air with more accuracy, a half-chewed amphibian snack smacking Bethany in the face. The troll blew its horn for the final time as the platform started to descend with a shudder. Delphi turned to our hero, trying to hide the smirk on her face.

"I'm so very sorry…"

Bethany wasn't listening – she was lost in her thoughts and her fear. She knew things were going to get even worse.

Nine

I T WAS SAFE TO CONCLUDE THAT OUR HERO'S
situation had deteriorated dramatically, not that her time
in Goldensmorg had been anything but terrible in the first
place. Upon arriving back into the antechamber below the
smargs' court, she was quickly clapped in more chains. Along
with her wrist restraints, her ankles were now manacled with
a ball and chain. Other chains and links were quickly fastened
around her body by grubbs and orc guards. Delphi the goblin
had whisked herself away, accompanied by her servants, and
had disappeared into the darkness of one of the corridors, a
bounce in her step. Bethany herself was quickly ushered down
another route by her orc gaoler. The journey was long and cold,
the weight of her shackles slowing her to an exhausted shuffle.
Bethany could only assume that they were going farther and
farther into the vast prison complex as they descended flight
after flight of granite stairs. The deeper they went, the greater
the darkness grew. It got dirtier and damper, with pipes

dripping and moss growing, the tunnels in increasing disrepair. She began to see brightly coloured mushrooms growing from moist corners. She saw the light-emitting slugs again too, these ones thin and shrivelled, as if they were starving, and so only dimly illuminating her surroundings.

When they had walked down enough prison hallways and descended enough flights of stairs, and when her surroundings couldn't become any more grim and depressing, she finally reached her destination. They stopped in front of a huge iron door, rusting away at the corners with age and neglect. The gaoler set about sifting through its keys again. After a few moments of searching and clattering, it found the oldest and most beaten key on the ring and placed it in the keyhole of the heavy chamber door. With a grunt and then a straining creak, it was unlocked. With even greater effort, the orc pulled the door open, which swung with a tired, metallic moan that pierced the silence, bouncing from wall to wall. With a point and a grunted command, she was instructed to enter the chamber, which she did. It was dark inside, darker than anything she'd ever known, only illuminated by the dim and dying light of the malnourished slugs outside. The orc gaoler used all its efforts to swing the door shut behind her. It slammed with a piercing creak and a heavy crash, after which came the clicking of lock mechanisms. With the door closed it was even darker, as if the light were too frightened to enter. Unable to see a thing, and overwhelmed by her predicament, our hero slumped onto the cold granite floor, utterly dejected.

She sat there for what seemed like an eternity. Both the darkness of the room and the silence were all encompassing, as if she were somehow trapped in a vacuum, separated from existence. Whether her eyes were open or closed, she was greeted by the same blackness and emptiness of her cell. Her mind and body were exhausted. If she had had the energy, she would have done something, thought something, cried or shouted out in rage, but she just felt numb. Everything had gone dramatically wrong, and the situation seemed unlikely to recover. Her only thoughts were of dejection and acceptance, for this was clearly the end; this darkness, exhaustion, and loneliness must have been the very makeup of death itself. However, what Bethany did not know was that she was not alone in her cell.

"My, my, you've met with a most dreadful fate, haven't you?" came a light voice from the darkness, like a favourite primary school teacher gently dissolving a bad situation.

Bethany's skeleton almost departed the confines of her skin (or should that be the skin of her new gropscrub body). She scanned the room in surprise.

Just behind her in the cell, somehow illuminating itself, was a mysterious figure. It looked human; male, of medium height and slim build, it – or perhaps he – had a round head with pale milky skin, big eyes, long eyelashes, and a grinning face. Altogether it seemed a somewhat friendly face, though something about this character struck Bethany as rather off. Apart from his apparent ability to illuminate himself, he was also bald. Now, being hairless is not a sign of someone being inhuman, but the tattoo-style flame patterns that plastered the top of his head seemed to have an unnatural aura, moving and squirming of their own accord. Despite his nose, cheeks, and mouth being very much human in design, his ears were pointed, like those of a traditional elf or fairy. Indeed, his whole facial appearance was pixyish. Just above his rosy red cheeks were his eyes, which were rather large, though not unusually so for a human, and changed colour at regular intervals. His suit did the same; made of a rich velvety material, it shimmered into different colour palettes at the blink of the eye. Apart from that, however, his attire was familiar and professional –

a suit and tie, jacket, shirt, smart trousers, and polished shoes, which would all have seemed rather normal if they hadn't been shifting seamlessly from one colour to the next. In his right hand he held a smooth walking stick, and a brown leather satchel hung by his left side, the straps wrapping across his body and resting on his right shoulder.

Bethany still sat in silence, eyes transfixed upon this new character. More than anyone else she'd met, this being seemed beyond belief. He casually strode towards her, the silence only broken by the clicking of smart shoes upon a granite floor.

"I can imagine you feel at quite a loss. You haven't been greeted with any warmth since you arrived here. I can imagine you don't quite feel yourself either, is that correct?"

By now the suited character had reached our hero, standing a few paces in front of her. He gently offered her a hand. Bethany nodded a reply and stretched out her own hand to take it. He lifted her to her feet, the touch of his skin surprisingly warm.

"Well, let me be the first to change that, and properly welcome such an amazing character as yourself to this most interesting galaxy of Edimor."

Bethany was now standing, tilting her head only slightly upwards to look at this peculiar character. The vibrant colours and general warmth of this being, whatever he was, were contagious, and she started to feel herself again. Her exhaustion was fading in favour of a certain curiosity.

"Who are you?"

He tilted his head and gave a cheeky wink and smile. His eyes transformed from yellow to blue.

"I'm afraid I can't provide you with that information – not currently, anyway." His voice was smooth and reassuring, despite his refusal to answer her question. "What I can tell you is that I am a kind of businessman, and I am here to offer you a proposition. I am sure it will help monumentally with your current situation."

She knew it. Despite everything, there were good people here who would be very happy to assist her. But where had he come from? Before she could think further, he continued in the same charming manner.

"I guess I'm right in thinking that things haven't gone quite right for you, have they?"

Bethany sheepishly nodded in agreement. The suited gentleman paced around the chamber, gesticulating with his arms and examining the room intently. Bethany, anxious not to lose him, followed.

"Lost in a vast sewer complex, deserted by the world, abandoned, and then wrongly accused by a corrupt body of officials who have no responsibility to judge. 'Twas not your fault. Edimor has changed. There is nothing new here, nothing exciting, no adventures to be had. It's stagnant. Since the appearance of that purple hole, things have changed even more. Everyone, whatever race, is now just angry, ready to let out their frustrations on any vulnerable creature coming their way. Not just because of their potential imminent destruction, but also because they are bored and frustrated that we are, in a way, stuck. This used to be a happy place, full of song and laughter. But now, well, there's nowhere left to go, nothing left to do. Nothing great to achieve that hasn't been done before. Nothing is special here anymore. Maybe it would be best if everything was just torn down, and we started all over again."

He stopped in deathly silence with his back to our hero. Nervously she looked on at him, no words coming to her as she moved back and forth, trying to reconnect with her visitor. In one sudden movement, he turned on the spot and stood unnervingly still, his eyes red and his smile gone. The light that radiated from him dulled, and the room felt colder than before.

"You saw him, didn't you?" he said coldly, his friendly manner vanishing.

"Who?" she replied, though she was confident of whom her visitor was referring to.

"I think you know who I mean," came the impatient response, as with slow, deliberate steps he advanced towards her. Bethany tried to find a response, but she was beaten to it.

"In the sewers. You saw him? Him and his carer?" He was still coming closer, as if he were a smartly dressed predator stalking his prey, ready to strike at any moment.

Despite the tension, Bethany managed to find her words. "Well, I did bump into two… rather peculiar characters whilst down there—"

"That's them!" came the response, silencing her. He stood still, his eyes flaming red as he stared down at Bethany. He raised his cane and pointed threateningly in her direction. "You met them! Down there in that sewer. And you left this…"

Bethany's bag appeared from nowhere in her visitor's hand, replacing the cane. His eyes burned with an ever-increasing frustration. Bethany felt truly frightened, but could do nothing. She was frozen, ready to receive her fate.

"This here! Which contains within it the most powerful item in existence." The bag then transformed into the locket that Grollp had guarded with his life. "I cannot tell you how disastrous it would have been if it had fallen into their hands, especially the little boy's. For he is more dangerous than anyone who has existed before!"

The locket disappeared again, as quickly as it had appeared, and the cane was back in his hand, pointing accusingly at our hero. He looked more and more frustrated, his once-pale skin glowing fiery red.

"If it had been lost or destroyed, it would mean our total destruction. It is our only tool against him. He is the one responsible for everything that has gone wrong here. Everything that has changed, been destroyed, been lost. The corruption, the stagnation, the greed, the hole itself! And you almost lost it!"

The tension hung in the air. Bethany prepared for her potential demise, accepting all the abuse being sent her way, stunned into silence. But as quickly as his fury had appeared, it disappeared, and he returned to his original friendly manner. His eyes became green, and his whole body glowed again with warm light. The tension drained away as he lowered his cane.

"That is why I am going to need your assistance."

Bethany tried to relax. She wasn't quite sure what to make of the gentleman. Still, she made sure to stay attentive.

"My friends and I are very keen to keep this locket safe. There are big plans afoot for Edimor, and the destruction of the item would ruin them entirely. It is therefore of the utmost importance that you fully commit to our cause. Will you do that for me?"

He waited expectantly for some kind of response, a wide grin on his pixielike face. Realising that it was highly unlikely she would ever escape her cell without his assistance, Bethany swallowed her concern and duly nodded. Her visitor's smile grew even larger and wider than before, and his eyes became a warm yellow.

"Good. Shall we shake on it? A sign to mark your promise to commit to the cause that belongs to me and my friends?"

The cane disappeared again as he offered his hand. With even greater caution, she took it. It felt even warmer than before as they shook. When he took his hand away, Bethany still felt that warmth. Curious, she looked at her palm, to find a small silhouette of a house marked upon it. Before she could think too much about it, her visitor had begun to talk again, this time rather pacier than before.

"Wonderful. Now, here is what I need you to do."

Her bag was suddenly sitting in her hands. The manacles and chains that had been attached to her had vanished. It was really quite a pleasant surprise.

"I need you to look after that locket with your life. Keep it in that bag of yours and don't show it to anyone. More importantly, don't open it yourself. You understand?"

Bethany nodded almost unthinkingly as she tried to keep up.

"Wonderful," came the response, and he carried on in his usual enthusiastic manner, the soft, gentle tone of his voice starting to bubble up with excitement. "Whilst keeping the item safe, I need you to travel, by whatever means, across Edimor towards the Heart of Unreason. Around said location are a cluster of twelve planets, planetoids, and moons held in stasis. You must reach Skallathraxus, Planet of the Dead. From there, you must travel to where the child and his carer are staying, the Isle of Whispers. Is that understood?"

Bethany nodded again. She didn't quite understand everything he had said, but she had taken it all in and stored the information in a secure part of her brain to decipher at a later date.

"Wonderful. It will be tricky and somewhat dangerous at times, but you are a very special person, Bethany, and I know you can pull through." He nodded to her and then started to walk away, though Bethany couldn't see anything in the direction he was heading. "Good luck, my friend! May your travels be safe and uneventful."

Bethany swung the bag on her back, anxious to get out. But she saw no means of doing so.

"How do I get out of here?"

He turned on the spot and faced her again. His eyes were now a dull green.

"Oh yes, I forgot to mention. I should really leave it all as a surprise. Don't worry, my friend, you will escape the confines of this cell – and soon, might I add."

He pointed into the darkness, towards the opposite corner of the prison cell. Bethany turned to look, but there was nothing there.

"Just don't stand in that corner."

Bethany was still rather confused. She couldn't see any corners of her cell, especially in the pitch black. She turned back to her visitor, only to find that he had gone. She walked forward a few paces and found, with outstretched hands, just the cold, hard corner of the chamber. The stranger was nowhere to be found, and she was yet again in total darkness.

"Hello? Are you still there?" Her voice bounced off the walls of her chamber.

Silence. She turned to look back in the direction her visitor had pointed. She did not dare approach it. The cell was cold again and still dark.

KKKKKAAAAABBBBBOOOOOMMM!

The corner she was staring at had exploded. Granite and rubble was thrown through the air, accompanied by a thick cloud of dust. She clutched her ears, sheltering them from the sudden roar as best she could as she was thrown to the floor. It hurt, and a dull throbbing pain greeted her right side. Despite this, she pulled herself up, brushing herself off, as her whole body was coated in a layer of dust. As she blinked, she looked through it and saw the remains of the chamber cell corner, a bright light shining from a small ball floating in the air. Three different characters stepped through the hole into her chamber. It was time for our hero to be rescued.

Ten

THROUGH THE DUST CLOUDS OF DESTROYED MASONRY came three strange figures. First came a faun, a half-goat, half-human creature, and then a gnome, short and bearded. Both were dressed like eighteenth-century pirates, with frilled shirts, hose, necklaces, rings, bandanas, and big swashbuckling boots. The goat creature was an imposing figure with curling, ram-like horns who stood almost two feet taller than our hero, with a muscled but slender figure clothed in a dark green captain-style coat with brass buttons, an ornate sabre by its side. The gnome was much shorter than Bethany, dressed in a worn leather waistcoat and armed with a collection of pistols and what appeared to be bombs, all strapped across his chest and a small pot belly with leather straps and buckles. The third figure looked rather out of place – it was a large bear, who stood quite comfortably upright on its hind legs and was dressed like a court magician, with baggy Arabian-style trousers, an ornate leather belt, a fez hat, and a frilly shirt. In its left hand it held a long wooden staff. Our hero watched in fascination as they approached, still dusting herself down.

"Don't you think that was a bit much?" said the bear hesitantly in a gruff but slightly high-pitched voice.

"Got us through, didn't it?" the gnome pirate replied in an even gruffer voice. He sounded to Bethany like a West Country farmer.

They waded across the room, stepping through the rubble. The gnome went on.

"An' if you hadn't a' handed in de girl to dem authorities, we wouldn't be in dis mess."

They continued their approach. Only the faun pirate was looking at Bethany, an expression of both surprise and delight upon its face. The other two kept bickering.

"Well, how many times have I gotta say sorry? I was told it was going to be a hooman thing, not a gropscrub. To be honest, I don't know what a hooman thing looks—"

"Silence, you two!" came the faun's sharp response, halting their bickering immediately.

"Sorry…" the bear replied sheepishly. The gnome simply grumbled to himself, folding his arms indignantly.

Satisfied that the argument was over, the faun pirate turned back to face our hero, with a warm smile on its face and its hands resting at its sides.

"Sorry to keep you waiting. Things didn't quite turn out as planned. But now we're here to rescue you. Ms Bethany Hannah Morgan, yes?"

Bethany was taken aback by the faun's confident and rather brash approach, though she couldn't deny she was impressed. And how did everyone seem to know her name in this place? Our hero, remembering her manners – as well as the key points of safety and security around strangers – thought it best to get to know her rescuers before she did anything else.

"Yes, I am. Who might you be?"

The faun shifted slightly, winking at Bethany, still smiling. Its companions seemed less interested; the gnome went to stand with his ear next to the door, a flintlock pistol in each hand. The bear continued to mumble to itself, inspecting the room with its staff.

"Well, that grumpy little gnome over there is my quartermaster, Orin Wheatals. Engineer and demolitions expert, though I must say he's a grumpy sort, aren't ya, Wheatals." The gnome gave an incoherent grumbling response. The faun carried on.

"This bear here is our apprentice magician—"

"And pilot, might I add," the bear nervously interjected. The faun didn't miss a beat.

"Yes, trainee pilot too, the wonderful Ms Gruffennia Kolchi!"

"Cheers!" came the bear's response, a sheepish grin now creeping onto her face as she continued inspecting the chamber, looking for traps and surveillance points.

"And finally, of course, *moi*! I am Mistress Isabella Cortai, adventurer extraordinaire. Excellent fighter, silver tongued, and as you can see, daringly beautiful. I am the new captain of the mighty pirate ship the *Evanescence*."

"The *Evanescence*!" Bethany interjected in awe. That was Grollp's ship.

"I'm guessing you've heard of it—"

Before Isabella could continue bragging and Bethany could fan her ego, Bethany heard another voice, entirely unattached to any of the characters in the chamber.

"Excuse me, ma'am," the deep, wizened voice said. Bethany had no idea where it came from. Indeed, it felt like, rather than entering her ear as sound, it was bouncing around without origin in the middle of her brain.

"Oh, don't be alarmed, that's just Tassarin," Isabella explained. "He's an Andarin. Mysterious beings, magically gifted too. That voice of his, well, he's broadcasting it to you psychically. Only way they can talk, see. Go on, my boatswain, sir!"

"Sorry to interrupt, but I don't think this is the time for such formal introductions."

The faun captain waved it off, pacing, her hand toying with the hilt of her sabre. "Nah. No need to worry. We're in the deepest, darkest part of Goldensmorg, the restricted zone. Even with that explosion, no one's going to hear us down here."

There was a brief awkward silence as she and her companions stared upwards, as if expecting a response from their psychic friend.

"I am sorry to inform you, ma'am, but the guards have been alerted to our presence. I suspect the Inquisitor has been informed too. This Bethany Hannah Morgan is of the highest priority. I advise you extradite yourself from your current location and rendezvous at my location as rapidly as you can."

As if on cue, an alarm could be heard faintly from outside Bethany's chamber. It was all that these three adventurers needed. They headed towards the opening blasted in the cell corner.

"Understood, my friend. Let's go! Stay with me, Bethany, all right?"

She nodded as she followed her three rescuers quickly through the hole. To her surprise, she was greeted by the gloom and stench of the Goldensmorg sewers. Her colleagues seemed unaffected as they advanced down the tunnel to the right of the blast hole with some pace. Knowing that her freedom depended on it, she quickly followed into the semi-illuminated darkness. Kolchi led the way, her staff shining brightly in front of her, whilst the faun captain made sure she accompanied Bethany, shouting out encouragement to her as she went.

"Don't worry, my friend, we'll soon be out of here. I'll stake my life that you'll be safely out of here in no time at all!"

The gnome pirate brought up the rear, pistols in hand and grumbling.

As we have already seen, the sewer complex of Goldensmorg is a vast labyrinth of tunnels that is only traversable with any confidence by the few individuals with a key understanding of its layout. Most unfortunates who find themselves within it become hopelessly lost. Indeed, this would have been the case for our hero and her rescuers if not for the strong psychic ability of their Andarin friend Tassarin. Whenever they came to a crossroads, antechamber, or what have you, the group would go through the same routine. Isabella would bark out orders to Tassarin, who would reply in his deep and wizened voice. They would then proceed in the direction their psychic friend would provide. At first Bethany found his voice unnerving, appearing as it did rather suddenly within her head. After a while, however, she began to find it reassuring. Each instruction seemed to bring her closer to freedom.

They carried on in this manner for some time and they made good progress, staying together and advancing through the claustrophobic tunnels of the sewer. Our hero had forgotten her exhaustion in her eagerness to finally escape. Their pursuers, however, were tailing them closely. No matter how quickly they went, the alarm could still be heard behind them, slowly but surely getting louder and louder, as if it were drawing closer to their position. Still, they were moving quickly, and Bethany hoped that if they continued this way they would reach their destination before anything or anyone could catch up with them.

It was impossible to keep a sense of time in the tunnels. Though they hadn't been running, Bethany was exhausted, and the others didn't look much better. Sweat dripped down their faces, and the heat and stench of the tunnels was getting to them. She knew, however, that soon they'd be free – she could sense it. Tassarin's directions were becoming more encouraging. Isabella turned to her, breathing heavily in her weariness.

"Just a few clicks now. You'll see. We'll come out the side of the Sixpenny Ridge, then a quick hop on the *Evanescence* and away we go."

Bethany could do little but respond in her hopeful exhaustion, "Really? Where will we go from there?"

"Once we're on the ship, we'll make a beeline across Goldensmorg. Go as fast as we can, you see. Be like we're flying straight off this godforsaken rock. Then comes the interesting bit—"

Before she could continue, they had turned a corner, and she was interrupted nervously by their bear friend.

"Captain!"

The faun lost much of her jovial manner and snapped into business mode. She turned her attention to Kolchi ahead of her. "What is it?" Her voice was blunt.

Though it was soon quite evident what the problem was.

"This ain't meant to be here..." replied the bear. She stood pointing at a huge iron gate that barred their way.

Bethany was not quite sure what this meant, but clearly it wasn't good. Isabella's demeanour changed dramatically. Where she had been jovial and boisterous, she now appeared serious, determined, and commanding. Orin had stopped grumbling and now stared wide eyed in bemusement at the gate that barred their way.

"Tassarin!" came Isabella's barked order.

"Yes, Captain?" duly came the response.

"We have a problem here. One of the sluice gates has closed. We can't go further if it's down."

The sounds of their pursuers were now becoming audible from behind. They were only a few corners away. Moments went by before any response came from the Andarin.

"I deeply apologise that it slipped past my notice. The Inquisitor's powers are distorting the effectiveness of my abilities. He must have guessed your route and closed it accordingly. May I recommend you blast your way through?"

With that, Orin perked up. His eyes widened and shone as a grin appeared on his face.

"O'course! 'Xplosives would do it. Let me have a crack at this, miz!" He seemed to bounce on the spot.

The sound of their pursuers was closer still. After a few seconds of what appeared to be deep contemplation, Isabella replied, "All right. But get to it! We ain't got much time. I can't hold them off forever."

"I'll get right at it den!" He scurried towards the gate, pulling his goggles down from the top of his head over his eyes as he grabbed bombs and tools from various straps and pockets.

"Kolchi! Help him."

With an anxious mumble, the huge bear did as she was bid. The captain then turned her attention to Bethany, drawing a flintlock pistol from a leather strap across her front.

"You know how to use one of these?"

"No…" came Bethany's stuttered response as the weapon was placed in her hands. It was heavy and cold, and she felt awkward holding it.

"Don't worry, you'll get the hang of it. All I need you to do is cover me, all right?"

Bethany nervously nodded her response.

"That's my girl! Now follow me."

Isabella drew a long, cogged brass rifle from the holster on her back. It was an ornate item, made from both fine wood and patterned metal. Attached to its underbelly was a cartridge chamber similar to that of a classic Western revolver that she'd seen in films. Bethany noticed it had eight shots. With a few gazelle-like bounds on hoofed feet, the faun captain leapt over the canal of sewage and was on the other side, where she knelt behind a corner of masonry. She aimed her rifle in the direction of the noise. Bethany stumbled into position, leaning her back against their nearest corner and poking her head round it, peering into the gloom. Her body was shivering as if from cold. She'd never held a gun before, let alone been in any kind of fight. Indeed, she realised she could be rather ineffectual in a confrontation. Their pursuers were growing closer. Light seemed to bob around in the distance, travelling along the corridor they had come from. She took a deep breath, trying to calm her nerves. Isabella was still kneeling, gun raised. The noise of the enemy got louder. They waited to receive the onslaught.

It wasn't long before the first of their pursuers came into view. Approaching our hero, they came in single file either side of the sewer canal, their large, orcish frames impeding them slightly. With them were a number of grogs, similar to their green cousins but slightly smaller, hairier, and with boar-like faces. With burning torches and weapons raised, they approached our hero's hiding place with bloodlust in their eyes. She hid herself back around the corner before peeking out once again. They were approaching fast. The grogs sniffed the air eagerly, then stopping momentarily the lead grog pointed roughly in her direction – they knew she was there. With boastful grunts they sped up, eager to get to grips with their foe. Our hero could do nothing. She stood in position, frozen, the pistol in her hand, as if watching the beginning of a great train wreck. They were only a few metres away. Bethany could smell the stench of boiled leather and sweat.

Before they could reach her, Isabella fired. A bright green light smashed into the wall beside the lead grog. It exploded, flinging it and the orc behind across the tunnel. Masonry flew with them as they landed in the canal of sewage. Before they could react, she fired again. This time she hit the orc on her gangway, flinging the beast backwards into its mates behind it. Another orc stumbled and fell into the river of sewage. She aimed again.

"Come on, you scurvy beasts!"

She fired, hitting a grog who was in the process of raising its musket. Then she turned to hide behind her corner. Bethany did the same as their pursuers returned fire. Flashes of green, blue, and red light flew past them, blasting pieces off the walls. Isabella laughed to herself.

"See, my friend, they couldn't hit a giant from five paces. You try a shot, aye?"

Bethany nodded nervously.

"Right, they're reloading let's go!" Said Isabella.

They both appeared from their respective corners. Isabella fired first, sending three bolts of light towards the enemy on her side. Two missed as the respective orcs ducked out the way. The third, however, caught a grog in the shoulder, sending the beast flying to the floor. Bethany tried as well, but stepping awkwardly she tripped over her own feet. The pistol lurched back with great force as she pulled the trigger. The shot itself was wide, hitting the ceiling above a pair of orcs, but it hit it with such force that chunks of masonry were ripped from it and fell upon the two orcs beneath, knocking them out. Isabella couldn't help but laugh.

"Well done, me girl! You better reload now. Turn that crank."

They hid themselves again behind their respective corners as the return fire came. There were still plenty of them out there. They seemed to be getting more accurate, too, as more bolts of energy crashed against their corners, sending lumps of rubble this way and that. Bethany found the crank on the side of her flintlock-style pistol and quickly got to work reloading. The ball inside it began to glow.

"It's lighting up!" she called across the din of the next enemy volley.

"Good. That's what you need. Now cock back the hammer!"

She did as she was told, using the whole of her strength to do so.

"Done!"

Isabella gave her another encouraging nod. After the next enemy volley, she responded.

"Let's go then!"

Their enemy was closer and their numbers had grown. Towering above the group of orcs and grogs was a huge troll, heavily armoured and brandishing what appeared to be a cannon. Before she could take a proper look, Bethany fired her pistol. Her aim was wide and she missed. Isabella fired her last three shots in quick succession, hitting a grog on Bethany's side and not much else. They hid again behind their corners and began reloading. Bethany noticed a worried look on Isabella's face.

"How long, Orin?"

"Nut much time now, miz!"

"Well, hurry it up, all right! Heavily armed troll coming our way!"

The gnome got back to his work, grumbling audibly. Kolchi tried to help as best she could, though it looked to Bethany like she was really more of a hindrance.

Another volley of blasts flew in their direction. It was at this point that Bethany saw something behind Isabella. In the darkness in the tunnel that branched off from their position were two pairs of red eyes. Bethany thought she heard a low, menacing growl. The captain was too busy reloading to notice as they grew close.

"Behind you!" cried Bethany, pointing.

Two large hyena-like creatures leapt from the darkness. They were ugly and twisted, with beastly horns protruding from their heads. They growled as they flew through the air, pouncing upon the captain. Bethany raised her pistol and fired. The bolt of light hit one of the creatures in mid-air, throwing its body aside with its force. The other creature managed to reach Isabella as she turned to face them, biting into her shoulder. She yelled in pain as the beast's teeth sank into her. She threw her rifle butt around, smashing the creature in the face. It yowled in agony as she threw it from her shoulder and into the river of sewage. She collapsed to her knees, panting in pain.

"Hurry up!" she yelled, clutching the bleeding wound.

This was it, Bethany thought. Isabella was in no fit state to fight on, and there was little chance she'd be able to fight off this endless horde of orcs, grogs, and other malicious beasts on her own. She hid behind her corner as another volley ripped further chunks of it away. Closing her eyes, she reloaded as she waited for the inevitable ordnance from the troll to make its impact. But before it came, a familiar voice burst from among her pursuers.

"Halt!"

It was the Inquisitor. A dim hush descended. Even Orin stopped and looked up, before continuing with his work.

"I must congratulate you for your resistance, but it should be clear that this is all utterly futile."

Isabella was still breathing heavily, but she grabbed hold of her rifle again and continued to reload.

"We have you surrounded. There is no escape. That is, unless you hand in the girl to us. Give her over and I can guarantee favourable treatment, or at the very least gift you with a quick, painless death."

Isabella was now staring at Orin expectantly, who was staring right back at her, a grin on his face. She gave him a nod, to which he rubbed his hands with glee.

"Show yourselves now! Such resistance will only see you suffer."

Our hero and her companions made no reply. Orin and Kolchi shuffled into a better position next to her. He leant over to whisper.

"I wud recommend you cover your ears."

"She is an enemy of the Alpharian Confederation – indeed, of reality itself – and therefore you must surrender her so justice and order can be resu—"

The Inquisitor didn't finish his sentence.

KKKKKAAAAABBBBBOOOOOMMMMM!

The earth itself shook. Bethany held on to her ears as best she could, trying to blot out the deafening noise. Though her ears were safe, the force of the blast put her in a precarious position, throwing her across the tunnel. Her whole body was scrambled, as if turned to jelly. What she could tell was that she was about to fall right into the raw sewage of the canal. The prospect of such a demise did not excite her, but there was little she could do. Time seemed to slow down as she plummeted to her stench-filled end.

Luckily for Bethany, Isabella had noticed too. Though she was injured, she still found the energy to leap forward, vaulting over the gap between them with all the strength and grace of a horse. She plucked Bethany from the air with her right arm and continued to sail across to the other side, landing with ease and precision, dodging the occasional musket blasts from their assailants.

"Run!" she shouted as the dust was settling.

Run they did, charging with great speed through the now-destroyed sluice gate that had barred them. Isabella scooped up Orin with her left arm as they went, as the poor gnome's feet could barely go that fast. They were going upwards, racing along a gentle slope, which after a few moments was devoid of sewage. In fact, our hero was soon greeted by the refreshing bite of cold, fresh air. She was still getting her bearings, but she quickly realized they were actually outside, standing upon a platform high above the city itself. It was night, but still it was far brighter than anything she had experienced inside the sewers and dungeons of Goldensmorg.

Isabella placed her on the ground. She couldn't believe it – she was finally free and outside on Goldensmorg, and it was glorious. But there was little time to take it all in, as she was soon ushered forwards to something quite marvellous in front of her. Hovering just a foot from the platform was a ship right out of the eighteenth century. It had cannons, sails, and three tall masts, even a crow's nest. An aura of bright, golden, magical energy glistened around the vessel. Bethany could only stand in wonder. Isabella placed a four-fingered clipped hand on her shoulder.

"I'm glad you like it, Bethany. I think you might've heard of this fine vessel before. This here is the *Evanescence!*"

Eleven

"MADAME, I DON'T MEAN TO HARASS YOU, BUT it is of the utmost importance that you board the *Evanescence* this moment so that we may depart and make our escape," Tassarin instructed.

Both Bethany and the faun captain awoke from their almost hypnotic admiration of the ship. He was right. The rumblings of their pursuers were growing louder behind them.

"Yes, yes. Right you lot, all aboard!"

It was all they needed, and Orin and Kolchi scrambled up the boarding plank onto the deck of the ship. Bethany did likewise, following the gnome across, making sure to keep her balance. As she made the journey, she hazarded a glance downwards and could see in the haze and darkness of the night the city of Goldensmorg below, all glistening from the shine of a thousand lights and windows. She took it in quickly with delight. It was like seeing a Christmas tree for the first time.

With a few bounds she was upon the deck of the ship. It looked just how she had expected an eighteenth-century wooden ship of the line would look, but with a number of peculiar, ornate brass contraptions that pulsed frequently with light. What caught her attention, however, was the crew. From what she could see, it was made up of roughly two dozen colourful grubbs and no one else. They were all dressed as stereotypical pirates with eye patches, wooden legs, hooks, and even smaller grubbs that sat on their shoulders imitating parrots. They growled and roared in typical pirate fashion, and murmured about grog and pieces of eight almost constantly. Bethany felt a tinge of mockery coming from the creatures.

For everyone else it was business as usual, and the captain, once she had arrived on the ship, started to bellow commands.

"All right, you swabs! Time for us to set off. All hands to your duties! Master Orin, to your mechanisms."

The gnome needed no such instruction, as he was already pushing through the grubbs, grumbling as usual. The mischievous sprites, which were only slightly shorter than him, seemed to get louder with their mock pirate noises as he passed. Soon the gnome headed down some steps into the hull of the ship.

"Boatswain Kolchi!"

The bear made herself apparent to the captain, staff in hand, with a quick salute.

"Yes, captain?"

Isabella gave a quick nod. "The enemy's coming in fast, with a lot of fire power. We're going to need you as secondary ship artificer. Get to it!"

"As you command, miz!"

With a quick salute, she rushed into the centre of the ship, staff raised and muttering to herself.

The captain was right – the enemy was close behind them.

Bethany had stopped listening to Isabella's commands and had moved to a position where she could see the dungeon entrance they had just passed through. A nervous tension gripped her gropscrub body. Grubbs had now scattered across the deck at a further command in a flurry of activity, arghing as they went. Our hero paid them little attention, focusing instead on the approaching enemy. They burst through from the darkness of the tunnels, torches and weapons in hand. Those grogs and orcs with muskets began to fire freely, but their shots either went wide or simply scratched the paint of the ship's hull. Next came the troll, armed with its cannon, who promptly took aim. Finally came the most menacing of all, the Inquisitor, his black cloak blowing in the wind, his eyes full of anger as he stared at her position. All this happened in what felt like a series of long and nerve-wracking minutes, when in reality it was mere seconds, for with a jolt the ship burst into action.

Our hero was thrown to the floor as the ship roared rather unexpectedly to life. They were away, and with great speed too as the vessel soared through the sky as light as a bird, with all the agility of a fox. The troll fired its cannon with a roar, but the *Evanescence* quickly redirected, and the missile passed harmlessly by. In a few short moments they had made great distance, and Bethany could hardly see her assailants anymore. Relieved, she felt it was time to let herself relax and enjoy. She was free and flying through the air on a great pirate ship over a mysterious city full of lights and adventure. True, she was still stuck inside a gropscrub's body, and the mysterious man who had visited her in her cell had given her a rather difficult task to accomplish. But her bag was still securely on her back, with the locket in its front pocket. Confident of its security, she let these problems disappear from her mind, at least for the moment, and began to enjoy her ride on the *Evanescence*.

Bethany ran across the deck, leaning over the sides to get a better look at the world she had yet to properly see. Down below it was dark, but she was still mesmerised by the twinkling lights of the city beneath them. She could make out the shapes of all sorts of buildings; some seemed very similar to 1½ Cordling Drive, whilst others seemed totally different. What they all shared, though, was that they were obscenely tall, for she could barely make out any streets or front doors. As she continued to look, it became apparent to her that Goldensmorg was almost entirely covered with buildings and nothing else – it was as if the whole planet was just one huge city. But that didn't dampen her spirits. Indeed, it made her more fascinated. She bounced from one side to the other in excitement, at times stopping to feel the wind brush into her face as the ship raced through the air. She only wished she had another thousand eyes, as well as daylight, so that she could take every single last bit of detail in.

After a while, it became clear that they were ascending ever upwards, as if they were intending to burst right out into space.

"Enjoying yourself there, young lady?" shouted Isabella in delight from behind the ship's wheel.

Bethany nodded excitedly in response.

"Nothing beats flying a hearty vessel like the *Evanescence* here. Especially in the heat of a chase!"

Bethany could hardly contain herself. She was almost dancing with delight. "It's amazing!" she shouted.

Isabella could not help but laugh. Even Kolchi stifled a bit of laughter. It looked like she had relaxed somewhat too, confident that they were now safe.

"Well, if you think this is good, you ain't seen nothing yet! Boatswain Kolchi, you ready to assist?"

The bear nodded, looking nervous again. "Ready as I'll ever be…"

"Right then! Tassarin, continue ascending and increase speed!"

The ship began to speed up even more, so much so that the city below with all its lights became a blur. Bethany had never travelled this fast before. All she felt she could do was hold on as best she could. They rose and rose, crashing through the clouds above them. A twinge of panic gripped our hero.

"Don't you worry there, Ms Bethany. All under control!"

She hazarded a glance around the deck of the ship. To her surprise, everyone seemed calm, just getting on with their duties. The ship continued to rise, hurtling through the sky. The city and all her lights lay out of sight below them.

"Where are we going?" Bethany shouted above the din of rushing wind and the buzz of the ship's machinery.

"At this present moment? Well, into space! But where we're actually going? That'd ruin the surprise!"

The ship was starting to burst through the planet's atmosphere, shuddering. Our transformed hero held on for dear life to the side railings, taking a deep breath in preparation for their entry into space. The ship seemed to be running on a course to its own destruction, and despite her newfound fondness for these characters, she hadn't eliminated the possibility that they were crazy or suicidal, maybe even both. It didn't help that Isabella frequently hooted or laughed in delight at the thrill of their current speed and trajectory.

"Here we go, friends! Hahahahahahaha – brace yourselves!"

By that point, Bethany had been bracing herself for what seemed like an eternity. The rest of the crew on deck finally did likewise, though it looked like they did so more out of respect for their captain's orders than from actual fear. A number of the grubbs actually growled or giggled to themselves in delight. This affirmed Bethany's opinion: they were all stark raving mad. With a tremendous shudder and a clatter, the ship burst through Goldensmorg's atmosphere, throwing a number of the magical pirate sprites to the deck. Bethany closed her eyes tightly.

The clattering stopped, and the ship gently glided on its way once more. Bethany was still in one piece, and breathing too. In fact it was all rather anti-climactic. So realising that nothing bad was going to happen she sheepishly peeled her eyes open and found to her surprise that they were now zooming though the great blackness of space. She turned to look back at Goldensmorg, now a ball that was gradually getting smaller, disappearing behind them. The crew had gone back to their duties, with little bother or celebration. With some hesitance, she then let herself free from the railing she had attached herself to and directed herself towards the captain. The ship itself still seemed to be going monstrously fast.

"Was that it?"

Isabella gave a huge hearty laugh in response. Some of the grubbs joined in with their mock piratical giggles.

"Well, I guess we're in space now. But that ain't the good part. Watch this!"

Bethany hesitantly clasped a hand onto the railing again in preparation.

"Kolchi, are you ready?"

With a gulp and a nod, the bear responded, then she began to mutter to herself again, this time with greater intensity and desperation.

"Right then! Master Tassarin, cease all power to the main capacitors…"

Bethany gripped the railing with both hands.

"…NOW!"

The energy that encompassed the ship and compelled it forward subsided. The bizarre machinery that protruded from the *Evanescence* stopped buzzing too, though the ship continued hurtling through space at the same speed.

"Now, my friend, put all power in reverse motion!"

"As you command."

The ship then began to slowly but surely decrease in speed. Bethany's hands loosened again from around the railing, though our hero had somewhat forgotten how to breathe as she waited expectantly for the next event. But all that happened was that the ship continued to slow down, as if being blocked by an almost equally strong push in the other direction. Just as the ship was stopping, Bethany noticed Kolchi's eyes had started to glisten, her chanting growing to a new intensity. Something very interesting was about to happen.

Before Bethany could blink, however, she again felt herself being broken into millions of little pieces. A familiar white light shone, and it felt as if she was hurtling at great speed across a vast distance with an unnerving hissing noise screeching in her ear. The whole experience was almost entirely like her journey via the wizard door, but this time she felt that there was a lot more travelling with her. Thankfully, she knew it would be brief, and in a few short moments all the tiny particles that had once made up her and those around her began to reconstruct themselves. The hissing subsided and the light again dimmed and disappeared. When it finally ended, she found herself back together again and very much herself, albeit in the body of a gropscrub, standing upon the deck of the *Evanescence*. There were Kolchi and Isabella, looking the same as they had been before. The grubb crew, however, seemed to be somewhat of a mess. Where before they were in pirate clothes, they now appeared to be dressed as typical Georgian gentlemen and gentlewomen in formal attire, with white powdered make-up and wigs, as well as coats, puffy dresses, and stockings and hose. They bowed to each other ceremonially and mockingly greeted each other in an arrogant manner, with the obligatory sniggers and giggles lurking behind their smiles.

They were now somewhere entirely different. Rather than high up in space above the planet of Goldensmorg, they all appeared to be in a huge, grand dining hall, in some kind of large country house, with a smashed chandelier and a crushed banquet table that had clearly met its end with the sudden arrival of the *Evanescence*.

"Where are we?"

With a few steps and a quick, graceful leap, the faun Isabella appeared next to her.

"We, my friend, are on Goldensmorg, in the house of the—"

Before she could finish, a Bethany-sized elderly man, with thick glasses, and long grey beard, dressed in what looked to her like traditional scarlet wizard robes, burst through the dining room door. His face was burning red with rage.

"How many times have I told you! Never apparate into the DINING ROOM!"

With that, Bethany finally let go of the railing and remembered how to breathe again.

Twelve

With Orin appearing again from below, the whole crew, minus the grubbs and Tassarin, stood sheepishly on deck. The diminutive wizard's anger had a remarkable impact on them. The Georgian-styled grubbs watched eagerly, with smiles on their faces and suppressed giggles behind their teeth.

"Much apologies for that, I must say, Alarabus. We did intend to apparate in the hangar, but something must have gone amiss," said Isabella.

Even to Bethany, it was clear that the captain knew exactly who was at fault, but she imagined it was pirate honour not to expose someone in such a manner. Orin, of course, tutted and grumbled to himself, eying up his bear companion, whose face was the very image of guilt.

"I'm… s-sorry, sir… I didn't m-mean to… just in th-the moment…" stuttered Kolchi, lost for words.

It did little to calm the wizard, whose face was going an angry red; it seemed like he'd explode at any moment.

"Please forgive the young Kolchi," interjected the sombre, wizened voice of the Andarin. "She is still young and has much to learn. I believe in the panic of the escape, she must have focused too much on your house, much to the detriment of your furniture. I too must apologise for the mistake, as I should have taken on the momentous task rather than expecting the inexperienced acolyte here to accomplish it, especially under stressful conditions."

This explanation did its job. Tassarin's soothing tones relaxed the little wizard, who went from a boiling rage to a more manageable level of frustration. He batted away the comments with his hand.

"Well, well, what am I to do," his small, squeaky voice went, as he took off his spectacles and polished them with his large sleeves. "I do hope we have been successful in our mission. Disembark, and let's sort this all out."

He placed his glasses back on his face, magnifying his tiny green eyes once again, huffing his displeasure as he did so. The crew laid the gangplank and then scrambled down it, landing on the broken wreckage of the dining table before climbing onto the marbled flooring. It was in that moment that Tassarin first appeared from within the bowels of the ship. The Andarin was quite a sight and unlike any being Bethany had ever met. Their race, as she had been told, were wraith like creatures of pure emotion and amazing magical ability. They existed to find good experiences and lasting bonds, driven as they were by their love for life, which they valued above almost everything else. This being, however, did not look like a creature of joy, but rather of sadness and war. Tassarin was tall, Bethany guessed around seven feet. He was powerfully built, though slim, like a swimmer or dancer, but with far broader shoulders. He was shrouded in a fine cloak and hood. The fabric was lined with runes and text, all in dark purples and blacks. Underneath this layer, she could see elegant plates of dark golden armour and a long blade, sheathed in an equally elaborate scabbard. What was perhaps most interesting was his face. It was like a mask of stone, still and expressionless, shaped like a skull minus the bottom jaw. Its surface was smooth and it was elegant in design, bearing an artistic simplicity. It was covered in a great series of cracks that gave the impression that it could easily shatter. In the middle of which were eyes that took the form of two blue lights. Nothing much else could be deciphered of the creature, as everything was clothed, gloved, or otherwise covered up.

Bethany realised she was staring and looked away awkwardly.

"Do not be embarrassed or ashamed, my friend. I understand my race is very much unlike any you would have met. Though I think it is proper that we present ourselves to the wizard."

She nodded and did as she was told, clambering down the gangplank to the floor. As she went, she noticed the Andarin moving behind her. He did so with a magical grace, almost as if he were floating, each move deliberate and precise, covering the ground with great ease. An aura of power and strength underlined each movement, like that of a big cat hunting in its prime. Out of the corner of her eye, she could tell Isabella, who was attending to her injured shoulder, and the other crew had been muttering to the wizard. As she reached the floor, she felt the eyes of the man locked upon her.

"My, my, you must be Ms Bethany Hannah Morgan," he said inquisitively.

"I am, yes."

Bethany could think of no other response. An excited smile appeared on the wizard's face.

"We have been expecting you! It's a shame that things did not quite go to plan. But here we are. You're not looking how you should, but you need not worry. I will soon sort that for you."

The wizard seemed giddy with happiness, almost bouncing in the air. Bethany could not help but raise a smile. He was clearly delighted to see her.

"But enough of this chatter, let us get you back to normal. Tassarin, deal with the ship, please."

"As you wish."

With a nod and a gesture of the Andarin's gloved hand, the *Evanescence* disappeared, with all the grubbs still giggling on board. Before she could think, Alarabus was off through the great doors and into the rest of the house. Bethany did her best to keep up, but he was surprisingly fast, his energy and excitement clearly enhancing his speed as he tottered away. Orin, Kolchi, and Isabella also followed. They passed through a series of ornate corridors and rooms, immaculately dressed and decorated, no two of them the same. With gestures, great doors opened before him. The house was surprisingly empty. Isabella tried her best to communicate with Alarabus, clutching her shoulder as she went.

"See here, we did it. A few more problems than we expected. Landed ourselves in a lot of trouble. But we did as planned, pulled off our trick too. They'll end up searching high and low for us. Even the Inquisitor—"

"Well, they won't think of looking for you here on Goldensmorg – if you did it properly, that is. Given us plenty of time to prepare. Well done for getting the girl, better late than never."

It was difficult to get his attention as he raced through the house, taking little heed of the captain, his mind apparently focused on something more important. Before long they were climbing flights of stairs, going further and further upwards into the seemingly never-ending building. The architecture itself had become high Gothic, the decorations grimmer. The gargoyles that our hero passed seemed to be everywhere, and she occasionally caught some of them shuffling around. At the top of a great stairwell, two large doors with finely carved wooden panels stood in front of them. The characters on them moved of their own accord, and with the arrival of their master, they swiftly gave all their attention to the tiny wizard.

He stopped, brushed himself down quickly, and turned on the spot towards our hero a few steps behind him, his red velvet wizard robes swishing.

"Now, Bethany, I must say I am sorry that you have had to go through so much trouble to get here. It was never my intention. You were meant to be picked up in the sewers. It is imperative that we get things moving. But there is a great deal I must tell you first."

With a stern look, he peered over Bethany's shoulders at the pirate crew. They were awkwardly looking to one another, waiting for the wizard to continue. Alarabus gave a sharp and impatient cough. Tassarin had just caught up, his travel graceful, purposeful, but slow.

"I understand that our wizard master here does not want us present," he said. "I believe he desires to speak to Bethany alone."

Orin gave a grunt of disgust. "Too good for us, are you?"

Kolchi seemed uneasy as the standoff continued. Tassarin stood emotionless in the silence, watching. This would have continued but for the intervention of the captain.

"Don't worry, friends. Let's give them some privacy. I think it's time for some grub!" Isabella eagerly said, trying her best to defuse the situation.

They all turned and began to descend the staircase, Orin leading the way, grumbling as always.

"I'll see you later, all right?"

The captain winked at our hero and, first with hesitant steps, then with an eager gallop, followed the rest of the crew downwards. Bethany watched until they were out of sight. She was alone with the eccentric little wizard.

"Pirates. Funny bunch they are. A good team too, not like some of the ne'er-do-wells I've had the unpleasant experience of dealing with. That captain is rather fond of you."

A small smile formed on Bethany's face as she turned back to the wizard.

"She'll take care of you, I know she will."

An eager little smile was on his face too, wrinkling the corners of his eyes.

"But now on to the matters at hand. We are about to enter my office, and there are only a few special people who have entered it. You, Bethany, are indeed a very special person."

Bethany awkwardly fidgeted in response. She could hardly see why everyone thought she was so special; she was just a rather eccentric person who wasn't really good at much. (As you can tell, she had never learnt how to receive compliments.) The wizard turned on the spot and faced the great doors to his office with his arms outstretched. The animated figures on the wood panels waited intently.

"Open!" came his demand.

There was a flurry of activity. Each of the wooden figures promptly searched for its own key, placed it in a keyhole, and turned. With a great moan, the two doors opened, revealing the office inside. It was huge, with bookshelves and papers everywhere. Everything was made of rich polished oak. Here and there were tools and devices of all descriptions that seemed to be operating entirely on their own. Typewriters and floating quills autonomously wrote notes on parchment. Great ancient books floated through the air, past statues, pieces of art, and piles of paperwork. Furniture was littered liberally across the room, interspersing the collection of eccentric objects, artefacts, and detritus. The room was busy with movement and an utter mess.

Our hero followed the wizard inside, walking along a rich red carpet, momentarily distracted by a vast map on the wall to her left.

"Welcome to my office. I hope I don't offend you with its current state. I am a very busy wizard. Never a moment's rest! I guess that happens when you take on the role of Grand High Wizard. Have I told you that yet?"

Bethany shook her head and then proceeded to duck a book that was floating a bit too low. "No, you haven't…"

The wizard stopped, turning his head to look back at her. Everything in the office stopped momentarily.

"Well, I am, you know. A very important job, it is. Now, where was I…" He scratched the side of his head contemplatively.

"You were welcoming me to your office—"

"Ah, yes!"

His office came back to life as he continued on his way, Bethany close behind. They were heading towards the tidiest desk in the middle of the room, which was accompanied by three chairs.

"This wonderful chamber is where I work and learn. Would you like a hot Cripsen brew?"

"A Cripsen brew?"

They came to a stop again as they reached the semi-tidy furniture.

"Oh yes, you won't know what one of them is." He gave his head a scratch again. "I guess it is similar to what you call tea. Yes. Very popular here. Before it was discovered, everyone had the funny habit of heating up water and drinking it with a bit of milk and sugar. It's not really from Cripsen either, funny that..."

He continued to witter on. As he did, he gestured towards the chairs, beckoning her to sit. With a swish of his hand, all the unnecessary clutter on the table whisked up in the air and flew across the room, finding a new place to rest. They sat, and the wizard, still lost in his thoughts, clicked his fingers. A small, elegant teapot and two matching teacups and saucers, as well as a jug, sugar pot, and spoon, flew through the air and landed in front of them on the table.

"...but there you go. 'Tis a funny old galaxy, isn't it?"

Bethany was too distracted by the tea set to properly listen. The tea had been poured, milk had been added, and it had presented itself on the table just in front of her.

"Yes, I guess it is..."

She could suddenly feel a cold metal prod. She looked down to see the sugar pot was indignantly using a spoon to get her attention.

"Oh, it wants to know how many spoons of sugar you have."

"Right... erm..." Looking awkwardly at the piece of crockery, she responded, "Two, please."

The object did as it was told, ladling two spoonfuls of sugar into her teacup, stirring, and then making itself scarce again. Bethany found the whole thing rather delightful. The wizard had begun drinking his tea, legs dangling off the edge of the chair, being too short to rest them on the ground.

"I can imagine you are probably wondering what is going on, and how you figure into all of this?"

Bethany nodded as she struggled to pick up the teacup in her gropscrub hands.

"This galaxy is having a bit of bother. It's stagnated, you might say. Some even go on to say there's no more room, no more adventures. This is simply not the case. There is still life to be had, wonders to be discovered."

Bethany listened intently, her tea untouched.

"The Alpharian Confederation is indeed corrupt and a bit evil at times, but that could easily change if we put our minds to it. What the real problem is, well, it's that boy and his minder. I think you might have met them already, yes?"

A cold shiver ran down her spine as she remembered her current form and how unnatural and uncomfortable she felt in it. Alarabus continued.

"They have done wicked things, which I think you know first-hand. It wasn't always like that. Indeed, that boy, what was his name again… begins with an 'F' or something. Well, he did wonders for our world, a proper hero he was. Had a magic beyond even my comprehension."

The wizard gulped down his tea in short order. He looked cold and sad, his energy somewhat drained as a flush of melancholia seemed to take over.

"But then everything changed. Something, and I do not know what, happened, and it changed him forever. He disappeared for a long time. When he did finally reappear, he was different. Everywhere he went, he was always accompanied by his minder. Only sorrow and destruction were sown. That black hole, the Heart of Unreason, well purple really, the one in space, well, we presume that was created by him too. Any day now, it could activate and bring all life here in Edimor to a terrifying end."

The little wizard now looked truly sad. It was contagious – the books and papers themselves seemed to slow as if afflicted by the same sorrow. Bethany too felt a shiver of worry, even slight terror, grip her. She had heard it all before, of course, but it had never truly felt like it meant anything then.

"But all is not lost yet." The wizard perked himself up again, regaining some of his energy. "There is an item. A tiny item from your world with unimaginable power, or so the legends say. So special that, if used properly, it could end all our problems."

Bethany could visualise the locket hidden in the back of her bag, but she was hesitant to reveal it. The smiling man had warned her to be cautious.

"When, after lengthy study, I managed to confirm its existence and ascertain its location, I sent my good friend Grollp and his crew on an adventure to find it. Unfortunately, others learnt of its existence and did all they could to stop them. It was all in vain, though, and they were able to obtain the item. On his return they stopped at port, and that was when Grollp was ambushed by the crew of the *Abomination*. He made quick his desperate escape, despite some injuries, and appeared in your world. I think we both know what happened next."

Bethany nodded her head silently. She missed the troll captain.

"Most of the crew made themselves scarce after that; they were scared. Only Tassarin, Kolchi, Orin, and Isabella remain. Lacking crew members, they now have to summon those annoying magical sprites to help. In a bit of a pickle, I went for some advice, and I was informed by reliable sources that all was not lost – that despite the initial failure of the plan, you would appear and prove yourself to be our saviour, Bethany."

Her ears pricked at the sound of her name, though she certainly didn't consider herself a saviour of any kind. All she'd done so far was muddle her way through from one mess to the next. Only now did she seem to have had any luck, largely due to the kindness of Isabella and her crew. She'd thought her part in the story was purely accidental. Maybe that wasn't the case.

"I spoke to the Dramatimancers. They predicted your appearance, and here you are. You even arrived in the sewers, exactly as they said. They told me more, of all the changes that you will make and how integral to our galaxy's story you are. How you, in fact, would arrive in our world with the very item I had been searching for."

Bethany became somewhat nervous again, her heart pounding away. He leaned inquisitively over the table, his eyes magnified by the glasses, peered at her.

"I would very much like to see that item."

Bethany didn't know what to say. He was still leaning across the table expectantly. The crockery seemed to do the same, waiting for the great reveal. But it didn't come. Bethany, being a very stubborn person, and heeding the advice of the smiling man, decided she should keep hold of it. She didn't want to disobey the first helpful individual she'd met on Edimor, despite how mysterious he was.

"I'm sorry, Mr Alarabus, I'd prefer not to..."

His disappointment was evident with a confused indignant wrinkle of his face. In a few moments, however, the whole room went back to its normal behaviour. Alarabus himself relaxed again, leaning back into his chair.

"Very well then. The Dramatimancers are very confident in your ability. As I trust their judgment, I will therefore trust yours. Indeed, I do not expect anything malicious in the slightest from you. I am confident you will prove a very competent and successful character in our great story. However, there is something we should correct first." He jumped off his chair and began again on his merry way. "Follow me!"

She did as she was ordered and they went deeper into his magnificent office. They passed further utensils, tools, globes, maps, ornaments, and furniture, all elaborate in design. As they went Bethany couldn't help but notice a large glimmering mirror that seemed to pulse with magical energy. For a few moments she couldn't help but stare at it. Alarabus impatiently interjected.

"That thing? Well that, too, is a very special item. It is what is known as an eternity door. It can take you anywhere across the galaxy – well, as long as you know what you are doing, that is. Ancient things, they are, and truly powerful; there are only a few in existence nowadays. But that is neither here nor there right now, so please continue to follow me."

They resumed their journey, reaching a relatively large circular platform ringed by steps. The pair proceeded to climb them until they were at the top. Upon it was a series of carved runes and decorations, none of which our hero could understand.

"Please stand there. This should only take a moment."

He scurried off to one side, where there was a lectern. Climbing it, he was greeted by an exceptionally old and thick book that had flown through the air and placed itself open in front of him. After a bit of muttering and examining the page, the wizard looked up to get Bethany in his gaze.

"Now, stay calm, please. The following sensation might be a bit peculiar for you, but it will be over in a few moments."

Before Bethany could respond, the wizard shouted something that sounded like a spell. Bolts of warm yellow light flashed from his hands. They reached Bethany and wrapped themselves around her like tentacles, lifting her into the air. Bethany could feel the energy flow through and around her whole transformed body. She felt her person change once again, as if her old body was triumphantly re-emerging from deep within her. Her heart began to flutter with excitement. Looking down at her hands, she discovered that within the warm yellow vines of light, the stubby wooden ones that belonged to a gropscrub had gone, and in their place were those that belonged to her. She inspected the rest of her body, and to her delight she found she was back to her normal self. The magic came to an end, and the arms of light lowered her to the floor again with ease. She patted her face inquisitively to find her very recognisable features and her long, black, messy hair all intact. She was back to normal. The wizard hesitantly appeared from behind his lectern.

"I hope you do enjoy your own form again."

She leapt forward and hugged the little wizard tightly. A tear formed in her right eye.

"Thank you!"

After a few seconds, she broke the embrace.

"It was easy, Bethany. Anything to help you."

The tension drained out of the bottom of her feet into the floor beneath her, as the full weight of her weariness crashed in on her. She then remembered how tired she actually was.

"You are under my care here at the house. You are my honoured guest and we shall see to it that your every need is taken care of, though unfortunately you must stay within the confines of these walls until we can come up with a plan. We must ensure your safety."

Though slightly disappointed that she couldn't explore the outside world as of yet, she was grateful for the offer. She did a weary but spirited twirl as she inspected her returned form with joy.

"Now, Bethany, what do you desire to do at this very moment?"

Bethany gave a huge yawn. It was quite clear to her what she actually wanted. "I think I would quite like to have a good night's sleep..."

Alarabus nodded cheerily and granted her wish. "So shall it be, Ms Bethany Hannah Morgan."

Thirteen

ETHANY'S FIRST NIGHT'S SLEEP IN ALARABUS'
house was magnificent. She'd been given the fifth
guest room of twenty. It was an extremely lavish space with
comfy furniture, a massive squishy bed, and all the many other
wonderful comforts that one would expect of a grand, stately
Victorian home. It wasn't something she was used to, though
she soon grew comfortable with her dwelling and slept that
first night till the afternoon of the next day, missing breakfast.
When she woke, she had never felt so well rested before in
her life. During the next two weeks, however, her bedtimes
became more and more restless. She'd often wake up late at
night, dripping with sweat or with tears in the corner of her
eyes waiting to be shed. A friendly old man with a song in
his heart was appearing in her dreams, accompanied by an
uncomfortable feeling of loss. There were other terrifying
sensations, mostly that she was running away and forgetting
something. Sometimes her dreams felt incredibly real – she'd
awake and appear back at 1½ Cordling Drive. At other times

it was even worse; she'd seem to wake up in a hospital bed, with tubes attached to her body and medical staff looking down at her in concern. Unable to understand any of this, she'd allow herself to get angry before trying to get back to sleep or making the best of the day.

On the whole though, Bethany found her stay rather enjoyable. The wizard's house was fascinating to explore. For the first few days, she roamed its many halls and great chambers, often getting lost. When finally she thought she knew her way through the house, it would suddenly change, both in layout and design. The first time this happened she found it rather baffling, but she soon understood this was a common occurrence, for as the house was controlled by Alarabus himself, it could transform according to his whims and fancies. At times the house took on a style that our hero could recognise from her own world – Renaissance, Romanesque, or Gothic, for example – whilst other times what she woke to find was completely alien or surreal. Despite these almost daily changes, the house maintained two particular qualities: it was peculiar and incredibly comfortable, both attributes that Bethany very much enjoyed.

She was also enjoying being back in her original body again. People do not appreciate the tiny details and functioning of their own bodies unless they have had the displeasure of inhabiting a different one. Like removing your feet from someone else's shoes that are too big or too small and returning them to your own, this change was a wonderful relief. It was something Bethany would not take for granted again. Unfortunately she was unable to express her gratitude to the wizard, as she rarely saw him. When she did, he was always incredibly busy, and hardly a word passed between them. Most of the time he would be locked away in his office, which, unlike the rest of the house, always appeared in the same place. Whenever she tried to visit him, the wooden figures would maintain their posts and she would be unable to enter.

Despite being unable to see the wizard, Bethany still managed to find company in the great house. The non-grubb crew of the *Evanescence* were housebound just like her and had taken up residence in some of the other guest rooms. Normally she'd find them at mealtimes in the dining room. This was the only other room that went unchanged; that is, apart from the old crushed table and chandelier, which were replaced with newer, unbroken models. At first they were quite surprised at her appearance, with the exception of Tassarin, who she had always felt knew what she really looked like. They knew she was a human, but none of them had ever seen one before, though they all agreed that this body suited her more than that of a gropscrub. Isabella was her usual boisterous, loud, and happy self, and Kolchi too seemed to have found a quiet happiness, safe in the confines of the house whilst practising her spells. Orin the gnome, however, continued to complain, mostly to himself, and tinkered away with his gadgets, inventions, and bombs, which at times made meals particularly uneasy for Bethany. It was quite clear that something important was bothering the small bearded pirate, but she could not guess what it was. The Andarin continued as he normally did, rather still, contemplative, and outwardly emotionless. Sometimes it even felt like he was not really in the room. Everyone was eager to get out of the house. They were incredibly restive, and Isabella was vocal about her need for adventure. House arrest was really not to the liking of these pirate adventurers.

What they all enjoyed, with the exception of Tassarin, were mealtimes. They were extravagant affairs: the dining table, at the same times each day, would be magically covered with all sorts of dishes, beverages, and sweet things. The crew would then set about it in reckless abandon, groaning in pleasure as they consumed items from the almost endless buffet. After about an hour, the contents of the table would disappear as magically and as suddenly as they had appeared, leaving some very full diners. Only Tassarin did not eat. He spent his time sitting at the table and observing, as well as taking part in any tableside conversations. Bethany marvelled at the food that would appear in front of her, for she had never seen a spread like it. Despite this, she was cautious with what she ate at first, only choosing items that looked familiar to her. She'd always been a picky eater, and this initially impeded her food adventurism. When Isabella finally convinced her to try a new and unusual item, though, the seal was broken, and she took every opportunity to try new things. She consumed dustmarch stew, Oggblabian cake, Antarian bean bread, Mamoran sausages, rich Tilean wines, gumpwit pies, hornwelk steak, and many other remarkable dishes, thoroughly enjoying the experience.

What was particularly odd at mealtimes was a custom that the crew of the Evanescence always carried out. At first she didn't notice it, often arriving slightly too late. But once she had got accustomed to the internal clock of the house and began arriving on time, she couldn't help but see. Every mealtime, the crew would lay an extra place at the table and fill its plate with food. Then they would individually set another four places, whilst singing what seemed to be a rather melancholic sea shanty led by the captain herself.

Its time you go now
Haul away your anchor
Haul away your anchor
It's our farewell time

Set your dreams upon her
Drop away your anger
Drop away your anger
It's our farewell time

The stars are surging over
Sail on through the darkness
Sail on through the darkness
It's our farewell time

When your journey's over
Sail away for Ior
Sail away for Ior
God be at your side

Then they would sit, eat, and be their normal selves. At first Bethany thought that perhaps the extra places were for the wizard and maybe some other occupants of the house she hadn't met. But this idea was soon proven wrong as neither the wizard nor any others joined them to dine. After about a week, Bethany began joining in, thinking that perhaps it was some kind of local custom, setting her own extra place at the table. It seemed the right thing to do, though she did not know why. The first time she joined them, laying her extra space, Isabella put her hand upon her shoulder and said "I'm sorry," in a most sombre way.

Despite the lavish surroundings, Bethany soon became restless too. She desperately desired to see the outside world and explore – find interesting new creatures, try other foods, and learn new customs and cultures. There was only so much the mealtimes were going to appease this appetite. When she did manage to corner the wizard and plead her wishes, the answer was always the same. No. This did not help. Her appetite for adventure only got worse, a longing that could not be quenched. She would join her friends in complaining at mealtimes, her frustrations so strong she would almost explode in an emotional mess. Luckily, she eventually discovered a particularly interesting and well-stocked room of the house: the library.

Fourteen

ONE MORNING, HAVING JUST FINISHED HER breakfast, Bethany had decided to go for a little bit of a wander, as she usually did. Despite her restlessness, she still enjoyed exploring the house after one of its frequent transformations. However, on this particular morning, she came across a set of ornate wooden doors that she hadn't seen before. Letting her curiosity get the better of her again, she decided to investigate. To her surprise, the doors opened as she approached to reveal the largest collection of books she had ever seen. Bethany loved libraries of all shapes and sizes. The chance to get hold of a book and have a quiet read was always a real pleasure. To discover such a treasure for the first time was magnificent.

Tentatively, she entered the library.

"Hello?" she called out. No reply came, so she let herself explore.

It was exactly the library she had always dreamed of having, though she knew that in her world to possess one would require mountains of money. Polished wooden bookshelves stretched almost endlessly to the ceiling, with ladders and spiral staircases attached to them and raised platforms bedecked with worn, squishy furniture. Of course there were also countless books, as if every single one in existence had found its way, somehow, into this room and then decided to never leave. Whilst most sat on the shelves in neat rows, a good number were strewn around the room messily in great piles that almost reached the arched ceiling. Books flew through the air, reorganising themselves, struggling to sort themselves back into their ordained places. It was beautiful and chaotic, exactly the library that the wizard would own and exactly the one that was perfect for our hero. Bethany had found her new home.

So for a number of weeks, Bethany spent the good part of her days in her new paradise. Selecting a new book each day, she'd find a spot to sit in and then lose herself within its words. Sometimes she was rewarded with what appeared to be Edimorian high tea, lunches, and other snacks, all very different to what she usually ate, but all delicious. The books she chose were mainly those that could provide further information about the galaxy she now inhabited and the creatures that lived there. Though she still longed for adventure in the outside world, this at least temporarily satiated this hunger. She quickly learnt a lot, immersing herself in research.

Magic was generally where she began, for she had yet to discover how it actually worked. But despite her best studies, she could not find a definitive answer. Her favourite quote was from Madame Idris Manacia, a particularly eccentric witch, who said:

"Magic is the ability to create and do whatever one pleases. It is the pure energy of one's imagination, which, when properly harnessed, can give the user the ability to achieve anything that they desire..."

To some degree, this felt correct. The magic users she had bumped into seemed able to achieve near impossible things, like sailing a ship into space, or attempting to organise an office. In fact, the great struggle in regard to magic seemed to come from trying to make sense of it and to categorise it by type or an individual's ability.

To her surprise, she discovered that anyone could be a magic user; they simply had to be born with the gift. For some species, like the Andarins or the Magi, it was rare to be born without any such abilities at all. The Magi were of particular interest, for Alarabus was one of them. Wizard was the terminology used for a male Magi, and they always bore the characteristics of the stereotypical Merlin character, being old, bearded, and in possession of eccentric robes. This was not a set of characteristics that they grew into, they were born this way, albeit a lot smaller and with the tendency to cry and defecate themselves. The female terminology for a Magi was witch. These, as Bethany came to expect, held all the characteristics of the traditional witch, being old and ugly with a taste for black pointy hats, broomsticks, and cackling. Not all witches were evil and not all wizards were good, but both were almost immortal, for when one is born old, there really isn't anywhere for the body to physically go. They did have great difficulty reproducing and increasing their numbers, for as G. P. Sline keenly wrote in his book *Beards and Pimples: The Decline of a Species*:

"Because both genders of this race of beings find the other to be utterly hideous, they have doomed their kind, and to some extent all others, to extinction."

Bethany was intrigued to find a pamphlet in this book about a charity for Magi copulation, which Alarabus had mercilessly covered with graffiti.

The Andarins were far more mysterious. Everything she read about their race was confusing, unspecific, or contradictory. Orc scholar Grungots Iron Hide XI said in his book *Fightins Around da Edimor*:

"Dose Andarins are powerful so keep back. Only try to take one ons if yous particularly big an tuff likes me. Dey as magics, bigs magic, gibben to dem by da gods. Dey wait for the perfect time to strike, den der will be nuthin left but dem. Be warned dey is up to sumtin."

Whilst Athagarex Treekin, the last treeman, wrote in his melancholic book *So This Is the End*:

"They are beings that know of our impending doom, for as I have mentioned before, everything must one day come to an end, like a warm summer day, or a bountiful spring shower. From this emotion comes their power, for it is clearly understood that their magic has only become apparent since the decline of all life. Now they watch as sentinels, cautious with their powers, watching us all as we descend into our putrid…"

Bethany could not stomach much of the treeman's ramblings. It was clear that Tassarin's race was still much of a mystery, despite the best efforts of a number of scholars. From what she gathered, no one had ever been to their home planet, nor even knew its location. To see one was immensely rare. She pondered long and hard about Tassarin and his role in her adventures. There were so many questions, but she failed time and time again to pluck up the courage to ask, even though the Andarin always seemed to be ready for them.

Bethany also did her research on the other races that made up the crew of the *Evanescence*. Fauns, the half-human, half-goat creatures, were originally found on Goldensmorg. Generally dashing and adventurous, they were highly in tune with nature, and so naturally had departed the planet once it started to become heavily industrialised. The majority had found a new home on the verdant forest world of Elderwood, whilst others had journeyed out into space, making great sailors, sea captains, and rangers. Most of the descriptions she discovered seemed to agree that the majority of this race was brave and stubborn, with a do-or-die attitude that often saw them bargaining with fate itself. Sadly, their new homeworld had been encroached upon by the Alpharian Confederation, who had discovered vast mineral deposits under the planet's surface. After a brutal war, the dissidents had been suppressed and the planet occupied and industrialised by its new masters. The once-great forests had been chopped down and replaced by large, smoke-belching chimneys, the faun inhabitants becoming servants of the Confederation or fleeing for refuge out amongst the stars.

Gnomes were also interesting creatures, and one of the very few that frequently travelled to her world. All of their kind were short, between three to four and a half feet, and in possession of a bushy beard, even if they were female. Peaceful creatures, they loved nothing more than forming strong friendship bonds with other living things, becoming almost inseparable from their chosen companions. When they happily found themselves with such friends, they lived peaceful lives fishing, gardening, and making highly explosive gadgets. However, once such a bond with a chosen companion was broken, they'd transform dramatically, responding to the loss with great rage.

Bears were also intriguing; where once the wise races had believed that dolphins, pigs, or cockroaches would be the first to find sentience and civilisation, they were surprised to discover it was actually the bear that would do so. Breaking from millennia of servitude in the entertainment business as dancers and combatants for angry attack dogs, they had since tried to scrape a living in Edimor, though often consumed with depression, unable to forget the tragedies of their people's past. All three of these races could be born with magical abilities, though their capabilities in this varied because of education and the type of character the individual possessed.

On the other end of the scale were the races that had no magical abilities at all. Creatures who, no matter how much they were tutored, could never learn anything of the sort. Among the list of such there were only two she recognised – goblins and smargs – which frankly didn't surprise her much.

It was the beings in the middle, however, those who could learn and possess magical abilities despite lacking a natural ability for it that fascinated her the most. Kolchi was clearly being tutored to master her abilities, but what that involved was beyond Bethany's understanding. In fact, Bethany discovered that the market for magical academia was vast, for there were plenty who possessed the gift, as it was called, and who wanted to learn to control their powers. These academic centres took the form of colleges, most of which were run by a particularly capable or eccentric Magi. At one point there had been schools for those of a younger age, particularly those going through adolescence, but the rampant sexual and emotional issues, as well as utter ignorance of any health and safety protocols, had seen the education governing bodies close them down. Pirilious Flittin, a goblin, was famous for saying in criticism of one particular school, Boarspots Academy:

"Among the clear violations of health and safety at this school were the housing of an incredibly powerful magical item, a barbaric competition which sees students captured and submerged in dangerous waters or fighting dangerous beasts, and an admissions faculty run by a drunk talking sock. All of which gave me just cause to close the school down. More remarkable was what I discovered at a later date: that security was especially lax, despite the annual attempts of unknown dark forces to murder pupils in residence. Also, sadly, there were serious recreational drug problems."

They had since all been closed down.

The colleges, however, survived and were open to all those who had the relevant magical potential and grades. Most of them were found on Goldensmorg, and they were almost as peculiar and ornate as the house she now resided in, or so the Committee of Magical Colleges said. These centres of learning each focused on a particular branch of magic use. Those who managed to master them all were truly admired by the Alpharian Confederation. Bethany was stunned to discover how many there were, each with their own books and pamphlets, which she read but failed to interpret during her stays in the library. There were the colleges of pyromancy, the study of fire and energy; necromancy, a controversial bunch who spent a lot of their time around graveyards; astromancy, the study of the stars in relation to magic, who spent most of their days looking upwards; and many others besides. There were even those called Scienomancers, a group that believed magic didn't exist and instead thought that Edimor was controlled by the laws of science. They were particularly unpopular.

Most significant and peculiar to Bethany was the College of the Dramatimancers, originally created when the Litomancers and Theatomancers combined and created a particularly bizarre school of magic. They believed that the whole world was ruled by the magical laws of dramatic effect. Important things could only happen at their most dramatic point, such as the last few seconds of a bomb's fuse, or when a lover's companion is about to depart and their feelings for one another have not been expressed. When said event doesn't happen in proper dramatic manner, it is clear that those involved are not significant characters in the great story of existence. Their demise or failure is therefore but a side note to the greater story and the progression of the true dramatic heroes. The magic users who studied at this school hoped to achieve some control over their surroundings by harnessing the magic of these perceived laws. These were the people Alarabus had mentioned, those who had predicted her appearance in their galaxy's great story. She tried to discover more, but there was little to be found in the library. They were almost as great an enigma as the Andarins – another of Edimor's great mysteries.

Apart from magic, what fascinated Bethany most was space travel. In her own world, of course, this was something particularly difficult to master. The best humanity had achieved so far was visiting their back garden, the moon, and then going back inside once they realised something good was on the TV. She was keen to discover how, here in Edimor, they seemed to have achieved what they had to such a great extent. The answer, naturally, turned out to be magic, which didn't quite satisfy her curiosity. Space travel depended on the Navigators, particular magic users who could command vessels and travel from planet to planet through the void of space. While there were better ways to travel, such as wizard doors, not everyone trusted these. This was also why ships continued to be made in their traditional way, to maintain the confidence and sanity of those who did not have the powers to travel themselves. It was unnecessary for the *Evanescence* to be built like a late-eighteenth-century pirate ship; it could just as well have been shaped like a massive ball, as the ship's structure had little impact on its ability to fly. But people preferred it that way, for in their understanding, to shape a spacefaring vessel like a seafaring one made more sense.

There were countless books on the subject, for it was generally understood to have been a key component of Edimorian history for the past five thousand years. The first individual to travel into space had been a wizard named Altharius Demarchay, who with one spell had transported himself to Goldensmorg's second moon, Joanna. It would be two hundred and fifty years before anyone else learned of his success, when his body was finally found, devoid of life. His big mistake had been failing to recognise the importance of oxygen, and that a severe lack of it was fatal. There were plenty of other interesting, bizarre, and sometimes downright odd stories our hero came across when studying this topic. For example, in the unofficial diaries of the great adventurer Matthias Angle-Switch, which were only published after his death, he described why the Dread Zone was so called:

"I must admit the Dread Zone is only really frightful in name. In reality, the whole cluster of planets is anything but: one of my greatest and most brilliant lies. The planets found in this zone are primarily inhabited by the Zygronians, a particularly interesting race purely because they are the nicest creatures in all existence. They are the perfect hosts; the worlds they inhabit are wonderful paradises, catering to one's every whim. In my greed, I ashamedly concocted the whole idea of the Dread Zone purely to dissuade anyone else from visiting it and enjoying its great pleasures. You can therefore understand why I so frequently adventured to the Dread Zone and why my fellow explorer Alpius Bedius was not actually killed by monsters but murdered by my wife and I. He wanted to reveal the truth. My spouse was lost to the planets as well, having fallen in love with one of the delightful Zygronians. I die therefore with great regret in my heart…"

When the diaries were published upon the famous space traveller's death, the Dread Zone was overcome with visitors.

To everyone's surprise, the Zygronians had actually been playing a ruse all along and horrifically consumed every single individual who visited, plunging the galaxy into a merciless fifty-year war. This had only ended with the total destruction of the Dread Zone by the Alpharian Confederation.

The stories and information were endless: there was so much that even Bethany, with her thirst for knowledge, was overwhelmed. It was impossible to learn everything there was to know about space travel, so she decided to change subjects again. First she went on to the races of Edimor, but there was little she hadn't already learnt from Grollp. She then attempted to find something, anything, about the boy and his carer. Only one book she found mentioned these beings: the diary of space adventurer Altaria Vulk, a faun. Her final entry had been written just before she headed away on her journey to the Heart of Unreason in an attempt to make contact with the two. There was nothing else after this chapter except a note from the editor, saying:

"Regrettably, we here at Rockhopper Publishing are unable to provide suitable material to bring the writer's diary to end. This is because the author herself has never returned from her adventure mentioned in this book and is presumed dead. If further material is found, we will provide an updated version of this book upon display of your original copy."

Rockhopper Publishing sadly had gone bankrupt due to customer disappointment in Altaria's last literary instalment.

She continued to change subjects. Foolishly, she ended up in the section of the library about Goldensmorg. This only made her hunger for the outside world even more. The planet itself had always been the heart of Edimor. Once the home of some supposed creators and the land of adventure for heroes, it had slowly but surely become overpopulated, forcing them to travel among the stars. Forests had been felled and mountains crushed as more and more structures had to be built. Factories with tall smog-belching chimneys had been erected, evidence of the greatness of their civilisation. Navigators had desperately attempted to find new sustainable planets across the galaxy. There had been many who travelled with them to colonise new worlds. These they had inhabited either by taking empty space or removing, supressing, enslaving, or enlightening the natives to the Alpharian Confederation's way of thinking, much in the manner of the fauns on Elderwood. Those planets with enough foresight had obediently integrated their worlds into the Confederation before any more government officials, settlers, or soldiers could arrive. The planet of Goldensmorg had been the centre of all this, the beating heart from which the smargs and their friends could attempt to rule over everything they considered their jurisdiction, which was all of Edimor. The city world was therefore brimming with life from all over the galaxy. A vast cornucopia of smog, cultures, and wealth.

It all seemed utterly horrific. She understood why Grollp, Isabella, and perhaps even the great wizard himself despised the planet and the whole Confederation. And yet at the same time she found it all so terribly fascinating. There was so much to see and do, a whole galaxy to explore and villains to defeat. She needed her freedom again: to go out into the galaxy and help defeat her new adversary the Alpharian Confederation. It was her own villain for her own story. She needed to adventure into this terrifying world. To right wrongs, see the stars, and visit exotic places. If only she could be allowed out. Even into the streets of Goldensmorg for one day. But it was not to be. Every time she got a chance to ask, Alarabus simply declined her request. After which she would return to the library, frustrated and somewhat angry, sometimes without eating. Day in and day out, it all seemed the same. Even the books could not quench her appetite forever. She desperately needed to continue her adventure, for she knew that the smiling man's mission was of the greatest importance. Just as she was starting to lose her mind and beginning to plot her escape, she was visited in the library by Isabella, who had a huge smile on her face.

"Would you like to go on an adventure with me?"

Fifteen

OUR HERO FOLLOWED ISABELLA EAGERLY through the corridors of the wizard's house to a part she had yet to visit. The faun captain herself moved with a distinct bounce in her step, the injury to her shoulder healed.

"We came upon it quite by accident. Though of course we knew there was likely to be one in here somewhere. But we thought it'd be very much under the wizard's watchful eye."

Bethany tried her best to keep up. "What is it?"

Still moving, the captain glanced back towards her and gave a quick cheeky wink, chuckling to herself. "You'll find out soon enough! Look, there's the rest of them waiting for us."

She was right – just down the corridor, standing next to a door, were the other three members of the crew. Orin paced on the spot whilst Kolchi fidgeted, her arms full of long green cloaks. Tassarin stood motionless, watching them as they drew closer.

"I know how much you've been wanting to spend some time outside. Well, we might've found a good way of doing just that!"

They stopped in front of a very unassuming wooden door. Bethany looked it up and down before turning her attention back to the party. She had a good feeling what it was.

"It's a wizard's door?"

The gnome pirate was the first to pipe up. "Of course it's a wizard door, and we are aching to get to the other side. Not just you who's sick of bein' stuck in here," he grumbled. Isabella sharply turned, looking daggers at her short quartermaster, who for a split second looked sheepish before grumbling, "Only tellin' the truth, that's all. Always 'avin' to treat her all special like. What she done so far for us, aye? Anyways, let's get going then."

With that, he snatched a cloak from his bear friend, opened the door, and stepped inside.

"Come ons then!"

Bethany didn't want to move. Had she done something to annoy the gnome pirate? Indeed, he always seemed to be grumpy in her presence. The only times he seemed different were when he was eating or going through their mournful routine before meals. A familiar reassuring voice appeared in her head.

"Do not think you have done anything explicitly wrong, my friend. Orin has been very much like this since Grollp passed away."

Bethany noticed Kolchi nodding her head solemnly. Apparently she wasn't the only one being involved in the conversation. Isabella placed a reassuring hand on her shoulder.

"Indeed, he's right there. We all miss him. I think Orin has taken it the hardest."

Bethany looked up at the captain, then to Tassarin and Kolchi, tears forming in the corners of her eyes. "I really am sorry…"

With another reassuring slap on her shoulder, Isabella replied, "No need to apologise. Nothing wrong with being sad. It's a brilliant way of telling you how special something was. Whether it's a person, friend, lover, place, thing, or moment. If you are truly sad, when it inevitably has to come to an end, it tells you how special such a thing was. So there's never any real need to be sorry for such emotions."

A smile came across the captain's face. Bethany smiled too – slightly sad but warmed by her comforting words. Kolchi placed a reassuring paw on her shoulder whilst handing her one of the hooded green cloaks she was carrying.

"No point wasting any time. It's best if you wear one of these. I've enchanted these cloaks; there's trouble out there. But with these, no one will be able to tell it's us. They'll just see a group of orc guards, or goblins or what have you."

Bethany quickly wrapped it around herself. The hood was big and hung over her eyes. She adjusted it so her vision wasn't too obstructed. Isabella, Kolchi, and Tassarin did likewise. The Andarin looked particularly odd, having a droopy cloak over him. It seemed as if he had no understanding of how to wear such items of clothing. Orin burst from behind the door again.

"Can we 'urry this up, all right? You'll be yappin' here all day."

Isabella gave him a cold stare. "Right, let's go, everyone into the cupboard!"

All members of the party did as they were told. The cupboard itself soon felt rather cramped – fauns, Andarins, and bears not being the smallest of lifeforms.

"And now on to Goldensmorg!"

The captain spelt something out on the inside of the door. Then suddenly it all went white again. They were greeted with the all-too-familiar hissing sound and the sensation of travelling at great speeds in tiny pieces. Bethany was starting to get used to it all and only felt mildly queasy. Before they knew it, they had reached their destination, and stepping from the cupboard, they found themselves inside an old-style tavern bustling with activity.

The room was warm and loud, the air thick with sweat and gossip. There were all kinds of beings scattered around the bar and squashed around circular wooden tables. The ceiling was low, and though this did not bother Bethany, the hanging gas lamps were very much a problem for Kolchi, the captain, Tassarin, and many of the larger patrons of the tavern. Large, muscular lizardmen, trolls, and orcs gorged themselves on all sorts of snacks. Cyclopean ogres played cards with a group of goblins; rotscavs and grogs gossiped in the corner; a serving grubb or two skittered between the legs of the customers, laden with drinks and food, desperately trying not to get trodden on or crushed. A smartly dressed giant sat in the corner with an uncomfortable expression on its face. Along with these were all sorts of creatures great and small that Bethany could not recognise, all crammed into the confines of this low-ceilinged, timbered, wonky tavern, dressed in a variety of high-born and low-born attire. None of them paid any attention to the appearance of our hero and her friends.

"No need to worry, Bethany," Kolchi muttered to her. "Though they may seem rough and rather unsavoury, the patrons of this establishment don't pay any heed to strangers. We'd be safe even without our cloaks. Well, I think so, anyway—"

"Yeah, and the drink's cheap, too!" said the captain.

Isabella chuckled, enjoying her own observation. Tassarin was quick to interject.

"In truth, after studying the prices of beverages of the many taverns that I have visited being helmsman of the *Evanescence*,

I have concluded that the prices at the Albatross are no worse, nor any better, than the vast majority of establishments. In fact, in comparison to Galvinias II, the cost of a pint of ale here is astronomical. This is largely due to the widespread poverty and general aesthetic appeal of the—"

Isabella raised her hand to silence him. "I think... yep, that's quite enough. Let's get going. We didn't come here to hang around in such a place. Master Orin, lead the way!"

With an about-turn, he gave a mock salute to the captain and began to push his way through the throng of patrons, grumbling bitterly to himself. His pistols and blades clinked against each other as he went. It was a struggle, but in a few moments they had reached the front door in one piece, albeit slightly breathless from the journey. Kolchi was right – not one patron, not even those they had happened to bump into, had cast but a fleeting glance or a grumble in their direction. Isabella guided our hero through the door, ceremoniously opening it.

"Welcome, my friend, to Goldensmorg!"

She couldn't believe it. There in front of her was the most amazing sight she had ever seen. She rubbed her eyes in a vain attempt to focus. Spreading out before her was a huge, bustling city, full of life and activity. The buildings all looked like her own 1½ Cordling Drive, leaning precariously this way and that, stretching upwards towards the sky like a dying plant grasping for sunlight. Most seemed to be made of timber or brick and were in a similar style to what she knew as late Victorian, although with far less architectural integrity. The consequence, she thought, of having magic users dominating the building market was that nothing really had to follow any rules. Some looked like they were hammered haphazardly together, using whatever bits and pieces could be found, whether ceramic tiles or tin. The street was painted in a colourful palette of chalky oranges, pinks, reds, and greens that all seemed faded from poor upkeep and age; indeed, many of the windows were covered in a thick layer of dust. Despite their differences, every single building stretched endlessly into the sky. All were jam-packed together, squashed like the patrons of the Albatross, for space, no matter how small, was at a premium here. The uneven cobbled streets, which led off to all kinds of tiny backstreets, cellars, and passageways, were remarkably narrow and chock full of goblins, orcs, lizardmen, and other fascinating creatures.

"This is it, Bethany! The splendour of Goldensmorg. It's a crazy busy place, this is, but just follow us and you'll be fine! Where to first?"

Bethany was so overwhelmed she didn't know how to respond. Trying to take in all the new sights and smells, she had little room left to make decisions. To her distaste, the air seemed almost as thick and unpleasant as that of the tavern. It was Orin who spoke.

"She ain't gonna answer. Look at her!"

"Can it! You miserable old fool!" Isabella bit back. Her teeth were clenched in anger.

"Just saying what I sees," he rebutted in mock apology. "I got business in Grand Market Thirty-Two A. If you wants to join me, then do."

With that, he walked away in a huff.

"I guess that's a good place to start..." Isabella replied, trying to soothe the situation. "Don't listen to him, alright? There's nothing wrong with you. Now let's get going. Grand Market Thirty-Two A is the greatest one in existence. Well, apart from One to Thirty-One... But hey! It's only a few skips over in that direction. Let's go!"

They started their journey, scrambling through the winding streets of Goldensmorg. Orin's words sat heavy in

Bethany's mind. Refusing to let it ruin her day, she continued to follow her friends, trying her best to take everything in. They passed countless shops with great wooden signs hanging just above their front doors, swaying in the occasional breeze. They walked past a myriad of buskers, beggars, and all sorts trying to fetch a few coins. At other times, they passed orc and grog guards on patrol. Most wonderful for our hero were a family of ten beaked, fluffy green creatures of various sizes, all wearing little waistcoats, carefully navigating the bustling streets. Not one of these creatures paid any heed to their party.

There was so much to look at that she wanted to stop and let all her senses take over as the world passed by around her. The delightful smell of gingerbread danced from a bakery into her nose. It was coming from a batch of freshly baked biscuits shaped liked reptilian monsters, and for a moment she stood confused, half remembering something or someone dear to her. She was quickly snapped from her thoughts by what sounded like the patter of feet keeping step with them, and the gaze of a pair of eyes. She started to feel as if they were being watched, maybe even followed.

Isabella had become something of a tour guide, though she did not care who was listening and simply spoke on and on about the city. The gnome continued to grumble as he led the way, sometimes having to brush someone aside to clear the path. Kolchi looked around warily, ever vigilant to potential dangers, particularly from the city's law enforcement. Bethany, however, was not listening to her guide, nor really looking at anything but the mysterious cloaked figure that seemed to be following them. At first she passed it off as a coincidence – it was so busy, she concluded, that it was probably a series of similar-looking individuals she was seeing. There could be any number of Goldensmorg citizens who possessed the same cloak and walked with a similar hunched and mysterious manner. But it wasn't long before she realised this was entirely wrong. It was the same figure each time, and it was clearly following them intently. In her imagination it had every intention to catch up and do something horrible to her or one of her friends. It followed them through every busy street, around every corner, and through each crowd they passed, even stopping when they did at crossings or points that Isabella found interesting. It was also getting closer and closer every minute and every second that they walked. Just as she was about to shout out in distress, the cloaked figure only an arm's length away, she was interrupted.

"Are you all right, Ms Bethany?"

It was Tassarin. His soothing voice immediately calmed her.

"There's someone, something there. And it's following us."

She pointed, but the cloaked figure was gone. The Andarin moved purposefully, his armour reflecting the hazy light, placing a hand ready on his sheathed blade. If the cloaked figure returned, Bethany was confident that Tassarin, with his powerful physique and skill, could manage the hunched creature. After what seemed like a moment of deep contemplation, he turned back to her.

"No need to worry, no harm will come to you. Not at the hands of that one. Let us catch up with the others now."

It was then that she noticed they had fallen behind the rest of their party. The others had continued their journey, heedless of what was going on and almost lost in the crowds ahead.

"Yes, I think we should."

They hurried through the crowds, catching up with their friends. Bethany quickly swung her backpack around and checked its contents. To her relief, the locket was exactly where it was meant to be. She swung it back onto her back, checking her surroundings again for danger. Before she could think any further on the matter, they were stopped again by their self-appointed tour guide.

"And now, my friend Bethany, prepare to behold Grand Market Thirty-Two A!"

Yet again she was dumbfounded by what she saw. It was magnificent.

They had emerged from their narrow cobbled street into a vast square bustling with shops, noise, and creatures. The air was still thick, and she could see a blanket of yellowish smog, punctuated by a vast cube-shaped market complex made from wooden scaffolding, planking, and miles upon miles of canvas and fabric. It rose up high, even higher than the buildings themselves, and was abuzz with activity as vendors and customers of all shapes and sizes conducted their business. Almost endless lines of beings disappeared into the construct, many pulling wagons of produce or with arms laden with things to buy or sell, whilst another endless chain of beings was leaving the structure. Musicians played, and weird prophets yelled lectures to no one in particular. This one square upon Goldensmorg was utterly swarming with life.

"Fascinating, isn't it?" Isabella bragged, enjoying herself, watching the dumbstruck look on her friend's face. Bethany did little but nod, trying to take in every detail. Noticing that the unlit lampposts were monstrously tall, she thought that the lamplighters would have to be giants. The captain couldn't stop herself from laughing in delight.

"Well, I can tell you're impressed. You can get anything here. Well, here and the other forty-one grand markets. Made aeons ago. Back then they were far smaller – still large, might I add. Huge stone commercial blocks, where shopkeepers could sell their wares. Thing is, everyone kept wanting to add their own shop to it. Problem was the designer took the plans for the complex to the grave, so the only thing they could do to expand was add all the scaffolding and wooden stuff. Would take you a good while to get to the centre nowadays. Very dark in there too!"

It was at that point that she noticed Orin walking on ahead. Going in his usual grumpy way, he had impolitely barged past a number of shoppers and was about to disappear into the market complex. The captain gave her bear companion a knowing look.

"Kolchi, do you mind keeping an eye on our miserable gnome friend? He seems to be in one of his moods. Probably looking for that gadget guy who takes advantage of him. Make sure he don't make a fool out of himself as usual."

She let out a quick chuckle, enjoying her own joke. The bear, stammering for words, gave up on them and disappeared into the market in pursuit of Orin.

"Right, I think it's time we went shopping! Let's find you something nice!"

Bethany couldn't let her nerves get the better of her, for the captain, full of energy, grabbed her by the hand and, with equal parts force and encouragement, dragged her into the market complex too. She was hit by a wall of muffled sound, heat, and smells, as if she had smashed through the atmosphere of a different world. The first shop she noticed as they entered was run by an old grog in a string vest selling what were clearly tacky Goldensmorg souvenirs. She was quickly dragged past it.

"Where to start, where to start..." the captain repeated to herself as she powered through the crowds, her vassal in tow. "What sort of stuff you into, Ms Bethany?"

They passed a squid-faced creature whose stall sold elaborate ink pens and who was clearly uneasy, surrounded by six fishmongers. She was assailed by the stench of fish, both fresh and otherwise, as well as sweat, which hung unpleasantly in her nose. They also passed what looked to be an ogre barber's, where a wolf creature sat next to a huge pile of cut hair. Bethany tried to respond to the captain.

"Lots of things. But I don't know where—"

Isabella stopped and pointed over to a stall covered in gold, silver, and all sorts of beautiful shining stones.

"What about jewellery?"

Bethany had never really been interested in jewellery, preferring books, theatre, and art. Even so, she was utterly fascinated by the magnificence and beauty of the items that gleamed from the stall in front of her. The dim light of a solitary lamp caught the precious articles in such a way that they hung glistening like elegant Christmas lights.

"Well, I certainly like that stuff, yes..."

Passing through a number of shoppers, they reached the stall. They were greeted by a surprisingly friendly-faced rotscav. He was old, with a wrinkled rat face, patchy grey fur, tiny glasses, and a black, brush-like moustache. A series of shining diamonds sat in front of him on the counter, accompanied by a magnifying glass and a row of cloths and polish.

"Whatsss can I dosssss for youssssss, young friend?"

Bethany couldn't help but flinch a little – his hissing voice reminded her of the creature that had murdered Grollp. She berated herself mentally; it was wrong to profile this creature just because of his race. Her gaze roamed around his wares, the light now glittering off her eyes too in amazement.

"I... really don't know."

The rat gave a chuckling squeak to himself, similar to that of a friendly old shopkeeper, but of course far more rodentlike and high pitched.

"Well, youssssss mightily impressed, I can tellss, makessss me feel right stoked, it doesssssss."

She turned this way and that in the small confines of the stall and was greeted by all sorts of splendour. There were broaches, necklaces, rings, and earrings, some made with glimmering gold and silver, whilst others twinkled in colours and ways that Bethany had never seen before. The craftsmanship was magnificent, with jewels of all sorts shaped like glass into delicate birds, flowers, and beautiful abstract swirls and shapes. Some of the ones moulded into animals seemed to flicker with life.

"You made these?" she asked.

"Every ssssingle piece. Learnt my trade from a massster artificer from Galliussss Prime. Use the besssst gold, sssssilver, adarix, quacialon, and even precioussssssss etiraux, when I get my handsssss on itssssss."

Isabella stepped into the small shop too, her size making it quite difficult for her to move. Carefully she placed herself so that she wouldn't knock any of the now obviously priceless pieces from the holsters and hangers.

"Which one will itsss be, then?"

Bethany contemplated his stall as she continued to examine the talented ratman's wares. Though it was all utterly beautiful, nothing caught her eye straight away. She liked what she saw – all of it, in fact – but she couldn't find anything that suited her. It was then, out of the corner of her eye, that she saw a small, blue-stoned penguin necklace. It reminded her of one of her favourite imaginary friends.

"That one. That one's my favourite. Though you really don't need to—"

Before she could continue, Isabella had grabbed hold of a bag of coins she had with her and dropped it on the shopkeeper's counter with a heavy thud and clatter, shaking the confines of the stall. A few thickset gold pieces burst out the top, marked with pretty geometric patterns, skulls, scratched runes, and horrific-looking beasts – the rule of course being, when it comes to gold, the older, the scarier, and the greater the risk of cursing, the greater the value of said currency. The ratman's green eyes sparkled with excitement, and he proceeded to polish his glasses in surprise with a rag cloth before placing them back on the end of his nose. Without missing a beat, the captain continued.

"Will that be enough?"

The answer was of course a yes. The old ratman nodded ecstatically before he lifted the bag of gold coins with a struggle and placed it behind his counter.

"It'sssssss yourssss!"

Bethany immediately tied the rope of the necklace around her own neck and admired it up close, placing it in her hand.

"You happy then, Ms Bethany?"

She replied not with words, but with a huge hug.

"I'll take that as a yes, then," she said, chuckling to herself heartily.

For the next couple of hours, Bethany enjoyed her time with the captain, exploring the huge market complex and doing their best window shopping, while Tassarin followed keeping watch. Bethany loved presents, but she always felt guilty when she received them, especially when she could not reciprocate. So she spent most of her time dissuading Isabella from getting her anything else. The captain seemed to be incredibly wealthy, though with little interest in the fact. She regaled our hero with the reason for her pirating.

"Not for the money, no! That's one of the irrefutable evils in the world. Many a good folk has gone stark raving mad in their pursuit for what in the end is a load of emotionless lumps of metal. No, I do it all for the thrill of adventure. To break free and feel alive."

Our hero guessed quite rightly that, much like Grollp, she had acquired her money from her voyages, though unlike the late captain she had learnt to save it, not out of any wish to do anything worthwhile with it, but because she had little interest in spending it. Though of course she'd spend it on things she liked – all her captain's attire was of the greatest quality and extravagance, as sometimes it's good to treat oneself.

The market complex seemed endless, and Bethany grew weary exploring it, climbing stairs, walking passageways, and entering overburdened stalls. At each turn, Bethany's senses would be bombarded with new experiences, which she found both exhilarating and tiring. She was fascinated to see every kind of stall that could possibly exist in this one location. There were spice stalls laden with mysterious powders, orange bult powder and deathly sweet dyrolian sugars. Many of the owners would hand out tasters, which exploded in her mouth. There were sweet shops too, many like those she knew her grandparents would have visited in their youth, with huge jars full of all kinds of colourful and sugary concoctions. To her surprise, some of these, like the Ozzorbe Fizzbug, darted around in their containers, whilst the striped DibDongs pulsated with fluorescent light. Isabella dissuaded her from eating any of them, saying there was a good chance she wouldn't survive the experience. Still, Bethany was tempted away by Squisheish, which tasted very much like the common marshmallow and was completely harmless. Perhaps the most interesting stalls were those that seemed to have anything and everything, from peculiar furniture to eight-horned musical instruments. In Galagesh's Emporium, she came across an illegal vinyl record of the Giant Iron Music Band, Everlasting Ragnarok. Such music was made illegal after the first festival featuring it saw the destruction of the entire host planet when the first chord was strummed by the band. The art form had therefore gone underground, where it could only be played at the lowest volumes. These hidden groups were now only discovered when the earthquakes caused by their music revealed their locations.

Eventually their adventurous window shopping grew too much, and Isabella thought it was a good time to go for lunch. The dining quarter, found within the ornate stone part of the market, right at the centre, was as crowded as the rest of it. Yet again, Bethany's senses were stormed by sensory delights as countless street vendors and chefs cooked their various ethnic dishes. Orcs sliced and chargrilled large hunks of meat and goblins boiled great stews whilst bird people diced colourful wormy concoctions. A half-giant squashed into one kitchen seemed to be making the largest pizza imaginable. It was delightful, but with so many options, our hero did not know what to have. After what seemed like a good while, Isabella decided on what they would eat – traditional faun cuisine from Elderwood. She headed for a stall and returned moments later laden with bowls, plates, and all kinds of breads and cakes, so much so that Tassarin, who had followed them through the great market silently, had to carry some as well. With much ceremony, the captain placed the dishes in front of Bethany, who sat at a great wooden table on an adjoining wooden bench.

"Here we have it, my friend, the greatest of delights my people can provide. A big bowl of Elderwood hot crab and shrimp stew, an osteria salad with extra-creamy edamia, roast gork with honeyed ghoulin dressing. This is accompanied by warm gwendill bread, chestnut and bombardberry cake, and a good pint of elder grub ale."

Bethany was overwhelmed. It was a mountain of food and it looked delicious, with steam rising from it delectably.

"Well, no point sitting there gawping, tuck in!"

They ate, and her taste buds exploded with delight. The soup was hot, incredibly so, but it was delicious. So was everything else, all of it possessing a certain sweet spice which she soon discovered was the faun trademark. She had never eaten anything like it, and despite quickly growing full, Bethany continued to consume the morsels at a steady, ravenous rate. All the while, Tassarin stood watch, still wary of their stalker. They sat by a great ornate pillar, carved with smiling fairies and pixies playing in the sun, a good section of which was covered by posters old and new. Most startling of these was a wanted poster of what appeared to be the gropscrub version of herself, with a hefty reward. Next to this was a missing poster for another gropscrub, who looked like the one she'd found during her time in the sewers. The reward for information, however, was pitiful in comparison.

When they'd finally finished, Isabella announced the occasion with a huge burp. A few disgruntled diners turned and grumbled to themselves before continuing with their meals. Bethany couldn't help but giggle. She decided on a whim to beat her friend's recent vocal explosion with her own. To the surprise of herself, Isabella, Tassarin, and everybody around them, it was substantially louder. Quiet momentarily fell upon the dining quarter as people were shushed into revulsion, surprise, and admiration. It was broken by the captain, bursting with laughter, tears rolling down her cheeks.

"Why, dear Bethany! You might be small, but you have true power!"

She rolled around laughing, enjoying her own joke. Bethany couldn't help but join in. The rest of the diners returned to what they were doing, and the place buzzed with noise again. Isabella tried to fight through the giggles and tears.

"I trust you liked it, then?"

Before Bethany could respond, Tassarin interjected. Something was amiss.

"Orin is in trouble. I think we need to break off festivities and find them soon."

So they departed the dining quarter, following the Andarin. Their giggling stopped as they lugged their full bellies through the crowds of the busy market complex. It was difficult going, and Bethany immediately regretted eating so much. After descending two flights of steps and walking through four corridors, they reached their destination to find Orin bawling with fury at a reptilian shopkeeper, accompanied by Kolchi, who looked the epitome of worry.

The reptilian he was shouting at was a long snake-bodied saligar. Its slimy green skin glimmered beneath a nearby lamp. Under its round jittery eyes was a smirking smile, above which was a thin, straight, greasy black moustache. It wore a brownish waistcoat covered in pockets on top of a pair of multicoloured slim-fitted trousers. It was tutting to itself sarcastically, its arms crossed. This only seemed to rile up the gnome even more, who continued to shout in its direction, something about a faulty trigger and ignition. What was most worrying, however, was that Orin's magic cloak had been thrown onto the deck.

"The conditions weren't perfect, no! But you is clearly swindling me. Always start ignition?! My, what clobber is that! My ars—"

Isabella stepped forward as captain in an attempt to calm the situation, arms raised to silence them. "What seems to be the problem here?"

The reptilian turned to her with a wide, earnest smile on its face. "Nothing, my good friend."

Its voice was as smooth as silk and as tricky as toffee. A shudder went down Bethany's spine. There was something uncomfortable about the creature, but she couldn't quite pin it down.

"I was just having a discussion with my good pal Orin here."

They knew each other, that wasn't a good thing. One of the last things they wanted was to be discovered.

"Friend?" the gnome yelled, pulling at his beard in frustration as he shouted. "Who are you calling friend? I been your customer for nigh on eight years now. But every time I purchase something from you slimy git, I finds out later it's a heap o' junk. I 'ave a right mind to wallop you one, I 'ave!"

He tried to leap forward and throttle the shopkeeper, but Kolchi was there just in time to hold him back, her staff awkwardly tucked under her arm.

"Steady on now, Orin, mate!" the captain interjected. "Let's talk this out. What particular item is it?"

The shopkeeper ran its sticky tongue across its top lip, its eyes flittering from one individual to the next, before continuing the conversation. "The most recent item he happened to purchase from me."

His smile continued to grow, his two round eyes staring right at the captain, seemingly transfixing her in his gaze. Bethany looked away, uncomfortable. His sugary soft voice continued on.

"The Always Ignite. An old but successful brand that has proven indispensable for bomb makers and saboteurs. This particular item was slightly past its prime, mind—"

Orin had had enough. "See! See! This slimy reptilian knowingly sold me faulty goods! Let me at him!"

He struggled to get free of his bear friend, but her grasp on him was strong. A small crowd had started to form around them, watching the drama unfold.

"But I made this fully known to my friend here at purchase. Even gave him a discount as a chum of mine—"

The shopkeeper kept looking at them each in turn. His eyes were huge, with a fascinating green colouring to them. They were mesmerising; one could easily get lost in them. When his gaze met Bethany's, though it felt uncomfortable, she found it difficult to turn away.

"Liar!" blurted Orin, still struggling.

The reptile stared straight at the gnome, their eyes meeting again. He became sheepish, his body softening and his rage subsiding.

"Well... I guess, I might recall stuff like that being mentioned before... but..."

Isabella looked physically disappointed with her quartermaster. Kolchi began to loosen her grasp, letting her small friend slide, embarrassed, to the floor. The reptile continued his smirk and his steely gaze, eying each of their group in turn.

"I..." Orin stammered, "I... I's sorry, y'are a good friend. Things ain't been quite right recently, with Grollp's death and all."

Everyone seemed to be taken in with the apology. Bethany was nervous, and scanned their surroundings. Most of the shoppers were returning to their business, but still a small crowd lingered. She then froze as she noticed two guards appearing in the distance. They were approaching their position, and her body grew tense and alert. It was probably best that they disappeared, so she started pulling at Isabella's cloak for attention.

"Not now, Bethany, we've got to make sure this fool makes amends."

There was some distance between them and the guards, and a great number of shoppers too, but they were getting ever closer.

"Apology accepted, my friend. It happens to the best of us," the reptile said, sounding like the perfect citizen and friend. He was launching into a self-satisfying lecture when she noticed his tail. It seemed to be up to a more nefarious business, sliding slowly behind Isabella. It then reached up and started untying one of the bags of gold from her waist. This was all Bethany needed to see, and she leapt forward, slapping the lizard's tail as hard as she could.

"OOOOOOOOOWWWWWWW!" he yelped.

Her friends seemed to break out of a trance, rubbing their eyes wearily.

"Ow, my head hurts a bit..." Kolchi muttered.

The reptile stared at our hero, this time with anger in his eyes and teeth clenched.

"This shopkeeper was trying to trick you. I don't know what it was, hypnotism or something, but he was just about to make off with a bag of gold from you, Isabella."

The captain noticed its tail was flicking behind her in close vicinity of her bags of gold. Orin's eyes grew wide in realisation.

"He's a right slimy saligar, he is."

The reptile gave a shrug, but Orin knocked him over with one quick punch. The gathered crowd broke into commotion as they moved this way and that, shouting in terror. The guards put on a burst of speed.

"Old friend? Huh, well, that'll show ya!"

The gnome grabbed and pocketed a number of items from the stall whilst the shopkeeper sat on the floor rubbing his nose. Orin advanced on him, rubbing his hands meanly.

"That's enough, mate!" bellowed the captain. "I think it's time we made tracks."

Everyone's eyes fell upon the guards, who were a few metres away. Orin relented, relaxing his fist, and turned away from the cowering lizard.

"And put on that cloak, you fool!"

With a few short grumbles, the gnome put his cloak over his head again, vanishing into the fabric. Then they were away as one, disappearing into the crowds easily. Bethany glanced back before they were too far off and saw a bemused pair of guards talking to a mentally and physically bruised reptile shopkeeper. Their time at the market had come to an abrupt end.

Sixteen

ETHANY AND HER FRIENDS MOVED AWAY,
disappearing from the market square and losing
themselves in the narrow cobbled streets of Goldensmorg.
They agreed to go about quietly; even Orin didn't grumble. It
was afternoon and there was still plenty to see.

They first passed the Alpharian Galactic Museum, a
monumental building designed in a style Bethany knew on
Earth as neoclassical. A quick trip around the establishment
took Bethany on a whirlwind tour of the galaxy's history, as
edited by the ruling elite. Not much stuck in her mind, but
there were plenty of marble statues commemorating great
goblins and smargs. They then passed on to a collection of
Goldensmorg galleries, ranging from the Tipsonia's Galactic
Gallery to Captain Bogwig Fletch III's Artists' Extravaganza.
In these she found examples of traditional, Avant Garde, and
odd Edimorian art, the last of which defied all description.
Most perplexing of all was Madame Fiddlescut of Daneer,
whose masterpiece *Welcome* involved the ogre artist dressed

as some kind of big-breasted tropical bird spitting on viewers and shouting what Bethany could only guess were profanities. They didn't stay there long.

With the day growing late, Kolchi came up with the brilliant idea of visiting Goldensmorg's one and only galactic park. It was the only greenspace still found on the city world, and so to accommodate such a vast planetary population, it too was gargantuan in size. A full eighth of the planet had been designated as this green zone, and it required a veritable army of gardeners, who made sure it stayed beautiful throughout the year. On their journey, they passed the Alpharian Grand Court, the home of the Elder Smargs. It dominated the skyline, a vast iron fortress that sat upon a rocky clifftop. If the architect had intended to design a structure that looked menacing and powerful, they had clearly achieved this with the Grand Court. Bethany tried her best not to contemplate the Alpharian fortress for too long; just the thought of dingy black cells, orc guards, and bestial smargs sent shivers down her spine.

Before long, they had reached the park's east entrance. The sun had begun to descend and they found the large iron gate slightly ajar. In a small wooden shed to its right was an orc guard, older looking and asleep in its chair, snoring loudly, a cold cup of what looked like coffee beside it. With a great creak, Isabella pushed open the gate and they entered the park.

It was quiet. In fact, it was almost silent, especially in comparison to the hustle and bustle of the streets. All that could be heard were the trickle of streams and the call of nearby birds. For Bethany, it was like they had entered another world. She didn't dare say much, as she wanted to maintain the tranquillity of this empty and beautiful space. There was green as far as her eyes could see. Rows and rows of healthy bushes and trees. Vast seas of rich grass lay out in front of them, separated by long, neat slab paths. A small squirrel-like creature crossed their path armed with an oversized nut and then disappeared up one of the neatly trimmed trees. They walked onwards into the park, saying nothing, absorbing the peace and tranquillity of this surprising paradise. Only a few others could be seen in the distance, small, vague, and far away in their own little worlds. As if on cue, the wind gently blew against Bethany's face, tousling her messy black hair.

"Beautiful, isn't it?" Isabella said to her as they reached the edge of a pond. Large fish actually made from gold swam just beneath the surface. "You can thank the Alpharian Confederation for this. Put a lot of money into it. Meant to be a paradise for the people. Not that they generally visit. Don't think they need anything from here."

They moved on, following the gravel route down past a rainbow-coloured plot of flowers that seemed to hum as they went by. Orin skimmed a stone across the water before they left it, a sheepish expression still on his face. Tassarin looked out as if in thought, his bright eyes almost searching for something. Kolchi, however, kept her wits about her, checking this way and that. The path ran under a tunnel of shrubbery.

"None of it's real, mind," said Isabella. "Ain't what the wild's really like. This is a collection. A collection of all the natural things that they deemed beautiful, all brought into one place for their convenience. Some of this stuff doesn't exist outside of here anymore—"

Bethany could sense that something was bothering the captain.

"My homeworld was beautiful. Not like this. Not some constructed paradise, with neat rows of flowers and trees. It was beautiful, and naturally so. Chaotic and interesting, always an adventure to find. Monsters to hunt, good friends to meet, and hearty meals to be had. It was alive, that world. But now, not so..."

She trailed off, leading the way lazily through the lines of shrubbery. Bethany did her best to keep up. For the first time since she'd met her, the captain had gone quiet. Then she stopped, staring at nothing, lost in her thoughts.

"I'm sorry," Bethany said quietly, though she got no response straight away. The others began to catch up. Their footsteps were the only real noise to punctuate the tranquillity. Finally, the captain looked down at her, a surprisingly sad look upon her face.

"I think there's something I want to show you."

Isabella nodded and led the group down a path to their left. They waded through a rougher patch, all overgrown, with trees unkempt and full of grasping foliage. The bushes scratched against Bethany's face as they passed through the wall of branches and twigs. The path became a broken mess under her feet. Behind her, Orin and Kolchi struggled along, pushing through the branches. Tassarin brought up the rear, almost effortlessly as he always did, his powerful figure armoured in magical metals, snapping the branches as he passed through.

After a few moments of travelling through the undergrowth, they reached a clearing, the grass coarse and overgrown. It was silent, and all was still. The only noise that could be heard was a heavy yawning, like two pieces of bark repeatedly rubbing against each other. Isabella stepped aside and gestured towards an old, gnarled tree that sat rooted right in front of them.

"Take a look."

Bethany didn't immediately notice anything special. It was an old oak tree with a thick trunk. Its bark was cracked and dry, and there were no leaves hanging from the branches that stretched upwards thinly. A moment later, she realised that the tree, despite its appearance, was alive. The first thing Bethany noticed was its breathing. Its trunk heaved up and down like a ribcage with each weak intake of breath. As it exhaled, it made the wooden snoring she had heard before. It was then that she made out a mouth, roughly scrawled into its face, above which was a nobbled bit of wood that seemed to suggest a nose. With a creak, the living tree wriggled, smacking what appeared to be lips and scrunching its wrinkled and weary closed eyes, making more noise as it did.

"This is Athagarex Treekin. You might've heard about him?"

She had. Whilst wiling away her time in the library, she'd read many of his books. Most of them were either long verses of poetry or documentations of such things as the patterns of the sun and the behaviour of butterflies. All were mournful in nature.

"The last treeman…"

"That's right. Do you want to take a closer look?"

Bethany didn't need any prompting and started to advance, her right hand out in front of her. She couldn't believe her eyes; this was a treeman, a living tree. Paying no heed to where she was stepping, she stumbled on something below her in the undergrowth. It clattered and clinked against another object next to it. When she looked down, she was alarmed to see bottles, all empty and dirty. She picked out the word wine from a number of the decaying labels. Before she could look further, the treeman began to stir, waking from his slumber with a creak. His large mouth opened in a yawn, which sounded much like an old wooden horn. He stretched his long, thin branches in all directions, and Bethany took care to stay out of the way. His eyes screwed up, wrinkling the bark around them, and then they were open, revealing two dark hazelnut balls streaked with thin red lines. He looked immensely tired.

"What manner of being disturbs my slumber? Do you desire the sage advice of a being wiser than the world?" he droned in a low, weary voice, like an antique wooden bookshelf finally learning to talk. Bethany picked up a whiff of alcohol on its breath.

The treeman stared at her expectantly, squinting as he tried to focus. After a brief moment, she replied.

"Hello, Mr Athagarex Treekin. My name—"

The treeman interrupted her with a slow bellowing laugh. "Mr Athagarex Treekin is my father's name. Not that we really have parents. To call me Mister, too, is particularly inaccurate, for being sentient plant-based lifeforms, we don't have any real need for genders. That is, apart from trying vainly to attach meaning and order to our surroundings, making the consumption of the chaos and pitilessness of our existence far easier to stomach. As we all know, such practices always work out for the best."

Bethany detected a hint of sarcasm.

"I guess you haven't seen one of my type before, have you?"

Our hero replied with a shake of her head. Despite his – or should it be its – manner, Bethany could not help but be fascinated by the treeman in front of her. It seemed impossible that a tree, of all things, could move and behave in such a way. She had read Athagarex's books, and many others on the subject of the treeman race. But reading of such things compares little to actually meeting something so fascinating in the flesh, or in this case, bark.

"Thought as much. The majority of creatures have never ever bumped into one of us treemen. Not many of us left. Now, come forward, and let me have a better look at you. I'm old and my eyes don't see too well anymore."

With a few steps, she approached the moving tree, the stench of alcohol on his breath even more profound than before. Once she was close enough, a very confused expression became etched upon his face. This changed slowly into one of surprise.

"My, my, my… You're as rare around these parts as I am. A hoooman person. Only other one I've seen of your type was a very long time ago, in brighter, better times. What, might I ask, is your name?"

Bethany had no time to think or be scared and did as she was beckoned. "My name is Bethany Hannah Morgan, good treeperson… sir?"

The treeman was quite clearly surprised by her name, his brow furrowing as he arched his body back as much as he could.

"What a peculiar name. It sounds very similar to words belonging to the language of the Trysst. It translates into 'a willingness of one to defecate themselves'!"

He chuckled to himself once again, enjoying the joke. Even his laughter was low, deliberate, and slow, like an old wooden door creaking shut repeatedly. Bethany turned awkwardly back to Isabella and the rest of the crew. She saw a sense of bemusement in all of them, apart from Tassarin. Isabella shrugged. Bethany could not think of anything to do but ask Athagarex a question of her own.

"Who was the other human you have met?"

Bethany did not know where the question came from; she was just curious. In an instant, though, Athagarex stopped laughing, his demeanour turning to one of deep contemplation.

"Oh, that was a long time ago. Back when our galaxy was young, free, and full of adventure. Though adventures are quite impossible when one is rooted to the ground…" For a split second, anger seemed to appear on Athagarex's wrinkled face.

Then it disappeared. "But I digress. This other hoooman was younger than you, with shorter hair. Possessed great power. Always surrounded by these three mysterious friends. The hoooman travelled our galaxy, righting wrongs and helping all those in need. One time, he saved us treekin from all being chopped down. We had long talks, we did – sometimes the thing used to just lie below my branches."

Athagarex looked up as best he could at a bare branch he had lowered down towards his face. He was clearly displeased by the sight.

"All decorated with leaves, singing colourful songs, and dreaming the day away. The hoooman visited me a number of times, sometimes with his despicable companions. A very good friend, almost as close to me as my dear wife." He gestured to the rotten remains of a tree trunk next to where he stood. Tears began to form in the corners of his eyes. "Then one day the hoooman vanished and was never seen again. The galaxy seemed to slowly grow darker, as if all the lights were gradually being turned off."

Bethany went closer, eager to know more, and wanting to ease Athagarex's suffering if she could. "What happened next?"

It was then that things changed. Athagarex's mood abruptly boiled up into rage.

"Next? Next! I'll tell you what happened next. That's when our galaxy, lost like some idiot child, created the Alpharian Confederation and began to tear itself apart!"

The treeman spat the words out in bitterness. Balls of sap filled saliva flew through the air. Bethany hesitantly stepped backwards, confused. She'd clearly done something to offend him, to make the treeman seethe in this unbridled rage.

"Industrialisation came, which of course meant all us trees had to be taken care of. Money needs to be made, and a treeman doesn't make any, does it?"

Bethany did not know what to say. She tentatively shook her head in agreement.

"That's when we fought back. Murdered a good number of lumberjacks, we did. Started the Great Tree War. We stood no chance, but did we give up? No!" He was still boiling over with anger. "So we were sent a treaty. An olive branch, to end the hostilities. Told that it was all going to be sorted out. By thunder! It was a joke! Told us to meet at the Grand Court of Elsen II. Thing is, we treekin don't live on that godforsaken planet. Also, if you hadn't noticed, we can't move, can we? So how in Ior are we meant to meet there! As none attended, we were marked as violent hostiles, and we were murdered. Our race wiped out across the galaxy. All because it was more economically beneficial if we didn't exist. When it was decided peace was to be made, they approached me and my wife. They forced us to sign the papers, signing over our rights in the process."

Bethany still could not find the words to respond. She was bewildered and shocked, not only at the treeman's outburst but at the horrific story of the Alpharian Confederation. She wanted to go to Athagarex and comfort him, hug him, do something that showed she was listening, that she cared. Before she could decide what to do, the treeman continued.

"Then we were uprooted, my wife and I, and taken across the galaxy as trophies of war. Replanted into this godforsaken artificial green utopian bullshit they've created here. The flowers here sing! SING!"

His words just fuelled her more, but how does one help a most tragic and doomed treeman? Unable to do anything, she was suddenly tired, her emotions making her weary of the day, not just because of their activities but with her own adventure in this clearly miserable and pitiless galaxy. She wanted to lash out at something, but there was nothing close by, and her energy soon drained away.

"That's when my wife died. Couldn't cope with the replanting. Every waking moment, I watched my companion shrivel and fail before my very eyes. When the time finally came for my wife to leave this world, I guarded the remains. I thought it only fitting to have my first book of poetry printed on her body. 'Tis a bad life, being a treeperson."

He then went quiet as if, like our hero, the treeman had grown weary of his unbridled fury. He slumped as best he could into himself, lost in the sea of his misery and hatred.

"I-I'm sorry..."

Athagarex raised his eyes to stare directly at Bethany. A glimmer of tired disdain and bitterness appeared in his huge brown eyes.

"Do you know what paper is?"

Bethany knew the answer, but she dared not say it in the presence of this unstable and probably drunk treeperson.

"It's an everyday item used by you and your kind to write upon. You know what it's made from?"

She still didn't feel she could reply. She dropped her eyes, avoiding his gaze, wracked with guilt.

"It's made from my race's skin."

An uneasy silence hovered like an unpleasant fog in the air.

"Those book things you read, funny, aren't they? When you read one, well, you're just looking at weird symbols scrawled on the dead skin of a member of my race, which then inspires hallucinations of all sorts. That's a form of entertainment for things like you, isn't it? Hallucinations brought on by staring at my corpse?"

Our hero shuffled uncomfortably on the spot. She began to edge backwards towards Isabella and the rest of the crew.

"Tell me, Bethany Hannah Morgan, do you perchance dabble with this reading activity on occasion?"

Bethany responded with silence.

"Thought as much. You can leave me now. Go! Unless you have some drink for me? Then you can have all my sage advice!"

Bethany still did not respond and took deliberate steps away from the clearing and Athagarex. She was greeted back to the group by Isabella as she made her exit.

"I think it's best that we go now."

They left the treeman to his contemplations, making quick progress back towards the main path through the foliage. Tassarin led the way, followed by Orin, Kolchi, and then Bethany, who was accompanied by Isabella. All were silent. It was a few moments of scrambling through the undergrowth before Bethany broke the silence.

"Why did you bring me here?"

Isabella looked down apologetically at Bethany. "I'm sorry, my friend. It was something you had to see. This galaxy that we live in, it's an evil and dark place full of greedy, selfish, and ignorant beings. All structured by the ever-potent Alpharian Confederation. These are dark times for us here – our galaxy is falling apart. I needed to show you how far those monsters could go, how far anyone can go when pushed and shoved in the wrong ways."

Bethany looked up at Isabella, expecting more. Isabella and her crew were the only beings in this crazy world she felt she could trust.

"Thing is, it might look bad, disastrous and all. If the Alpharian Confederation doesn't do us in, that child is going to destroy everything. But there's still hope. There's stuff we can do, stuff that'll save not only us but everyone else here too. Then we will have better times, golden times, like the ones of old. The ones that have been lost, only heard as whispers on the breeze. It will be hard to accomplish, but I know if I've got a special group of friends around, we can do it. If I have you beside me, I know we can do anything. Will you do that for me? Stick by me through thick and thin?"

Bethany responded with a small nod. A smile crept onto her face unwillingly.

"Good. Now let's get back. The sun's going down and it's time for us to head home. Hope the old wizard ain't going to be in too much of a tizzy."

She was right – the sun was going down. Long shadows skulked through the forest as they struggled with the bracken. All seemed at peace, however, and a cool evening breeze blew through her messy black hair, accompanied by the last rays of sunlight of the aging day. Soon they were back in the main park and on the tended path. Bethany and the captain had trailed behind the rest of their party and were now surprised to find them standing in a semicircle with weapons in hand. Something was amiss. As they approached with quick steps, Tassarin turned his attention to them.

"I am sorry, Ms Bethany Hannah Morgan, I seem to have been a bit lax in my watch. It seems we have been followed by that cloaked figure, and now we are surrounded by the very creature and its friends."

He was right, standing all around them were fifteen cloaked strangers of all shapes and sizes. They stood still, their hands hidden within their robes. Bethany could feel the tension in the air. Her friends, weapons at the ready, were spoiling for a fight. Isabella drew her rifle and even Kolchi snarled, bearing her teeth menacingly at their assailants.

"Come at us, you mangy dogs! You ain't gonna do us in, and you certainly ain't gonna touch our Bethany 'ere!" Orin barked. Bethany's heart warmed to the gnome's defiance.

However Bethany suspected that something was amiss. These robed figures seemed to be shaking with nervous energy, perhaps afraid of the threats being thrown their way.

Indeed they didn't seem to be threatening them at all. So smothering her usual caution, Bethany stepped forward, her arms outstretched, hoping to calm the situation. The cloaked figures flinched as she approached, murmuring nervously between themselves. They certainly weren't there for a fight. Before Bethany could speak their leader stepped forward hesitantly to address them.

"Please. We mean you no harm, friends," it said in a weary but strong voice.

Bethany could see a long beard within the hunched figure's cloak. Then a wrinkled, leathery hand appeared and pointed straight at our hero.

"You are Bethany Hannah Morgan, yes?"

A murmur of anticipation rippled through the rest of the cloaked figures. Her friends' weapons were still drawn, but their arms began to droop. All but Tassarin were looking expectantly at her.

"I am… yes."

A great murmur of excitement pulsed through the cloaked figures. Even their ringleader seemed to straighten up, gracing himself with a newfound strength. This was still rather bemusing for our hero.

"And who might you be?"

There was a pause as the robed figures looked at each other, buzzing with energy. When the silence had lingered for what seemed like a dramatic enough period, their leader replied, "We are the Dramatimancers, and we want you to see our play."

Seventeen

"How did you know it was me?" Bethany asked cautiously, tugging at the corners of her cloak, realising to her shock that her hood was still down.

The leader of the Dramatimancers lowered his hood to reveal a goat face with a long, white beard, patchy grey hair, and thin wire glasses. There was also evidence of half-removed make-up.

"Our dramatimetres and dramatigraphs predicted your coming. Though our meeting here is a few seconds late from being conducted at full dramatic intensity, we must apply ourselves properly to the situation as it presents itself," the goat person said. His voice was still strong, in spite of his apparent age and frailty.

"But how do you know my name?"

The goat person stroked his chin quizzically. A murmur of excitement spread through the other robed figures.

"Don't trust 'em," Orin butted in. "These dramatic types be right queer folk. I think it'd be best if we move on, Mistress Bethany."

Bethany was still enjoying the gnome's sudden change of mood towards her. It was as if that one slap of a reptile's tail had expunged all her previous wrongdoing.

The goat man raised a hand, silencing the murmuring of his colleagues. "We come here in peace, with admiration for your cause. 'Tis of the utmost import that you quest in the manner you do. Your dramatic adventure will surely progress the plot of our troubled galaxy and lead us on to better things, and the ever-sought happily ever after."

As one, the other robed figures repeated "happily ever after", much to Bethany's astonishment. They seemed more a cult than a school of magic, though thankfully they appeared not to possess any ill will towards them. Her friends had now put their weapons away, though Orin still stood poised to draw them again at the smallest hint of danger.

"To properly answer your questions, however, I must tell you we have some powerful tools of dramatic detection and prophecation. Each letter of your name has been predicted and found in our own theatrical works during centuries of study and practice. When put together and rearranged, for the best possible dramatic effect of course, they spelt Bethany Hannah Morgan. To find you was easy. Our means of dramatic prophecation pointed to this very date on Goldensmorg, at the exact time a character of your category would tire of her surroundings and venture forth, with help from her new friendly-companion character types—"

"Who are you callin' a friendly-companion character type?" interrupted Orin.

Isabella quickly hushed him.

Bethany looked to her friends. With the exception of Tassarin, they all seemed somewhat bewildered, unable to offer even a show of encouragement. Apart from that quick exchange and the muffled grumbles emanating from Orin, they just stood in silence. The lead Dramatimancer went on, lost in his words, as if this were a dramatic monologue learned by heart and delivered in such a manner that it neither required the intended audience to listen nor even to exist at all. It was of course properly spoken, with interesting stresses and inclination, but lacked any of the qualities of a proper conversation between two people.

"Once you were out of the protection of the wizard's house, it was particularly easy for us to pick up your dramatic scent. My colleague Gulpinor" – the goat person gestured to one of his colleagues, who raised a furry brown hand – "managed to pick you up easily. Being of the vivacious race the hundst, gifted as they are with heightened smell, it possessed little challenge for him. Though his mission was made far easier due to the fact that this place of ours has not seen one of yours, a hooooman, for aeons. As a result, during your journey through the city centre, you stood out like the proverbial sore thumb."

This was quite a surprise to our hero. They had been following her, knowing who she was all along.

"But I was wearing this... H-how did you know?"

The goat man's little smile disappeared. He continued with reluctance, as if he were about to reveal some piece of scandalous information or get someone else in trouble.

"Unfortunately, those magic cloaks you have all been wearing had their magical charges removed and siphoned off when you used a magical means for travel."

Orin grumbled as he pulled his cloak off and threw it to the ground. Isabella did the same, shaking her head, visibly annoyed at the revelation. Kolchi rightly looked embarrassed, fidgeting and nervously pacing on the spot, as she attempted to avoid her colleagues' gaze. Tassarin promptly picked up the cloaks without a murmur and continued to hold them in much the manner of a butler politely holding his master's coat, unable to find a place to put it.

"But enough of all this chatter. I am the High Ordained Templar Ralphaius Tempeston of the Grand College of Dramatimancy. I am truly honoured to be graced with the presence of the great hero of our story."

He held out a hand, bowing slightly and lowering his head. Awkwardly, Bethany took his hand in her own, which was kissed by the aged goat man. With that, he released her from his grasp and ended his formal greeting. She blushed at the proceedings.

"I, my colleagues, and our predecessors have been waiting patiently for many centuries for your arrival. These friends of mine standing before you are examples of the greatest players of our college, masters of all manner of dramatic arts."

An excited murmur of agreement rushed through the robed figures.

"The day has grown old, and we must soon commence our nightly theatrical ablutions. Will you join us, Bethany Hannah Morgan, and do us the honour of watching our performance tonight? Will you partake in our theatrical endeavours?"

He was right; the night had really come on. For a moment it was silent, the goat man waiting expectantly for an answer. Bethany looked again to her friends. They offered no response, but looked expectantly at our hero, waiting for her to take the lead. From the sulky frown on Orin's face, it was clear that he was not in favour of watching a piece of theatre that night. After a few moments, though, Bethany found her voice.

"Why not? I will watch your play!"

The goat man jumped a short distance in the air, kicking his heels. The other robed figures gave a cheer, hugging each other in euphoria.

"Excellent! Now please, Bethany Hannah Morgan and friends, follow me!"

And with that he led them all away.

"Their magics didn't even reveal our names," Orin grumbled.

They were led out of the gardens and back into the streets of Goldensmorg. It was dark now, and the streets with their layer of smog were illuminated by what appeared to be gas streetlamps, tended by tiny pug creatures in overalls, perched on extremely tall ladders. The air was cold and still, the streets empty but for the occasional beggar, guard, or vendor desperately trying to sell the last of his wares. It was quiet, too. The only noise came from the buildings they passed, all of which seemed crammed with occupants and full of light. The moon shone down upon the cobbled streets, making their damp surfaces glisten like polished gems. They made quick progress, the Dramatimancers clearly eager to hurry them to their destination, excited to perform, boasting about the night's production as they went. The crew of the *Evanescence*, however, hardly passed a word between themselves, the conversation dominated by the chatter of their hosts.

Before long, they had arrived at their destination. It was a theatre with ornate neoclassical pillars and archways, and a light shone through its many-windowed front doors. An illuminated sign above the entrance said Tonight's Performance: "When the World Falls Down!", and placards and photos plastered the walls on either side, listing the starring actors in the play. It was, however, clearly underfunded and seemed to have fallen into some disrepair; the paintwork was severely faded and chipped, the lights in front were broken, and the marble-slabbed steps and flooring were loose and cracked in a number of places. The goat man stood in front of them expectantly.

"We've already told the box office of your arrival. We knew you'd come. You've got the best seats in the house. Just go up and they'll give you your tickets. But yes, it's almost the hour call, so we'll see you later."

They quickly disappeared around a corner and down an alleyway, towards the stage door. She and her companions were left on their own, standing sheepishly on the steps of the theatre entrance.

"Shall we go in, then?" Isabella queried with a surprising hesitancy.

It was clear yet again that they were all waiting for Bethany to lead the way, so with a strong and positive but altogether hesitant nod, she replied. "I don't see why not..."

She pushed through the heavy front doors and walked into the light of the theatre interior, her hands latched around the straps of her backpack.

The foyer was empty and quiet. The walls were painted in a deep purple, faded and scratched in many places. Posters old and new, as well as black-and-white headshots, coated it like wallpaper, separated by gold-painted pillars half submerged into the walls at regular intervals. They too looked old and poorly kept, with chipped paintwork and dust on their ridges. The ceiling was high and decorated with picturesque landscapes that had also seen better days. Below them, the floor was made from the same marbled tiles as outside, covered in most places with dusty red carpets. The place seemed utterly deserted. To her right was an old wooden alcove and what appeared to be a box office, all covered in dust and posters and stuffed with papers and old tickets. Upon its scuffed desk sat a variety of rusted devices, wire trays, and all kinds of stationery that Bethany could hardly recognise.

She approached the box office, friends in tow. The place was silent except for the querying mutters from her group.

"Hello?" Her voice bounced off the walls.

"Just a minute…" came the quiet reply in what seemed to be a West Country accent. It originated from behind the box office desk.

Bethany approached it and looked over it to find the origin of the voice. It was a little mole-like creature dressed as a typical clerk, with a little brown waistcoat, brown and beige shirt with rolled-up sleeves, and grey, slightly oversized trousers. On its pointy mole nose sat a pair of thin wire glasses through which it looked up at our hero with squinting black eyes. It seemed to be struggling to get onto its chair.

"Jus' need to get ups on me chair…"

In a few moments, the mole creature was sitting in place, and with the pull of a lever it ascended to desk height, rubbing its nose as it went. A little pin badge on its right breast pocket said Joe.

"Now, 'ow may I 'elps you this evenin'?"

Bethany found the creature rather charming, though of course she didn't say anything of the sort. She didn't want to offend another living being by being condescending. It wasn't this race's fault, whatever it was, that they were so tiny and adorable.

"Well, my friends and I have been invited to tonight's performance. The Dramatimancers say they've put some tickets aside for me."

"Ah, yes!" came the reply, as Joe pulled another lever under the chair, which proceeded with a clunk to move towards a big metal box a few inches away. Fumbling for a key, the mole person opened it.

"Let me haves a look here, shall we? Don't get many pre-books, see. Most of the peoples that watch our shows turn up on the night. Though there ain't many of dem, really, an' most of dem tend to be other Dramatimancers or off-worlders with little clue of their work. What be your name, I pray, young maiden?"

With a slight hesitance, she replied, "Bethany, Bethany Hannah Morgan. Th-that's my name, yes."

With a serious nod, Joe began to search the box, which was empty of any tickets apart from a solitary envelope in the B section.

"Ah, here you are! Bethany Hannah Morgan, and four guests. I'm guessing these are yours?"

"That's me!"

The mole creature leaned as far forward as he could, stretching out his right paw, holding the collection of rectangular tickets he'd taken out of the envelope. Bethany could see he was struggling and quickly took the tickets.

"Thank you."

With that they headed to the bar and waited. The place was empty – there wasn't even a bartender. Isabella and Orin searched for one, leaning around the bar itself, eying up the barrels of beer. Getting impatient they slowly squeezed closer towards the drink, only to have Kolchi stop them before they could pinch anything. Bethany sat on a stool, half expecting for more people to turn up. They waited awkwardly, muttering to themselves, but no one arrived – they were on their own.

Eventually one of the wall panels to her left slid open all by itself, landing against another panel with a great thud. Joe had scampered from behind his desk and was standing in front of them in the bar, slightly out of breath. He pointed as best he could in the direction of the opening.

"The show is about to start. Over there, see. No interval tonight. Hope you enjoy the performance."

Thanking the mole creature again, she headed through the gap into the theatre's auditorium. Her friends followed her closely, uncomfortable with their surroundings.

Out in front of her were rows upon rows of cushioned theatre seats, all purple in colour and threadbare. The carpet underneath was the same. Above them were layers and layers of tiered auditorium circles, which reached high into the structure, much in the manner of a traditional theatre or opera house. The ceiling was white, with intricate gold trim and decorations embossed on its surface. Hanging from above was a huge chandelier that would surely block the view from the upper circles. It too appeared to be in disrepair, much of its glasswork cracked or missing. It was unlikely anyone from the upper circles would complain tonight, though, because there was no one in them, from what she could see. In fact, there was not one other soul in the auditorium. They headed for their seats, choosing at leisure their desired spots, ignoring their tickets. Bethany chose the best seats in the house: the very centre of the stalls. Taking off her bag, she placed it in front of her feet, quickly checking on the locket as she did so. Her friends did likewise with a noisy clatter as they set weapons and satchels beneath and around their seats.

In front of them was the stage. It had a traditional proscenium arch, in much the style of a late-nineteenth-century grand theatre. The gold adornments carried on, reaching like vines around the arch and threatening to encroach upon the stage itself. Ornaments and figures stretched out of this river of embellishment, looking desperate to escape their decorative existence. A gold goblin cherub in front of Bethany seemed to be missing its nose. The main space of the stage was hidden behind a red velvet curtain that looked immensely heavy and dusty. Just below the polished wooden flooring of the stage was an orchestra box, occupied by a solitary smartly dressed gropscrub and a collection of unrecognisable percussion, string, brass, and wind instruments.

They had only been sitting for a few moments when the panelled door they had entered through slid shut and the lights dimmed. The auditorium was incredibly dark; it reminded Bethany of the Inquisitor's cell she had occupied. Then the orchestra burst into life. Huge horns were blown, soon matched with a clash of drums. A thunderous cacophony of dramatic noises crashed in the darkness. A loud drumroll commenced and then stopped suddenly, signalling a quieter section of music featuring the string and wind instruments. It was a tune she'd never heard before, but before long, it changed again. She was blasted by song after song from these peculiar instruments as they sat in the dark. The music stopped at last and they were greeted by a solitary spotlight that shone on the very middle of the closed curtains.

A figure stepped through them with a great lunge. It was Ralphaius, the goat man, leader of the Dramatimancers. He clearly had a leading role. Focusing on a spot at the very back of the audience, he looked above the heads of our hero and her friends. He stood lost in his own world, dramatically posed and dressed in a grey business suit and trilby hat that would not have looked out of place in the 1920s. What was startling was that he appeared young too, the patches on his fur covered up, his glasses gone, and his make-up giving him this brighter, more youthful appearance. He also stood more upright and dynamically, as if he were impersonating a person far younger than himself. After a short dramatic pause, he began to speak. What came out of his mouth was all nonsense to our hero, for it seemed to be in an entirely unrecognisable language. Still, he attacked it with so much vigour and energy that he made the words, whatever they meant, seem immensely important. He used huge arm gestures, pointing towards parts of the auditorium, his eyes glazed over, lost in his character's thoughts. Here and there in his opening speech were pauses, some lasting only a millisecond whilst others stretched on for minutes. It was clear to Bethany that every moment of the performance had been carefully thought out and planned, and every syllable, every single stress, and every inclination had been carefully placed. Now that he was performing, he was going through these moments like clockwork. The result was a carefully crafted and structured dramatic monologue that also seemed completely artificial. After what seemed like forever, he bowed. Bethany nervously applauded, though it was soon clear the monologue wasn't meant to receive applause, as the action quickly rolled on. The curtains parted and the stage was flooded with light. The large cast that was arrayed on its boards then burst into a musical number as they danced upon a set that resembled a row of terraced houses, grim and grey in colour, befitting of a dreary day in an industrial English town.

Readers, I will not waste your time describing the rest of the Dramatimancers' play, for unfortunately, though it was performed with huge amounts of energy and enthusiasm, it was really quite dreadful. A full description would be tremendously painful, not only for you but for me as well. I shall continue this chapter by resuming our narrative from Bethany's perspective, highlighting any moments from their overdramatised chaotic rubbish that had any effect on her.

The play went on for four confusing hours. It was full of songs, monologues, jokes, and of course heightened dramatic moments. Throughout it all, the performers spoke and sang in this language unfamiliar to Bethany. It was a baffling, endless blur. Still, it was professionally done with huge amounts of skill, and as she knew they were very eager to perform to her, she tried her best to be attentive. At one point, Bethany was confident that all the characters had transformed into cheese graters and were endlessly shouting a word that sounded like "punt". However, despite some very confusing characters, random set transformations, endless dance breaks, and plenty of overacting, she managed to piece some sense from the endless chaos. The story centred on Ralphaius' character, who got progressively older during the course of the performance. This was something Bethany was impressed by; his mastery of his own physicality, with support from some rather ingenious prosthetics and make-up effects, made it genuinely seem like he was in fact aging before her eyes. His truly stunning performance was only offset by the overacting and overabundance of dramatic clichés that he and the entire cast seemed to rely on. His character was bursting with energy, incredibly friendly, and much loved, even when he had aged. Nearly every other member of the cast seemed to laugh at his jokes, even going as far as to dance with him in spectacularly extravagant but needlessly long dance breaks. The character then apparently fell in love, then fought off the advances of a particularly obvious villain before finally receiving a kiss. This happy moment was quickly over as the hero was separated from his lover and rushed off to some kind of war. When a character he'd become close with died, after singing a very slow and oversentimental song, which had three reprises, he went on to crash a vehicle into a body of water, consumed in a fit of rage. This was followed by a huge musical number with streamers, fireworks, and plenty of confetti, in which everyone was happy again, possibly because the war was over. Then there was what appeared to be a wedding as the two lovers reunited, though the joyful moment quickly disappeared again as he was tormented by a younger-looking version of his character, who was perpetually gripped with rage. This led rather swiftly on to his love interest lying in a bed and apparently dying too, leaving the lead on his own again.

His spirits dramatically improved with the arrival of a new, very young character, who possessed long, dark, messy black hair and had a fondness for baking biscuits. These two danced and played with each other merrily, enjoying each other's company. Two musical numbers later, there was sadness again as Ralphaius started to deteriorate with age. He grew slower and slower, spending a lot of his time on stage singing merry little tunes whilst sitting exhausted in a chair. The younger character tried to keep him active, but all efforts seemed in vain. As the climax came, in full dramatic effect, Ralphaius' character slumped down and died, accompanied by a new and startlingly different song. Of everything she had just experienced, this was the moment that affected Bethany the most. It was a sad song – the saddest she'd ever heard. A collection of musical instruments played a tune, conveying some great and enjoyable journey that only ends with grief, pain, a world falling apart, and finally nothingness. A small tear appeared in the corner of her eye. The sensations seemed familiar to her.

Before she could dwell too long, the play was over. The stage lights came up and the characters burst back to life. Ralphaius struggled to his feet, exhausted from his performance. The orchestra played upbeat reprises of the production's many songs, and the players bowed. Bethany diligently applauded. Looking to her sides, she saw Tassarin and Kolchi doing the same. Isabella and Orin, however, were fast asleep and gently snoring in their seats. After what seemed like an endless number of bows, the curtains were drawn, the orchestra finished with a dramatic crescendo, and the house lights came back on. After a few awkward moments, Bethany and Kolchi nudged the other two awake, and they all left the auditorium the way they had come in.

They were surprised to find the entire company of players waiting for them eagerly in the foyer, still in their make-up and costumes. Spots of sweat dripped down their hopeful faces. Ralphaius was at the front, still exhausted and surprisingly sitting in a wheelchair.

"Well... what do you think?" he asked in an alarmingly frail voice.

All attention was on Bethany. She struggled to find an answer; she neither felt like she had disliked it nor thoroughly enjoyed it. It all seemed so confusing. She didn't say that, of course – she didn't want to offend this group of magical actors who'd put so much time and effort into their project. So she replied in the best way someone can when trying to dodge answering truthfully.

"It was very interesting."

The Dramatimancers murmured amongst themselves, unsure of how to take the comment. Ralphaius looked at her inquisitively, stroking his chin expectantly. Then, eager for more feedback, he continued his questioning.

"What was your favourite bit?"

This she knew immediately. She couldn't say she had actually enjoyed it. It was certainly a fascinating part, however, that had woken something deeply emotional inside of her.

"The song."

The whole group of players went silent, waiting for her to continue.

"The song at the end. You know, the sad one when…" She didn't know the character's name. "…yeah, he died."

For a moment, the whole troupe of actors were lost in thought, murmuring to themselves.

"A very wise choice. You seem to have great taste." Ralphaius struggled forward as he leaned close to Bethany, almost coming right out of the wheelchair. "That song, like the rest of our play, is yet to be finished. It is a special piece, written by no one and found on the winds of destiny itself. We discovered its existence during our studies. It is the song of life's great story. A journey that you, the hero of our tale, have already embarked upon."

He fell back in his chair, exhausted. His attendants saw to his well-being as he struggled for breath.

"It is time for me to rest. That performance stripped me of a great part of my vitality," he gasped, though still managing to maintain his usual vocal excellence. "Good luck, my friend. Good luck, Bethany Hannah Morgan! Hopefully we will meet again."

They made their farewells, and our hero and the crew of the *Evanescence* promptly left the theatre and headed home. It was late and they were, with the exception of Tassarin of course, immensely tired. Orin was still in a bad mood, though this time aiming his frustration at something different.

"Well, tha' was a load of cra—"

"Not now, Orin!" Isabella replied.

All went quiet again as they made swift progress through the empty and silent streets of Goldensmorg. Before long, they were back in the tavern, which was still full of activity, and in the cupboard. A moment later, they were back in the wizard's house. Like adolescents breaking curfew, they snuck quietly through the house to bed, few words exchanged between them. Bethany, with her exhausted head full of thoughts, struggled to sleep. Eventually, though, the physical exertion of the day took over, and her racing mind fell into the realm of slumber. It was a sleep haunted by her recurring dreams, full of white rooms, drips, doctors, and the disinterested looks of her parents.

And a sense of loss she couldn't place.

Eighteen

THE NEXT FEW DAYS WERE MUCH THE SAME AS any others spent confined in the wizard's house. When Bethany was not eating and enjoying the company of Isabella and her crew, she was reading books in the library. She was very pleased to discover that Orin's attitude towards her continued to be more pleasant than before; indeed, he seemed to take great pleasure in seeing to her every need. The wizard, however, was still rarely seen. When he was caught, he said little, seemingly too busy and uninterested to respond or inquire into their well-being. He'd then disappear back into his office. As such, Bethany had no idea if he knew of their recent visit to Goldensmorg. Our hero and the crew of the *Evanescence* mutually agreed it was perhaps best for them to keep it amongst themselves, and this was how it was for the next few quiet days. That was until Bethany was actually summoned to the wizard's office.

The day began much like any other; having just had her midday meal, she had taken herself to the library to start a book about famous space pirates. She noticed at lunch that Tassarin was absent, and no one else knew of his whereabouts. But she thought little of it and rushed to the library to start her book. She had just finished reading a chapter about Meltom Prub, the first and most ineffectual pirate to exist (due to him being smaller than an ant), when she was interrupted from her studies by the Andarin himself, who had appeared unannounced in the library, much to Bethany's surprise.

"Mr Alarabus would like to see you, Bethany Morgan. Come with me."

"Why? Whatever is the matter?"

Tassarin made to go, stopping only to answer. The meeting seemed of great urgency and import.

"You will find out in due course."

He left the room with Bethany following dutifully, though hesitantly, taking her backpack with her. She was suspicious that something was bothering the Andarin, as his usual patient and courteous demeanour seemed strained. They made quick progress through the halls and rooms of the wizard's house, which that day had the appearance of a Roman country villa. They were soon outside the doors of the wizard's office. Without a word or gesture from them, the wooden figures sprang to life, finding their keys and opening the magical locks. The doors swung open to reveal the wizard's office inside.

Behind the doors stood not just the wizard, but also Isabella, Kolchi, and Orin, dressed in their usual pirate and magician garb.

"Ah, Bethany. We have been waiting for your arrival," Alarabus announced in a cheery tone.

She wondered whether he knew of their visit to Goldensmorg. He didn't seem angry, which of course was a good sign; she was surprised though to see that, unlike before, the air wasn't filled with flying books. They all seemed to sit in piles around the room or in the spaces on the bookshelves.

"There is much to talk about. Plans to be made. And it seems time is steadily running out."

She took her place beside Isabella, who threw a quick, friendly smile in her direction. Tassarin stood a few paces behind her, whilst Kolchi and Orin stood to the captain's left, their attention on the wizard.

"Whatever is the matter, Mr Alarabus?" Bethany cautiously asked.

"Plenty! But I think we already know what is troubling this galaxy of ours." He pulled a letter from his robes. The wax seal had been ripped apart. "I have received news from our friends the Dramatimancers about your visit the other night."

A nervous shiver ran down her spine and awkwardly placed itself right in the middle of her gut. She looked across to her friends, who shuffled anxiously, avoiding each other's gaze. Tassarin, of course, stood in his usual emotionless way, his oft-distant eyes now focused upon the wizard and our hero.

"The Dramatimancers?" She immediately regretted the brief reply.

"Why yes, the Dramatimancers. You watched their play the other day," the wizard replied in a matter-of-fact way.

Much to Bethany's surprise, he didn't seem annoyed in the slightest. Bethany felt guilty nonetheless; she had always been a thoughtful and caring person and hated the idea of upsetting someone.

"I'm sorry..."

"Sorry?" The wizard seemed confused. Then he gave a short, merry laugh. "Ah yes, sorry! No need to apologise. A person like you, travelling this far into an unknown world? I can understand why you would be curious and eager to explore. 'Tis my fault, really, keeping you all trapped in my house. Although I guess you could also blame Isabella and her crew..." He gave the assembled pirates a stern look. "They were your enablers. They are rather too fond of you. I told them to keep watch over you, but what did they do? They let you out at the first possibility. Anything could have happened!"

The wizard stopped. Collecting himself and taking a deep breath, he turned his attention back to Bethany.

"Thankfully, you were lucky, and nothing went wrong. In fact, your meeting with the Dramatimancers has been somewhat beneficial to our cause."

He'd clearly calmed down now. In fact, he began to buzz with excitement.

"They sent me this letter, in which they mention you in extremely good light. They believe, without a shadow of a doubt, that you are the fabled hero of our story. That you are the person we have been waiting for, the one who will change our galaxy!"

Alarabus put the letter back inside his robes. He straightened his hat, giving a quick, sharp cough. "Of course, it is wise to be cautious of what the Dramatimancers say. They are a particularly eccentric college. However, recently their predictions have all been correct, so I am willing to heed their message. Now, enough of this chit-chat, there is much to discuss and to plan. Follow me!"

With an about-turn, the little wizard started to make his way deeper into his office. He quickly shuffled forwards and then to the left between two bookshelves. The furniture on route jumped out of the way as he approached. Bethany, followed by the pirates, headed off in pursuit, and around the corner they came to a section full of maps, globes, and model solar systems. Some were made of paper, whilst others were huge copper pieces. They were placed in no particular order;

one might call it an organised mess. Each item seemed alive with energy, anxious and ready to move at a moment's notice. Alarabus inspected each in turn, running his fingers along very precise routes across a number of the maps and globes.

Bethany turned to Isabella. "What's going to happen?"

"I don't know for sure. What I do know is that the wizard has an idea of what to do next."

Pleased with his inspections, Alarabus stood in the middle of the antechamber, at the centre of a huge worn carpet decorated with the galaxy of Edimor.

"We are about to commence our great journey, my friends. The item that Bethany has in her possession is incredibly powerful. We cannot let it fall into the wrong hands."

Bethany was now mindful of her rucksack, which was empty save for a few items and the all-important locket. She had somewhat forgotten it was there at all, having become so accustomed to wearing the thing.

"As we know, our galaxy is in a terrible spot. Hate fills the hearts of many, and the Alpharian Confederation is doing despicable things. Then there is the child and his minder. They are the worst of all, for through their actions, we could see our utter oblivion. It is with this item that we have a chance to stop them. To stop all this madness and hate. To do so, however, will be quite a challenge."

At a raise of his arms, light shone through the carpet beneath him, throwing shadows of the galaxy upwards so that planets and stars gracefully floated through the air. At another gesture, the globes, maps, and other astrological items burst into life, adding to the mayhem of the improvised magical galaxy. Bethany couldn't believe her eyes. Stepping forward into the immersive moving map, she gazed around in wonder and delight, not just at the trick itself but at the true scale and magnificence of Edimor. It was vast – so many stars, so many planets floated around her, made from paper, brass balls, and shadows. The wizard pointed at a particular planet, which zoomed straight towards them.

"This is Goldensmorg, where we are now..."

Even the miniature version seemed to possess a layer of smog.

"...and this is where we need to get ourselves..."

At another gesture, Goldensmorg retreated and was replaced by a monstrous black hole, burning away with purple flames, ringed with planets. Even in this proxy form, Bethany found it terrifying.

"...the Heart of Unreason. Well, that is what we have called it, anyway."

The wizard adjusted his glasses, pausing for a response. Happy that there wasn't one, he continued.

"It is quite a distance for us to travel, and full of danger. Even to approach the Heart of Unreason would be calamitous, especially in the conventional way. Not to mention the *Evanescence* is a huge target; we would be hounded all the way by the Confederation, bounty hunters, and other pirates. There is a price on all our heads."

Isabella stepped forward, clearly getting impatient. "So what are we gonna do, then?"

"It is all quite simple really, once you have thought about it." There was a hint of boastfulness in Alarabus' voice.

At a sweep of his arms again, much like a conductor's, the map changed. Another planet came to the centre of their attention. It was smaller, more of a moon really, and was surrounded by a ring of rubble and asteroids.

"First, we must get to my friend the Great Astromancer, at the observatory on Cleeox. I plan to message him about our arrival. Once we have packed and tidied up here, we will take my eternity door. Whilst we do this, one of us must take the

Evanescence with great haste and lead the Confederate forces on a merry chase."

"I can do what is required of me," Tassarin interjected.

With a smile appearing on his face, the wizard addressed him, excitement exuding from the small bearded man. "Good! I know you can do it."

With an excitable point at the Andarin, he accidentally sent one of the facsimile shadow planets in his direction. It crashed onto his masklike face and disappeared without any bother.

"The ship is fast and can easily outrun any Confederate vessel! But yes, where was I..."

The wizard seemed slightly confused, scratching his head in contemplation. Bethany interjected to keep things going.

"You mentioned your friend the Astromancer—"

The wizard perked up, his old eyes wide and his energy back. "Of course! Once in his keeping, we will be safe. Then we will have more than enough time to procure a vessel, nothing lavish that could attract attention. We will use it to travel inconspicuously across the galaxy."

There was a murmur of agreement between Kolchi and Orin, who up until this point had been silent.

"Once we have our ship, we need to head here—"

Cleeox disappeared into the background and was replaced by another planet.

"This is Phaggia, not far from the Heart of Unreason. The Dramatimancers believe that there is a very old and very special eternity door on that planet. One that can transport us right into the Heart of Unreason."

The plan sounded plausible, though Bethany was still rather sceptical about the reliability of the Dramatimancers. There were grumblings from Kolchi and Orin; perhaps they shared her sentiments. The wizard carried on with his little performance.

"Using said door, we will arrive here..."

Phaggia was replaced by another planet, one which made up part of the ring that surrounded the black hole.

"...on Skallathraxus, Planet of the Dead."

Bethany could feel a communal sense of dread spreading through the group. It seemed to have a terrible name, but she wondered what could possibly be so frightening about the planet.

"I do not send us there lightly, my friends. It is the only way. It is the closest to the island which the boy and his minder call home. There is meant to be a means to traverse the void to reach it. I do not know what that is yet, but I am sure with the Dramatimancers help we will find it."

An angry grumble came from the direction of Orin, accompanied by a depressed murmur from the bear next to him.

"Once on the island, we will have reached our journey's end, and we will confront the child and his carer."

"What with?" blurted Orin. He'd clearly had enough.

"We're doomed. There's nothing we can do..." Kolchi added gloomily.

Isabella turned in one swift movement, the ends of her coat whipping through the air. She faced them with a snarl on her face. "I've had enough of you two! Shut it! Let the wizard finish."

The two averted their eyes, sheepishly looking here and there, mumbling quiet apologies in their captain's direction.

"This wizard here has a plan. Yeah, it sounds dangerous. But the crew of the *Evanescence* never shy away from a challenge. Heck, if we manage it, we'll change things, most likely for the good of every living thing in Edimor. Now, not another word from either of you."

She turned politely back towards Alarabus, who stood in patient shock. With a quick gesture, the faun captain encouraged him to continue, which after a short, awkward pause, he did.

"To answer your question, Master Orin, we will confront them with what Bethany has within the confines of her bag. It is said to possess great power. That is why I sent Grollp out to retrieve it – he was the only one who could. With its power, we can stop the machinations of those villainous beings. Then maybe we can try to find peace in Edimor."

At a final tired gesture of his arms, his display disappeared. The items and maps took their places again, and the light from the carpet faded away. The wizard paced around, checking everything was back in its place.

"When do we leave?" Isabella queried.

"As soon as possible – there is really no time to waste. The Inquisitor is a powerful being. Who knows how long it will be before he discovers our ruse and comes knocking on my door. In fact, I have wasted too much time already."

For a second he stopped, as if in deep contemplation. Then, with a jolt of energy, he continued on. "Anyway, I will be sending a letter to my friend tonight, informing him of the situation, our plan, and our imminent arrival. Once I have had a reply and all suitable preparations are completed – packing, for example – we will depart this house and begin our adventure. As you can see, I have a lot to do…"

He gestured to all the books, furniture, and whatnot that cluttered the office. Even by Bethany's standards, who had always had a talent for collecting and storing fascinating but unnecessary clutter, it was a lot to pack. She tried to work out how he'd manage such a monumental task. It surely couldn't all fit into suitcases.

"…but hopefully a couple of days will be all I need. You must do likewise. Prepare the ship as best you can, and make sure you take everything with you. We cannot leave a hint of our existence within this house. Do you understand?"

He pointed at them seriously, in what seemed like his best stern headmaster impression. The crew nodded.

"You can count on us, Mr Alarabus!" Isabella boasted, giving a salute. Kolchi and Orin did likewise, though with less enthusiasm. Tassarin did nothing of the sort and continued looking at the wizard, emotionless and almost lost in contemplation.

"Good! Now off with you. I have much to do. Oh, and tea should be ready soon."

The crew of the *Evanescence* turned and began to leave the office, heading towards the dining room. A bounce was in their steps, for despite the apparent hardships ahead, they had not lost their appetites. Tassarin of course followed in his usual manner. Bethany did likewise, turning on the spot to follow her friends.

"Ms Bethany? Before you go, can I have a word?"

She stopped in her tracks, turning back to the wizard. Isabella stopped too – Bethany had no idea why. Hesitantly, she responded, "Of course."

The wizard's attention turned to Isabella. Bethany's did too. There was a wary look upon the captain's face.

"Alone."

After an awkward second, Isabella became her normal, jovial self again. "Ah, right… of course. Leave you two muckers to it, then." There was another pause, in which Isabella didn't move. Then slowly she began to leave. "I'll see ya later then, Bethany, yeah?"

Bethany gave her a reassuring nod, and she slowly disappeared around the corner, muttering as she went. "Good. I'll leave you to it, then."

Bethany followed her departure; she was clearly reluctant to leave her there. The doors to the office swung shut. The wizard began again.

"Those pirates have grown incredibly fond of you. Even the gnome, which is really quite a surprise. Whatever happens, I am confident that they will protect you. Stick close – they are fighters, always have been. We are going to be bumping into some pretty scary stuff."

While he spoke, he summoned a pot of Crispen tea and a teacup, which flew through the air. They were joined moments later by a saucer, a spoon, a strainer, and of course the sugar pot. It seemed only the one of them would be having any tea.

"Remember, though, they are pirates. So please, I must ask you never to let your guard down."

Bethany nodded, somewhat reluctantly. Inside, she knew she had full confidence in them, though she tried her best not to let this objection be apparent to the wizard.

"Good."

At a gesture of his hand, the teapot poured the hot liquid through the strainer into the cup. The tea was a deep green and pulsed with an electric energy.

"I can imagine this might all be rather overwhelming for you. All this talk of adventure, space travel, and the like – you have never experienced anything like it before, have you?" He didn't give her time to answer. "Of course you haven't. We are used to it, pirates, wizards, and what have you. All natural adventurers. We have it pumping through our veins. But you are different. You should never have been wrapped up in this whole thing here. For that, I apologise for your misfortune and congratulate you for your conduct so far. The fact remains, though, you were never meant to stumble into this world."

Sugar was spooned into the cup, followed by a splash of milk, which had arrived late to the procession. Bethany suspected where this was going. Any moment now, the wizard would demand she hand over the locket to his protection. Then she'd be placed back into her own boring world. Of course she knew her answer, and it was a resounding no. The wizard continued.

"I must say, though, I wouldn't have it any other way."

Prepared to refuse, she froze in surprise.

"You are special, Ms Bethany Hannah Morgan. The Dramatimancers were right – you are the hero of our story. It wasn't chance that dropped you into this adventure here, it was fate." The teacup, ready, flew into the wizard's hands. He took a quick sip. "Fate, yes. In the great story of existence, some things are just meant to happen. Despite all your misfortune so far, you've made it through, and in one piece too! And here you are, ready to join me on a grand journey. Yes, I must say, you are one that will achieve great things."

Bethany felt herself blushing.

"You have so far seemed resistant to the powers of that item. Legend says that those who possess it are met with a most terrible fate. I don't think I need to remind you of what befell our mutual friend Grollp."

Bethany pictured the troll pirate with a huge grin on his face, enthusiastically blurting out his stories whilst intermittently gulping down whisky. She missed him.

"Thankfully, the same has not befallen you. Indeed, you have been able to escape, by some means or another, from situations which very well could have seen your early demise. It's truly remarkable!" Alarabus, buzzing once again, jolted slightly into a small jump. A drop of tea splashed out of the cup and onto the floor. "I really cannot quite believe it. Therefore, I think it is wise if you keep hold of it, Bethany. Hold on to it tight and do not let go. No one can see, not even me or the pirates. When the time comes, when we finally reach the end of our adventures, that's when you must reveal it. Show it only when we are in the presence of that boy and his carer. Will you promise to do that for me?"

"Of course," Bethany replied, starting to find her courage. This was her adventure, and she was confident she would not baulk at the challenges ahead.

"Brilliant!"

The wizard bounced in excitement again, spilling tea this time down the front of his robes. Noticing, he brushed it off as best he could and got control of himself, looking a touch embarrassed at his jolts of uncontrollable energy.

"Good, I mean. Just make sure you keep it somewhere safe. When you get the chance, take it from your bag and place it somewhere safer about you. Make it a necklace if you can and wear it like that. All right?"

Bethany nodded. It occurred to her she should have always worn it that way, especially after misplacing her bag in the sewers.

"Good. Now be on your way, your friends will be waiting for you. There is quite a lot for me to sort through."

He turned this way and that, inspecting his surroundings with concern.

"Okay, I'll be seeing you," Bethany responded, though no reply came from the wizard, who was now lost in his own world.

She turned and quickly made her way towards the exit, the doors opening as she approached with a great wooden moan. As she went, she noticed the eternity door again; it seemed to be pulsing now with some kind of magical energy. What, she wondered, would it be like using such an item for transport?

"Oh, I almost forgot," the wizard called, gaining our hero's attention again. "I was wondering if you had bumped into this rather peculiar fellow. He is difficult to describe, if you could even call him a he... How best to describe him? A smiling man, dressed smartly?"

She quickly looked at the house-shaped marking on her right palm. Yes, she knew of such a being, though she didn't think she could say anything. A queasy sensation formed in her stomach. She suddenly felt cold and ill, her body enveloped by nervousness. Hesitating to speak, she managed to find words to reply – though she couldn't understand why she replied in the manner she did.

"No."

She had lied. The ill feeling faded to guilt. She should have told the truth. But the man had been so adamant that she shouldn't say anything, or even hint at his existence. Heavens knew what could happen. Grollp was gone, and this galaxy was confusing and complex, full of dark things and sad ends. If she betrayed the smiling man who knows what he could do to her, or worse yet her friends. She didn't want any one of them hurt from a silly little mistake she'd made.

"Well, never mind. Off you go then. Relax, put your feet up, and join your friends."

The wizard then went back to his own business. Without needing any prompting, Bethany quickly left the room. The great doors shut behind her, the animate wooden figures relocking it. Instead of heading to the dining room to eat, though, she headed to her room to be alone. A sick, uncertain feeling lingered in her stomach. She'd lost any hint of an appetite and was disappointed with herself. Picking up her book about space pirates from the library, she isolated herself. She wanted to forget this unease and fill her head with adventure instead. Luckily for her, she was quickly lost in her imagination, thinking of pirates and ships soaring through space.

She made sure she skipped the chapters on Grollp.

Nineteen

THE NEXT FEW DAYS WERE RATHER UNEVENTFUL. Each morning she would clasp the locket around her neck, hiding it but for a small section of its silver chain just visible underneath her big purple jumper. Not even her friends had any inkling it was there. She liked its new place, sitting next to the penguin necklace Isabella had so kindly given her. She felt much more secure hiding such an important object on herself rather than in the depths of her threadbare rucksack.

Despite the return to routine, she was boiling with excitement. In just a few short days, she would be able to leave the confines of the house and head off Goldensmorg to begin travelling through the stars with her friends. She could become a pirate, maybe even a good one, embarking on epic quests, fighting monsters, and travelling to exciting places, to right wrongs and vanquish villainy. It would be but the first of many great adventures, and once everything was ready, it would begin.

It was two days since their meeting when things took a dramatic turn. Bethany was growing increasingly impatient with the wait, and to calm herself she had taken to the library. She had decided to study the finer details of space travel. As she had discovered long before, there were a huge number of books on this subject, many of which attempted to fully explain the intricate mechanics of how such magnificent ships made regular flights through the void of space, though none of them really made any sense. Indeed, at points she got the impression that the authors themselves had no idea what they were really writing about. Bethany eventually determined simply that it was all possible because of magic. After reaching this conclusion, she decided to find a new subject to study and set about placing all the books on space travel back in their original places. As she was struggling to put a large book back onto a high shelf, a massive explosion rocked the wizard's house.

BBBBBBBBOOOOOOOMMMMM!

The house shook as if it had been hit by an earthquake. Bethany was so completely taken by surprise that she threw her books up into the air, almost leaving the floor in the process. She shielded herself as best she could as with a crash they returned to the ground, only hitting her once on the very top of her head. She began to pick them all up again, grumbling to herself. While explosions such as this would normally be given a terrifying amount of attention, she blamed it on Alarabus or one of Orin's explosive contraptions and got back to her tidying. Her head was sore; she rubbed it gingerly to see if that would help.

BBBBBBBBBOOOOOOOOOMMMMMM!

The noise came again, but louder than before, and the house shook violently, throwing a piece of masonry to the floor a few metres away from our hero. Bethany jumped to her feet, forgetting her collection of books and looked all around. Perhaps this was something more problematic than her original assessment. She marched to the library door and opened it into the corridor outside. Today, the house had taken the form of the Russian Winter Palace circa 1917, but apart from that, nothing seemed particularly alarming. It was then that Bethany could hear the rumble of heated speech in the distance and the faint sound of crashing. For a few seconds she considered making a flight from the library to find her friends. In a panic though, she stood frozen above the pile of books, her body unable to move as her heart seemingly stopped momentarily in anticipation. Breathing deeply and deliberately, her brain scrambled to construct a plan of action – she really needed to find the source of the noise and make sure neither she nor her friends were in any danger.

BBBBBBBBOOOOOOOMMMMM!

This was the loudest yet. The house once again shook violently, throwing both Bethany and large chunks of the ceiling to the floor. With a thud and blunt pain, she landed. The noise seemed to be much closer now, and clearer, as if it were coming from just outside the house. Picking herself up with a groan, she headed to the large window behind her desk. She knew there wasn't much of a view from it, obstructed as it was by a thick layer of smog and the tops of houses, but she thought she should try. Peering through, she saw nothing of interest; it all looked rather tranquil. The sky was blue and filled with fluffy clouds, the ever-present smog looking noticeably thin. Remembering to breathe again, she let herself relax for a moment, lowering her guard. It was then that something genuinely frightening entered her view.

There in front of her was an iron ship, completely unlike the *Evanescence*. It seemed to be from an entirely different world that existed in an entirely different time period and made for an entirely different purpose. It was shaped like a tortoise shell, but one made of thick black metal, bristling with guns and with massive smog-belching chimneys protruding from the top of it. It looked similar to the ironclad vessels she'd seen pictures and drawings of in history books about warfare from the nineteenth century, though with the slight differences that this one looked evil and was flying. It was monstrously huge, and in an instant, Bethany knew that this ship was here to ruin her day.

Before she could do much more, one of the guns belched forth fire, sending a huge black ball hurtling through the air. It was headed straight towards her. She flung herself to the side a split second before the window exploded in a shower of glass. A shard slashed her lower left arm whilst another shot into her left cheek, leaving her with stabbing pains. She could feel blood beginning to drip down both her face and her arm, filling her with a queasy, numb sensation. The cannonball had continued on through the room, smashing into the opposite wall and crushing a bookshelf. A number of books burst into great explosions of paper and leather, their pages floating and landing around a shocked Bethany, still lying prone on the floor.

In quick succession the ship fired again and again.

BBBBBBBBOOOOOOOMMMMM!
BBBBBBBBOOOOOOOMMMMM!
BBBBBBBBOOOOOOOMMMMM!

The room shook with such ferocity that she thought the whole thing would collapse and crumble. Even the noise itself was frightening, bordering on deafening, and Bethany clasped her hands to her ears, desperately trying to block it out. Rolling to the side of the room, she hid herself as best she could under a wooden table, another shard of glass scratching her in the process. Luckily for our hero, not one of the huge cannon balls hit her, despite the room being torn apart by the unrelenting broadside. The flooring was ripped up and bookshelves shattered into tiny pieces. Loose pages fell from the sky, only to be kicked violently up again by another thunderous shot. The whole library was smashed to pieces as Bethany tried desperately to survive the storm.

Almost as soon as the ship had started its violent firestorm, it was off again, seemingly pleased with the destruction it had wrought. Bethany presumed it was off to do the same to another part of the house and so slowly made her way upright. Another cannon blast sent her to the floor yet again, though thankfully it appeared to be much farther away. Bethany picked herself up once more, brushing herself down as the shower of torn pages settled peacefully, as if in deathly slumber. The library was a battle zone, ripped apart by the gunfire, dust settling as the room returned to calm. The house was clearly under attack, so not wanting to waste more time, our hero grabbed a particularly heavy book to use as a weapon and sprinted out of the room, ignoring her wounds. She passed through the now-shattered doors and back out into the corridor, which was a mess of splintered wood and panelling. A huge black cannonball was lodged in the wall to her left. Despite being lifeless, it still looked intensely menacing, and Bethany chose not to approach it, instead turning right to try to find her friends.

The house was in pandemonium. Sounds of battle raged through the hallways as shots were fired and steel clashed, the world she had grown so accustomed to violently tearing itself apart. As she raced down the corridors, book under her arm, she passed more cannonballs wedged into the walls of the building, along with the broken detritus that accompanied them. At points she'd pass grubbs locked in deadly combat with orc, grog, goblin, and troll soldiers. The small magical creatures stood little chance, and each one she passed seemed to be quickly defeated by its enemy, whether by being chopped in half or blasted into thousands of tiny magical particles. Thankfully they provided a distraction, and Bethany was able to make her way through the house unmolested and pretty much unnoticed. The only creatures who acknowledged her existence were the grubbs themselves, who upon seeing her doubled their efforts to heroically sacrifice themselves so she'd be left to continue her journey. Bethany had no time to grieve their loss. She had to get to the dining hall and to her friends.

When she finally reached the dining room, she arrived in the middle of a huge battle scene. The room was a mess, with broken glass, rubble, and splintered wood everywhere. On either side were barricades facing each other, made from tables and upturned furniture, separated by a section of no-man's land. Behind one were the orcs, grogs, and goblins, who made pot shots at the other side manned entirely by grubbs, all dressed as World War I British soldiers circa 1916. There was no sign of her friends anywhere. The firing from both sides was intense, so she hid herself behind a large chunk of fallen masonry. With few options and no instructions, she thought it was best in the meantime to at least help the grubbs behind their barricade, as they were clearly on her side in this fight. In short bursts, she sprinted and leapt from cover to cover. The enemy soldiers seemed far too occupied by the grubbs' spirited but inaccurate return fire and paid little attention to her movement. She made good progress and was soon behind the friendly barricade.

She was approached by one of the magical sprites, who had taken on the role of commanding officer. The grubb was smartly dressed in the manner of a British officer, with a khaki uniform, peaked cap, riding boots, and the fanciest moustache she'd ever seen. Under one of its arms it held a swagger stick, and in its other hand was a misshapen revolver. It addressed Bethany smartly with a salute. She responded likewise.

"Ah, Ms Bethany Hannah Morgan, good of you to join us. As you can see, we're in a bit of a pickle here. Gerry has us pinned down pretty good, what what!" it said in its best gentlemanly English voice. Our hero was quite bemused, because from what she could remember, she had never met the sprite before. Despite the ever-present fear and danger, Bethany couldn't help but appreciate the wonderful caricature the grubb officer presented. Coming to her senses, she didn't let herself enjoy the performance too much, for of course, she reminded herself, there was a battle going on.

"We chaps here have lost contact with HQ despite our best efforts," it said, gesturing to its left, where there were a pile of dead carrier pigeons, each with a note tied around its leg, "and have decided on holding the line until further orders. What is your plan of action, Ms Bethany Hannah Morgan?"

Bethany, unable to think of any orders, just said, "Well, I was hoping to get in contact with my friends and find a way out, but I have—"

Before she could continue, the officer grubb gave her a quick salute and addressed the rest of its squadron. "Right lads, the time has come. Ms Bethany Hannah Morgan here needs to regain contact with her friends. It is our job to give her that chance. It may seem that Gerry has us pinned down here, what what, but we need to show them what for!"

The two dozen or so grubbs, armed with crooked bolt-action rifles, gave a cheer. Bethany was again thoroughly bemused, and hoped nothing dreadful was about to happen, though she feared the worst.

"Prepare for the charge, boys. Fix bayonets!"

It was exactly the dreadful thing she had feared. They did as they were ordered, or as best they could, as only a handful of the grubb soldiers seemed to actually have something resembling a bayonet. The rest instead possessed all sorts of cutlery, brushes, and even feather dusters, which they dutifully attached to their rifles either with glue, string, or tape. Bethany knew they didn't stand a chance. Smartly, and with a shade of mock military drill, they took their places facing the barricade, ready to vault it on cue and head out into no-man's land. Some even took quick sips from flasks, both real and imaginary, that they produced from pockets.

"Ready, boys!" the officer called out as it placed a whistle in its mouth. It looked at its pocket watch intently. The firing from the enemy had died down, probably waiting for the attack that was to come.

After a few painstaking moments, the grubb officer blew its whistle.

"Over the top, lads! CHARGE!"

As one, they leapt over their barricade with a roar and ran as quickly as they could towards the enemy, their bayonets levelled and ready. Bethany crawled up to the barricade and nervously peeked over the top to watch the proceedings. She couldn't help but feel a bit impressed as they charged, full of energy and brimming with gallantry. But it was all too clear what was about to happen next, and all she could do was helplessly watch the coming carnage. The grubb soldiers had only gone a few metres before the enemy responded. Flashes of colourful light burst from muskets, and in a few short moments, the cheering had stopped as every grubb was shot down.

Bethany's mind raced to construct some kind of plan. Now that the grubbs had been defeated, she was alone, outnumbered, and helpless, but she continued to peer over the barricade, watching for the enemy's next move. It abruptly dawned on her that she was exposed and presenting quite a target, so she quickly ducked back under the barricade. Unfortunately for her, it was too late.

"There she is!" cried an orc in its heavy, gruff voice.

Bethany could hear the heavy footsteps and the clank of arms and armour that told her the Alpharian soldiers were advancing on her position. Our hero frantically considered her next move. She was armed, but only with a book, so there was no chance she could take them in a fight. It was probably best to make a hasty retreat and continue the search for Isabella and the rest of her friends elsewhere. With quick steps, she did her best to creep back the way she had come, keeping her head low as she went. She softly darted back from cover to cover. Maybe, she thought, escape was imminent, and soon she'd be away from the brutes and in better company. As she reached the doorway, she turned and was greeted by the unpleasant sight of an orc and a grog soldier snarling menacingly. In front of them stood what appeared to be their commanding officer, a goblin dressed in a fine military coat with long tails, sporting a huge tricorn hat. Medals hung on its chest and an ornate sabre from its side. The goblin looked surprisingly slim and wiry, but short, standing just inches taller than our hero. Its face was gaunt and stern, and it looked like a perfect facsimile of Napoleon himself – if the emperor had been a goblin and actually the height rumours made him out to have been. The three advanced on her, the goblin leading the way, cackling evilly. Bethany backed away into the centre of the room, prodded occasionally by the end of the orc's rifle.

"Well, well, well, we finally meet again, and for the last time," the goblin said in a perfectly posh villain's voice, slowly pulling off its gloves.

Bethany couldn't remember the first time they'd met. But thinking of nothing witty to say, she just held on to her book as if it could shield her from what she imagined would be coming next.

"I knew it would finally come to this. The great Bethany Hannah Morgan and me! Mano a mano. The great duel of the century. Oh, and you seem to have come armed with naught but a purple jumper. Ill prepared, I must say."

The goblin gave a quick cackle, and there was a brief pause before the rest of the Alpharian soldiers joined in with their own hearty laughs. The dreadful chorus went on for an awkwardly long time, the continuing laughter making the goblin officer increasingly frustrated.

"Enough, enough!" it said, waving its arms around to no effect. "SILENCE!"

The orcs and grogs were suddenly quiet again, a number looking rather sheepish. The goblin re-postured in a huff. "Now, where was I—"

"Sorry!" interrupted a particularly embarrassed orc in its deep dull voice.

The goblin grimaced as if it were in pain. Making a sharp turn, it gave the beast a furious glare before it addressed Bethany again.

"Ah, yes! Ms Bethany Hannah Morgan, you have tried valiantly to evade us, but now it is time for you to finally face your judgment. It is only right that we do this properly."

With a quick move of its arm, the goblin slapped Bethany across the face with one of its leather gloves. It didn't hurt, but it was certainly an injury to her pride and self-esteem.

"I challenge you to a—"

Our hero had reached the end of her patience. Before it could finish, Bethany hit the goblin full in the face with her heavy book, knocking it off its feet and to the floor. For a moment she felt confident and satisfied with her brilliant act of defiance, though she quickly realised the folly of her actions. The once-snarling faces of the soldiers were now full of murderous rage. The goblin officer picked itself up, returning its hat to its place and straightened its coat. It was startled and horrendously offended.

"Really! How dare you behave in such a manner!" The goblin spat the words bitterly in Bethany's face, pride shaken and now somewhat nervous in her presence. "I would have given you an end worthy of a great story. A proper duel! But so be it." It clicked its fingers. "Bors!"

Bethany could hear clipped hoofed steps, as someone approached her menacingly from behind. When it stopped she could feel the creature's warm breath brush against the top of her head.

"Aye, sir!" it snorted.

Bethany turned to see it was a particularly large and muscular example of the boar-faced grog species. Its face was covered in scars, and one of its tusks was broken, making it a truly horrific sight.

An evil grimace spread across the goblin's face. "See to it that the hoooman girl here pays for her insolence!"

With a nod, the grog advanced on her, chuckling to itself. Cracking its knuckles, it reached out its arms to grab her. Bethany stood rooted to the spot defiantly, her book ready to be swung again. No flight for her, she'd go down fighting! Though she wasn't too keen on her chances.

Suddenly there was a flash of light and the crackle of a shot being fired. A moment later, the beast had been blasted off its feet and lay motionless on the floor in front of her. As one, the occupants of the room turned to look at the source of the gunshot. Bethany was overjoyed to discover it was Isabella, rifle in hand, smoke coming from its muzzle. She was standing in one of the doorways, flanked by Orin, Kolchi, and Tassarin. They were ready for battle, weapons drawn.

"I wouldn't lay a hand on her if I were you," Isabella warned.

The soldiers readied their weapons, a palpable excitement flowing through the group. With a grimace, the goblin pointed at Bethany's friends.

"FIRE!"

Every soldier in the room then raised their musket and fired at the rescue party. The air was awash with murderous bright lights. Kolchi was shouting something undistinguishable, raising her staff in one hand and waving the other in a ceremonial way as a force field appeared around them. It was just in time. The bolts of energy crackled harmlessly off of it.

"R-reload!" stuttered the goblin, but it was too late.

At a nod from Isabella, the shield came down. The captain fired six quick shots from her rifle, knocking down four of the soldiers still trying frantically to recharge their weapons. Orin did likewise, firing his repeater flintlock pistol and taking down a further three before lobbing a small orb through the air. As it flew, Tassarin leapt into action, his blade pulsing with deadly glowing energy. His eyes shone a wrathful blood red and his whole demeanour radiated anger and bloodlust. To Bethany, he was almost unrecognisable, the being of pure emotional energy transformed from a melancholic ghostlike knight to a bloodthirsty killer. The faces of the Alpharian soldiers were gripped with fear as they desperately tried reloading even faster. Many stood motionless, their eyes wide with shock as if witnessing the wrath of a demonic monster, before accepting their coming death. But before she could see the full extent of the carnage, the orb exploded, filling the room with thick smoke. Bethany tried with all her might to see what was happening, but all that was visible were arcs of red light as the Andarin swung his blade and his burning red eyes, which sent shivers of fear throughout her body. Tassarin seemed possessed. He got quickly to work as the blood-curdling cries of his helpless adversaries filled the room. Bethany stood rooted to the ground, her book still at the ready, not knowing if she'd soon need to use it to protect herself from her own friend. After a few moments, the smoke started to subside, and all fell still and quiet again. As it disappeared, Bethany could see the lifeless bodies of the soldiers lying strewn around the room. Tassarin's eyes now pulsed a duller red, throbbing from the exertion and adrenaline, and in his right hand he still held the goblin commander by the neck. Like a predator searching its prey for signs of life, he looked over the clearly lifeless body and threw it effortlessly across the room. Turning to Bethany, he looked her dead in the eyes, his body heaving up and down, panting. For a moment she was terrified that perhaps she was to be his next victim. But with a tilt of his masklike head, he seemed to recognise our hero again, and he returned to his usual ethereal state. His eyes changed back to their natural colour and he became the Tassarin that Bethany recognised, as if the daemon that had possessed him moments earlier had disappeared.

"I am sorry you had to see that, Bethany. I do not do such horrid things lightly. This, however, was a matter of the greatest urgency."

Bethany was still in shock. Though she did not believe he would harm her, she was cautious and nervous in his presence. She continued to look right into the Andarin's eyes, as if trapped in headlights, searching to make sure her friend had definitely returned. She noticed that new cracks had appeared on his skull-like mask of a face. Tassarin did not approach, aware of Bethany's unease. She wanted to say something, but before she could, she was embraced by the captain and lifted off the ground in her big arms, which squeezed all the air out of her.

"Thank goodness we found you! We were in a right panic when we couldn't find you with your books!"

Bethany couldn't help but notice Tassarin turning away from them, deeply distressed. Isabella squeezed tighter, crushing our small hero in her arms, who groaned in pain. The captain quickly released her, becoming aware of her own roughness, and carefully placed her back on the floor. Orin and Kolchi in turn patted her on the back, offering their reassurance. Bethany, with a confusing mix of relief and urgency, looked to the captain for answers.

"How did they find us?" she asked.

"I don't know... something has gone wrong. This house is swarming with those Alpharian brutes. We've only managed to make it this far cuz Tassarin here summoned all those grubbs. Poor things don't stand a chance."

Orin took off his bandana solemnly, holding it with both hands in front of himself as if attending a funeral. "Aye, brave sods they were. Even in the grips of death itself, they kept on the good fight." He gave a sniff before rubbing small tears from his eyes.

It was then that Bethany realised they were missing the wizard.

"Alarabus! Where is he?"

The crew looked to each other for answers. Kolchi was the one to speak up first.

"I guess he might be in his office. Though I don't like his chances. Probably been nabbed by the Alpharians by now. Tassarin said the Inquisitor's here too! We don't stand a chance against that monster."

A nervous ripple passed through the crew. Bethany decided to take the lead. The wizard had to escape with them.

"We've got to get to him. Then we've got to get out of here. Agreed?"

The crew nodded in affirmation, confident in her orders. Isabella, with a few bold steps, joined her friend

"She's right! We ain't leaving old Alarabus behind. He's one of us now, and we never leave one of our crew behind, do we?"

Kolchi and Orin shook their heads. Tassarin finally turned back to watch them again, in his usual passive way.

"That's right," the gnome announced firmly. "It's 'ow Grollp always did it, and it's 'ow we're doing it now. So what shall we do, Captain Isabella?" He finished with a salute.

With that, she took command and started to blurt out orders. Bethany could not help but be impressed.

"Right, it seems we're in the danger zone, my friends. Alarabus is stuck in the centre of it, and we've got to get out of here too. You three" – she gestured to everyone but Bethany – "are going to nab the ship. Clear away those fools, and let's repeat our prison-break trick. This time, though, we're going to do it straight into the wizard's office and out again!"

Kolchi gave a nervous nod. Isabella continued.

"Bethany and I are going to grab the wizard. Maybe we can beat the dastardly Inquisitor to him. You pick us up in the ship, then we're out of here."

There was no response but the quiet murmur of agreement from Kolchi and Orin.

"Let's do it, then!"

With a hearty cheer, the three of them departed. With concern, Bethany watched them as they went, dearly hoping this was not the last time she would see them. Isabella turned to our hero and gave her a quick reassuring wink.

"Don't worry, my friend, we'll pull through this. All of us will. We'll be out of here in no time. We might get a bit bruised up, but we'll do it. Now, no more time wastin', let's go!"

The battle continued to rage through the corridors, the grubbs desperately trying to fight the Alpharian soldiers, but failing. Still, our hero and her faun friend made quick progress, darting through the wreckage and rubble strewn throughout the house. Every now and again, Isabella would have to barge past a soldier, knocking it out with the butt of her gun. Bethany had to do likewise, swinging her book against the heads of any goblins or rotscavs that got in the way, and in no time at all, they found themselves outside the wizard's office.

They were too late. The Alpharians had arrived first. There was carnage as the crumbled remains of the gargoyles lay everywhere. The huge wooden doors had been ripped off their hinges and left scattered across the floor in splinters. The figures on their panelling, who had always seemed so full of life, were still, as though they were dead. Some great force had been used to blow through these doors, and perhaps the one responsible for the destruction was still lurking inside. Bethany's heart pounded, and a bead of sweat rolled down her forehead. She had never felt so nervous before in her life. Dread formed as a sickly lump in her stomach as she contemplated what was inside. What she did know for sure was that she had to do something to save the wizard. She gave a nod to Isabella, and they edged forwards to the door frame and its broken hinges. From within, they could hear a heated conversation between two voices, and with a sharp stab of fear, Bethany recognised them instantly. It was the wizard and the smooth voice of the Inquisitor.

Hushing themselves, they slowly crept into the office, stepping carefully over the rubble in their way. The office was half empty; the books and their shelves, along with a good deal of the furniture, had gone. In their places were old suitcases, full to the brim and ready to explode. Bethany supposed that all of the wizard's possessions must have been packed into them, though she didn't let her attention linger. There were other, more pressing matters to consider. The room was full of orc, grog, and troll soldiers, their eyes fixed on the centre of the room, where both the Inquisitor and the wizard stood. They didn't seem to have noticed the almost-silent arrival of the would-be rescue party. Alarabus himself was trapped, wrapped in thick, pulsating metal chains. At the other end of the chains stood two pink, round-bellied ogres, holding on to the wrought iron with huge, calloused hands. He squirmed in pain as if the Inquisitor, with his hand out in front of him, was inflicting some manner of magical torture. The Inquisitor seemed different; he was vibrating with some kind of dark energy. His once-effortless demeanour had transformed into restrained rage, like a predator moments away from leaping on its prey. In this case, the poor, defenceless animal was clearly the wizard. The sight of his anguish made Bethany feel sick in the stomach. She desperately wanted to do something, though before she could, Isabella shushed her. Bottling up her anger, she followed the captain, keeping to the walls and moving farther into the room.

"Where is it?" the shadowlike creature demanded, having lost all patience with the tiny wizard and struggling to contain his limitless rage. The dark energy around him pulsed like hungry flames.

Our hero and the captain crept closer. Bethany was desperate to do something, anything, to relieve the small wizard's suffering, but alone she didn't stand a chance against those gathered before her.

"Probably far away from here! That girl is a clever one. You underestimate her and that crew of pirates. Probably halfway

across the galaxy now. You're too late, you are, you evil fool!"
the wizard taunted, despite his apparent pain.

The Inquisitor tightened his outstretched fingers, his
rage burning stronger. The wizard gasped as the chains drew
uncomfortably tighter. The Inquisitor looked annoyed with
his prisoner, a snarl almost visible on his gaunt, lifeless face.
Isabella readied her rifle and gestured to a spot near a table,
which Bethany presumed would be their fire base. Our hero
readied her book and followed suit, keeping her body low
and her feet light. She was tense and alert, forgetting any
hint of fear, consumed with determination and a good bit of
adrenaline. Their chance to save the wizard was close.

"I will ask you again. Where is it?!"

Again the Inquisitor tightened his grip, choking the wizard
within the chains. His eyes locked on to the wizard, peering
aggressively into his soul. Distracted, it was then that Bethany
stumbled on a rogue piece of rubble and fell forward. As one,
every eye in the room was drawn to our hero and her friend.
For a moment there was an awkward pause. Isabella was the
first to act, instinctively raising her gun. A split second later
and before she could pull the trigger, five of the Inquisitor's
soldiers pounced on her, punching and kicking. Under their
weight, she collapsed, dropping her weapon and wincing with
pain. Bethany too was tackled to the ground, hitting her head
violently on the floor. Her world was thrown into a daze. The
Inquisitor walked towards them, the wild animal choosing
new prey, his long black robes trailing behind him, eyes fixed
on Bethany, full of thinly veiled hatred. His left arm stayed
outstretched in the wizard's direction, holding him firm in the
chains.

"Pick her up," he commanded.

The orc holding her down duly did so. Bethany had lost
her only weapon in the scuffle. The Inquisitor's eyes stayed

focused on her, much like in the courtroom, staring into her very soul. This time, he was furious.

"You!" he commanded, summoning another soldier, who promptly moved into position and saluted. "Get the item now."

The grog followed its orders and stepped towards her. Isabella squirmed beside her under the pile of soldiers holding her down.

"Leave her alone! She's got nothing to do with this!"

The soldiers responded by giving her a couple of swift kicks in the stomach. She groaned in pain, unable to speak but still squirming as best she could, desperately trying to break free. The grog reached out its arms, flexing its stubby fingers, as if ready to wrench the locket from her neck. Bethany struggled to escape from the orc soldier's huge rough hands, but to no avail. A gloom consumed our hero. She had failed in her quest. The very object that she had sworn to protect, that was of the utmost importance, was about to be taken from her and fall into the wrong hands. She closed her eyes, ready for the grog to grab her around the neck and remove the locket.

To her surprise, it grabbed her bag instead. She'd completely forgotten it was even there. She had put it on that morning by habit – indeed, it had become almost an extension of her body. This was a pleasant small victory, for they were taking, to her relief, just a bag filled with rubbish and a half-empty flask, and she tried her best to hide this enjoyment. With a rough tug, the grog soldier pulled the bag from her back, almost knocking Bethany to the floor, the stench of the boar creature's breath hitting her unpleasantly in the face. With the backpack in its hands, it proudly walked back and presented it to its master.

"Good," he said, inspecting the bag with an air of satisfaction, his ethereal rage subsiding somewhat. Then, with a quick movement, his attention was back on our hero, his eyes peering into her being. This time they did not search too long.

"Now kill them. Both of them."

The soldiers all at once drew their weapons, grimacing in cruel delight.

"Nnnnnooooooooooooo!" cried Isabella, trying even harder to squirm free, only to be greeted with a flurry of sharp, painful kicks.

The grog that had taken the bag from our hero approached menacingly, this time with a machete-like blade in hand. It seemed to salivate in delight at the thought of the murderous act it was about to commit. Our hero, feeling nothing but shock, fixated on the blade, stunned into a submissive stupor. The grog raised its weapon to strike with one huge cleave, and Bethany closed her eyes, ready to accept her end.

Now, I know what you might be thinking, dear reader: this surely can't be the end, can it? How could our hero, Bethany Hannah Morgan, meet such an ignominious death at the hands of an unnamed grog soldier? This is clearly the end of the book – a way out could not be hidden in these last few pages. To that, I must tell you to simmer down, all will progress in a suitable manner. Those of you with reliable sources will know that this is only the first book in the series. So with that information, this lead character whom we have spent so much time and energy on must clearly survive to appear in any sequels. That would be correct – she won't die here, not at all. "But how will she escape this grog's blade?" Well, just remember that Edimor is full of magic, so you must always consider the unexpected.

It was then, as if from nowhere, the *Evanescence* crashed into the room. It careened into the floor, ripping up floorboards. It passed mere inches in front of Bethany, mowing her potential executioner down with a violent smack. Soldiers of all kinds, seeing the huge ship, threw themselves out of its path. Bethany, Isabella, and even the Inquisitor did likewise, hurling themselves out of harm's way. Even the brutish ogres that were holding Alarabus' chains did the same, loosening them in their haste to hit the deck. It was complete carnage as the magical pirate ship ripped the room apart. Rubble tumbled from the ceiling as the top of the mast cut through it. With a crash and a screech, the vessel eventually came to a sudden stop a few metres from where the wizard was standing, chains limp and resting at his feet. Bethany picked herself up and looked towards the deck of the ship, to be greeted by the smiling faces of Orin and Kolchi.

"Right! Everyone aboard!" yelled the gnome pirate.

Bethany headed for the ship, on the way helping to pick up Isabella, who was struggling to find her footing. They hadn't gotten far before she noticed the soldiers around them were beginning to stir. She was also unable to catch sight of the wizard.

"Where is he?" she quickly asked the crew.

The situation was once again growing worse, as the soldiers, though still in a daze, picked themselves up and advanced on the crew's position with an angry glint in their eyes. Even the ogres moved towards them, free from their duties, aggressively thumping their hands together. Before they could get too close, a bolt of energy thrummed through the room, hitting a soldier and flinging it into a bookshelf with a loud crash. It was then that the wizard came into sight, pulsing with a golden energy that whirled around him in the air like streamers. He looked a mess, his cloak torn, beard ruffled, and hat missing. Bethany watched as his brow furrowed and anger flashed into his eyes, excited to see him demonstrate the true extent of his powers. The soldiers couldn't help but turn to him, full of terror and shock, mesmerised by the flowing streams of energy that surrounded his form. They were right to be scared, for Alarabus, Bethany finally realised, was an extremely powerful wizard.

At a gesture of his arms, the items still unpacked and undamaged in the room came to life. Books flew from the shelves, smashing themselves into the faces of orcs, grogs, and trolls alike. At another gesture, his suitcases burst open, pelting the Alpharian soldiers with all sorts of items and furniture. Then with a great sweep of his arm, the bookshelf to his left ripped itself from the wall and, with a huge swing, crashed into one of the ogres, knocking it across the room. A pair of grogs were thrown through the air, hit by another bolt of lightning, and hurled back through the door of the office. Bethany, Isabella, and the crew all gave a cheer, enjoying the destruction Alarabus was unleashing upon the enemy. With that, the soldiers seemed to have had enough of the battering and promptly fled in panic, yelling and squealing. Once the last of them had left the room, the magical energy began to disappear, and the wizard returned to his excitable and eccentric tiny magical self. He looked around awkwardly, as if searching for something he'd lost.

"Now, where's my hat?"

It was nowhere to be seen. Alarabus gave up, shrugged in annoyance, and tottered over to the crew. Bethany was gobsmacked. She'd been surprised earlier by Tassarin's murderous abilities, but this was truly something else.

"Well, I guess I can always get a new one. Plus some new glasses!" He gestured to a crack in his lenses, tutting. "Anyway, let's be off then." The wizard sounded both a bit put out and impatient as they headed towards the ship.

Roped rigging hung down the sides for them to climb. Isabella without a pause did just that, rapidly ascending and leaping onto the deck. After a quick embrace of each crew member, she reached down to Bethany.

"Come on, me old friend, let's be going." She turned to the wizard, who gave her a reassuring nod. "Well, here we go..." she said hesitantly.

"Indeed. It is time we begin our journey. Now, you get climbing and let us be off," the wizard replied.

Then, with an enthusiasm and strength that belied her injuries, Bethany happily climbed the rigging up to the deck. Her heart was full of joy and optimism. Against the odds, they'd already managed to defeat their enemies. They would soon be off, ready to start their adventures. The excitement almost consumed her, for it was time to travel the galaxy with her new wonderful friends, exactly what she had wanted to do since arriving in the house. She made quick work of her climb despite the effort and pain it cost her. When she was almost at the top, she reached out to take the captain's hand. Everything is now going to be wonderful, she thought to herself.

But her elation was short lived. All of a sudden, the ship and its crew were gone, nowhere to be seen. Bethany, with nothing to hold on to, plummeted to the floor, landing with a painful thud. Totally disorientated, she squirmed on her back, her body aching. She groaned at the pain. What had happened? Where had they gone? With difficulty, she pulled herself up onto her hands, positioning herself so she could see her remaining friend. The wizard was still with her, but his attention was locked on something across from him. By the worried look on his face, it was something dangerous. She followed his gaze and found to her shock the Inquisitor standing on the other side of the room, with streams of black energy swirling around him. Rubble had been flung through the air, as if it were fleeing from this chilling entity. The dark, burning energy that had flicked about him before was now an inferno. His body boiled with this magic, full of fury and rage. He approached them, like a wild tiger loose and determined to take its bloody vengeance. This was it, Bethany thought. Burning with energy, the Inquisitor looked more like a natural disaster than a living being. Bethany's heart sank.

Alarabus stood between our hero and the Inquisitor.

"Stay behind me," he said with an all-too-serious tone.

With a quick gesture, Alarabus began to attack his enemy. Bolts of lightning burst from his hands in the direction of the Inquisitor, who effortlessly batted and flicked them away. The Inquisitor, advancing relentlessly, responded by throwing a ball of furious black energy towards the tiny wizard. He too deflected it, sending it crashing into the wall and blasting splinters of wood that flew across the room. To Bethany's alarm, Alarabus looked weak – his face was pale, and he stumbled slightly as he took a battle stance. He clearly wasn't prepared for the fight ahead. Despite this, the wizard doggedly sent another flash of lightning at the Inquisitor, who again deflected it, advancing still. Alarabus tried again and again, becoming more and more frantic. Sweat appeared on his brow. But as before, his foe quite easily deflected the bolts. In a few moments, the Inquisitor had closed the gap between them, his eyes hungry and his body boiling over with raging energy. With one swift movement, he raised his right hand and out of nowhere the chains reappeared, rushing through the air and wrapping themselves around the wizard. Alarabus struggled desperately, but it was all in vain. The heavy chains enveloped him and began to tighten, until it seemed like the life would be squeezed right out of him. Satisfied, the Inquisitor's fury abated slightly and he turned his attention to Bethany again. Though weak and with a body full of pain, she remained defiant.

"What've you done to my friends!" she shouted.

"Your friends are gone. They were a nuisance, and I have thrown them across the galaxy. With any luck, they will have crashed into a sun and been burnt to cinders."

Bethany shuddered.

"Though I must congratulate you on your persistence, Ms Bethany Hannah Morgan," he said, returning to his usual smooth but threatening manner.

He stalked towards her, his wild hunger calming, giving him time to toy with his prey. Bethany desperately tried to pick herself up, but pain shot through her body and she hardly managed to move at all, feeling heavy and exhausted. With a mighty effort, she frantically pulled herself backwards, determined to make space between the two of them. Not far from where she lay, she could see the eternity door. It still appeared to be turned on and was surrounded by buckets full of paperwork.

"Despite the efforts of the Alpharian Confederation, you and your friends have been able to evade our grasp. What a shame it has all been for naught. As you can clearly see, I have the upper hand now. There is no chance that your feeble abilities could challenge the power that pulses through me!"

He was taking his time, relishing the moment. Alarabus was still enveloped in his chains, almost lifeless, and our hero felt truly helpless. He was right, she thought – there was absolutely nothing she could do but maybe accept her demise. Despite this, she continued to inch her tired body towards the magical door. If only she could get to it, she could be free. Though the space between her and it was tiny, the sheer effort it required to reach it and the pain that consumed her every part made it feel monumental.

"Therefore, you must relent. Your friends are gone, the wizard is defeated, and it was only because of them that you got this far. Luck has been on your side, but now it is time for you to accept your fate. You must be punished for your crimes."

Bethany thought that this must be the end. That was until she noticed a particularly heavy book that lay next to her amongst the rubble – *101 Ingenious Ways to Use Heavy Books*. Hiding it with her body, she quickly pulled it towards herself, a few ripped pages falling out of its bindings. The Inquisitor raised a hand again, and a ball of dark energy began to construct itself on the tips of his fingers. He swelled with triumphant rage, his dark magical aura bursting into angry flames again and his eyes full of primal hate.

"Your crimes would see the end of order and the Alpharian Confederation itself! Only chaos would reign. That is why you must be punished severely and by the harshest of means. Death!"

It was then, when her doom seemed almost certain, that she did something truly remarkable. With the last of her energy, she threw the heavy book as best she could in the direction of the Inquisitor. To her surprise, it hurtled through the air with some force. For a few moments, time seemed to slow as the book flew. Its destination was the centre of her foe's head. With a thud, it smashed him in the face. Time then resumed as normal and he stumbled backwards in pain, clutching the wound, and in this moment of respite, Bethany hauled herself up. She sprang into action, newfound adrenaline carrying her, stumbling towards the magical door as best she could. After a couple of steps, she could sense her nemesis behind her. He was back to his senses and bursting with dark fury, ready to end her. She heard a crackle of energy as he quickly prepared another spell. Bethany leapt through the air, throwing her body in the direction of the door. Both feet came off the floor, and for a moment she flew. The magical projectile was gaining on her, burning the very ends of her hair and the back of her head. But it thankfully passed, missing her, a few inches from being a fatal blow. Instead, it hit the corner of the eternity door, which began to crumble. The glass began to splinter as she grew closer in her flight, and her heart sank. Doubt now entered her mind – would the mirror be nothing but broken glass when she finally reached it? Would this, despite her best efforts, be her fate?

But her terror turned to relief as she passed through the door not a moment too soon. She felt herself quickly disappearing into nothingness. Through the eternity door, she was enveloped by its darkness, and everything went numb. The only sensation she had was of falling into an endless void, her body light as she descended into the endless gloom. Undistinguishable voices came from all around, as if they belonged to disembodied spirits. Our hero felt no relief or happiness, but neither did she feel fear or dread. Instead she was consumed by a deep and confusing sadness, a sense that she was running away from something, as if she were refusing to accept a tragic event. A tear formed in the corner of her eye as she struggled to figure out what this undefinable loss was. It was at that point, plummeting through darkness, that she realised her adventures had truly begun.

 Matador

For exclusive discounts on Matador titles,
sign up to our occasional newsletter at
troubador.co.uk/bookshop